Resistance

The Outlaw Lovers, Volume 5

Jan Springer

Published by Jan Springer, 2016.

Also by Jan Springer

Pleasure Bound
A Hero's Welcome
A Hero Escapes
A Hero Betrayed
A Hero's Kiss
A Hero Wanted
Captive Heroes

Pleasure Bound Boxed Set
Pleasure Bound : COMPLETE SERIES SciFi Erotic Romance Boxed
Set

Tentacles Shifter Erotic Romance
Taken by Him

The Key Club
A Merry Menage Christmas
Sophie's Menage
Jewel's Menage
Jaxie's Menage

The Outlaw Lovers
Jude Outlaw
The Claiming

Colter's Revenge
Tyler's Woman
Resistance
The Outlaw Lovers
Alpha Outlaws Boxed Set

Vampira
Sweet Heat
Dark Heat
Wet Heat
Crimson Heat

Standalone
A Touch of Menage Boxed Set
Shades of Menage Boxed Set
Nice Girl Naughty
Sinderella Sexy
The Biker and The Bride
The Fire Within
Bared to Him
Pleasure Bound : A Futuristic Adult Romance Boxed Set
Merry Menage Kisses Boxed Set
Inner Girl Rising
Stripped Naked
Risqué Girl Delights Boxed Set
A Holiday Menage
Ménage À Trois
A Hitman for Hannah
Billionaire Boyfriend
Edible Delights

Vampira
Toygasm
The Dark Side

Watch for more at www.janspringer.com.

Resistance

Outlaw Lovers 5

Jan Springer[1]

Fugitive female... Renegade Resistance leader Reena "Red" Wilde is in for the fight of her life when she experiences an erotic attraction to the two most dangerous men she's ever met.

Black ops assassin... Months ago, Will "Blade" Smith spent one sizzling evening in the arms of a red-haired seductress. Now she's his next assignment. One look into her gorgeous eyes and he's wrestling his heated cravings all over again.

Bounty Hunter... When Cade Outlaw nabs his bounty, sexy-as-sin Reena Wilde, his profession dictates she's hands-off. But he can't ignore the magnetic sparks between them...or that she is the biggest temptation of his life.

Resistance is futile... After Reena escapes Cade and Will and falls prey to a band of evil hunters, she's grateful her sexy hunks come to her rescue, and in return, saves their lives. Trapped in a solitary cabin during a wicked snowstorm, she can't resist her two well-hung studs, nor can she deny they've claimed her heart.

---

1. http://www.jasminejade.com/m-151-jan-springer.aspx

Outlaw Lovers Series

Jude ~ Book One
The Claiming ~ Book Two
Colter's Revenge ~ Book Three
Tyler's Woman ~ Book Four
Resistance ~ Book Five
Pleasure Burn ~ Book Six

~

Want to get updates on new releases?
Join Jan's newsletter ~
http://ymlp.com/xguembmugmgb
Other language newsletters ~
https://janspringerauthor.wordpress.com/newsletters/

Resistance
Published by Spunky Girl Publishing
Copyright 2016 Jan Springer
Edited by Julie Naughton
Coverart by Talina Perkins ~ Bookin' It Designs

License Notes

Author's Note

This is a work of fiction. Characters, places, settings and events presented in this book are purely of the author's imagination and bear no resemblance to any actual person, living or dead or to any actual events, places and/or settings.

Chapter One

Reena Wilde could barely stop her fingers from shaking. She stood in the hallway and unbuttoned the man's shirt she'd been given to wear while she stayed in the safe house. Baby-blue cotton, the shirt dwarfed her petite body and the hemline dropped to her knees. The sensual rugged scent of outdoorsy pine and soap on *his* shirt made her heart race. The owner of this piece of clothing was on the other side of the door and she was nervous to approach him.

She'd been here several days and nights having sex. Not with him, but with the men who'd rescued her from the brothel where she'd been held captive. Her rescuers belonged to a top secret government organization called SKULL.

Through her work in the Resistance, she'd heard of them. Skilled Kill Undercover Liaison Links was a Black Ops assassination organization for the government. During the Terrorist Wars, members had been doctors, nurses and other medical personnel—people drafted into the organization and forced to infiltrate any number of U.S. Military adversaries in order to kill targeted enemies.

The SKULL men she'd been staying with had been working on an unrelated assignment when they'd rescued her from the pleasure house she'd penetrated to gather intelligence for the Resistance.

Damn fools had screwed her plans. She'd *let* herself be captured by the pleasure house. SKULL had ruined the assignment. But she couldn't do anything about it now. She just hoped to hell they wouldn't discover her true identity, for if they did, they'd interrogate and then shoot her. Pretty much everybody wanted her out of the way. If not dead, tortured first—for the information she held—and then dead.

For the past few days, she'd had no option but to stay here. These men were dominant and so willing to give the sex she craved while she came off the sex drugs the pleasure house had pumped into her. The drugs had kept her aroused and willing to perform. The matter of her needing to orgasm every so often or she'd go mad also existed. This was due to the X-virus, a submissive virus released by terrorists intent on dominating all women. But the original strain had mutated into different forms—many of them deadly—thus killing off a majority of the world's female population and leaving most of those alive afflicted with various illnesses.

She had the O mutation of the X-virus. O for orgasm. Right now her body screamed for another climax. Not just with anyone. But with *him*. The man they called Will Blade, who just so happened to be on the other side of this door.

Avoiding her.

She knew why. Knew it in the hot way his yummy chocolate-pudding eyes studied her every movement since he'd shown up in this secluded house early this morning. She'd read the hunger on his face the several times the SKULL men had led her into the adjoining room.

She'd hoped he would join them. He never had. So she'd decided to hook up with him. Tonight. In his room. While the others slept.

She wanted a taste of him—just this once. Then she'd escape and she'd never have to see any of these men again. Never have to physically long for the man they called Blade.

Excitement lashed her as she twisted the doorknob, pushed the door open and quietly stole inside.

He was awake. She knew he would be. Or else he slept with the lights on...or maybe he'd been waiting for her.

At twenty-three years old, she was quite experienced in the sex department. She'd gained her skills during the last two years of the Terrorist Wars in the mandatory Rest & Relaxation Sexual Release Program—R & R for short—designed for the soldiers. Even her father, a top-ranking general, had been unable to keep her out—no matter how hard he'd tried to hide her overseas in a job as a teacher's assistant in the Teachers Without Borders program.

With all her sexual experience, she'd learned the power a woman has over men and was anxious to try her expertise on Blade.

As she stood in the doorway, Blade looked up from where he lay on his bed, an open book balanced on his chest. A succulent pine and soap scent drifted off the vibrant male and hung erotically in the room. His heated gaze made her jittery with an intense longing to be touched, especially her breasts and between her thighs. She was so wet, drenched, ready.

Maybe the arousal drugs were still in her system? No, her overwhelming urges for this stranger were natural. With the drugs, she'd been impatient, needy and desperate. With Blade, she just wanted his body heat wrapped around her. Wanted him to hold her in his arms, kiss her and bring his cock into her. Make love to her. Her desires were as plain and raw as that.

He remained silent as she closed the door behind her and crossed the room to stand beside his bed. He wore only a pair of skintight black jeans. He did nothing but return to his reading, as if dismissing her.

Disappointment rocked her and for a horrendous long moment she wondered if maybe he didn't desire her as she'd anticipated. Maybe he didn't want her because she'd been with so many of his co-workers. Maybe he still belonged to the old-fashioned world and stuck with the idea of wanting a pure, untouched woman. God, wouldn't that be something? And just her rotten luck too, because she really desired him.

He moved, catching her off guard, making her inhale sharply. Swinging his legs over the side of the bed, he sat up and gazed at her.

His tussled golden-blonde hair made her think of sleepless nights making love with him. The dark shadow he wore so well on his face made the insides of her thighs clench as she imagined his stubble rubbing her while he slurped her pussy into his mouth. Just thinking of having him between her legs brought a flush of heat to her cheeks and excitement raced through her system.

The slight bump on his nose—as if someone had recently broken it—on his otherwise flawless face made her wonder if he might be violent. She didn't know him. He could slap her around for daring to come into his room uninvited. But then why the heated looks for her when he'd first arrived? Did she burn for a man she'd misread? Or was this just wishful, old-fashioned thinking on her part, hoping he craved her as badly as she needed him thrusting into her?

No, she couldn't be wrong about him. He wanted her and, oh God, she wanted him.

He said nothing as she pulled the shirt open to reveal her breasts and her pussy. Instead he sat on the edge of the bed and looked into her eyes. Watching. Waiting. Seemingly unaffected by her exposure.

He didn't reach out to her as she'd hoped. Didn't touch her. Didn't do a thing.

Bastard.

Rejection slammed into her and she winced at the unexpected pain. Maybe she should just leave.

"Don't stop," he growled in a strangled voice.

"The man speaks," she replied, unable to stop her anger. If only he would have taken her into his arms.

A flare of irritation—or maybe surprise—at her uncontrolled outburst flashed in his eyes. She didn't care. She just wanted him to know she had an unexplained, overwhelming physical attraction toward him. She wanted to tell him she wished they'd met under different circumstances and hoped he'd join the ménages she experienced with the other members of SKULL.

Surely he'd had sex with other men in the same room? These days anything was the norm when it came to sex.

"Touch yourself," he ordered.

Any evidence of his earlier strangled voice had disappeared. Apparently he'd pulled a tight, controlled shield around himself. She'd just have to see how much persuasion was needed to break that wall, wouldn't she? Once again, sweet anticipation swept through her as she cupped her breasts.

"Why don't you *make* me touch myself, Blade?" she taunted.

A muscle spasmed in his jaw. His eyes darkened as he studied her.

"Perhaps you should spank me until I do what you want me to do. Or maybe you should hang heavy weights off all these rings of mine."

Without un-cupping herself, she inserted her thumbs through the large rings her previous jailors at the pleasure house had pierced through her nipples. She tugged on the rings, bringing her nipples and breasts outward. The sting of tenderness made her gasp, but she didn't ease off. The pleasure-pain excited her and from the flushed hunger on Blade's face, he was enjoying the show.

"You could zip a gold chain through the rings. String the chain down through my bellybutton ring."

She un-cupped her breasts and his gaze followed as she smoothed her hands leisurely over her stomach and fingered the gold ring in her bellybutton.

"Then you could loop the chain through my labia rings. Tighten the slack so I would experience pleasure-pain everywhere, all at once?"

Her voice became breathless, sexy as she erotically traced her fingers over her smooth, firm abdomen and between her thighs to toy with her labia rings. She pulled on them and whimpered at the pressure they created.

"Or perhaps you'd..." She cleared her dry throat. "Maybe you'd tie me against a wall and hang heavy weights from all my rings until I submitted to you...and let you fuck me."

She tensed as he rose.

He was a tall man—towered over her like a giant as he stood in front of her. Her eyes met his muscled, bronze chest. She gazed up. His pulse pounded in his corded neck and her own pulse picked up speed.

"You're wearing my shirt," he said in a quiet, husky voice.

"Maybe you should take it back," she teased.

Anticipation raced through her as he delicately grabbed the lapels of the open shirt and pulled the material farther apart. He stared down at her breasts and his soft gaze feathered across her flesh, making her nipples harden. She ached for him to loop his fingers through the rings and pull just as she'd suggested.

Disappointment once again rocked her when, instead, he brought the shirt up over her shoulders and let it fall and puddle at her feet. She trembled as she stood totally naked in front of him. A stranger. A big man whose powerful arms could snap her neck with one quick move.

She yelped when he grabbed her wrists. Tight. Like two handcuffs.

He led her hands upward to beneath her breasts. His eyes flashed with emotions she couldn't put names to.

His body scent wrapped around her like an aphrodisiac. Dark, alluring...dangerous. This man might not like it if she played games with him.

"I said touch yourself, Red," he commanded. "Play with your nipples."

Red. Because of her red hair? Or did he know Red was her code name as the leader of the Resistance? Uneasiness fluttered through her. Maybe he knew who she really was. No, not possible. He would have told the others. They would have interrogated her. Instead, they slept.

She liked the slow and sexy way he said *Red*.

She cried in surprise when he grabbed her hips and shoved her backward against the closed door. She hit it with a rough thud and held her breath as he dropped to his knees in front of her. She cupped her breasts, her hands smoothing over her curves. Plumping her tender nipples, she tried like crazy to keep her gaze focused on the big man on his knees before her. He reached up and slid his hands seductively along the curve of each hip. His palms burned her flesh as he held onto her.

"Open your legs. Wide."

He possessed a cool and controlled voice, his breath anything but as it fanned hot waves against her lower belly.

She did as he instructed and eagerly spread her legs very wide.

Her breath was shallow. Her senses fully alert as she awaited his next move. The tip of his tongue peeked out from between his lips and her knees melted, threatening to crumble at the erotic sight.

His nearness, his self-control, the intoxicating way he studied her pussy made her so aware—yet at the same time very shy too as blood hammered through her system.

Perhaps in her boldness toward him, she'd bitten off more than she could chew? Maybe he hadn't come after her for a reason? Maybe she wouldn't be able to handle him? He might be too rough with her.

She gasped at the heat of his palms as they branded her hips. He held her firm against the door and for a moment she forgot how to breathe as his head lowered. She cried out in both surprise and arousal as he sucked one labia—ring included—into his moist, warm mouth.

She struggled to keep touching her breasts. Fought to keep her body under control as the tip of his tongue lashed her clit. He sucked the ring between his teeth and pulled. The tug was erotic, way better than anything she'd ever done herself.

Oh yeah, this man knew what he was doing.

Her legs trembled. She leaned more heavily against the door and moaned softly as he devoured her other labia, doing the same naughty thing—lashing her with his tongue and pulling the ring with his teeth. He released her and ran his tongue between her wet folds and along her slit until a magnificent pulse of heat throbbed through her pussy. She tightened her thighs as her arousal mounted.

When his mouth fused over her entire pussy, she fought for a breath. Fought to keep standing.

She let go of her nipples and slapped her hands down upon his rock-hard back, trying to support her trembling legs. His palms caressed her hips, his touches electric upon her flesh, and she couldn't help but gyrate against his face.

She jerked as his tongue lashed her clit. He began a firm, rough lap. It was fast and intense, an up and down massage. *Oh God!*

He feasted on her pussy. Erotic slurping split the air as he sucked firmly on her wet flesh. With each swipe of his tongue, her restraint crumbled and she came closer to being whisked into a vortex of need and lust and pleasure.

He licked and stroked with his tongue, pushing her to the edge. The instant she wanted to let herself fly, he pulled back.

The tease! She cried out her frustration and he became intense again, feasting and urging her toward a wild desire that threatened to pull her under. Need built inside her. A need so powerful and raw, she knew this was what she'd required from a man. She strained her pussy against his face, demanding a harder pressure, needing to lose herself in the hungry pleasure wave that threatened to consume her senses and self-control.

He worked her close to an orgasm. So close! She burned for him. Yearned for release. Wanted him inside her.

She whimpered. She wanted him to fuck her. Now! But she couldn't say a word. He had her twisting inside a whirlwind that kept her gasping with arousal.

His mouth left her pussy. "You like this, don't you, Red," he growled up at her.

She moaned her agreement and tightened her grip on his shoulders. She couldn't remember when she'd stopped touching herself. Didn't remember placing her palms on his rugged muscular shoulders for support.

"Open your eyes, Red," he instructed.

His demand made her gasp as a familiar erotic wave of submission washed through her. She opened her heavy-lidded eyes and cried softly as he studied her.

Blade's lips were red, swollen and glistened with moisture from her pussy. He let go of one of her hips and moved his hand between her thighs. A hot finger teased her clit, stroked her until she trembled uncontrollably.

"You'd like me to fuck you," he said.

She gasped, her desperation turning into a physical ache. She needed him. God! How she needed him!

He bared his white, even teeth and her tummy hollowed out at the sexy satisfied smile he gave her so freely.

Yes, she wanted this man. Wanted him like no other. This was why she'd come to his room tonight. To be with him.

"You want me, don't you, Red?" His words stroked her senses. "You want me to make you come. To bring you what you crave. What you need."

Yes, bring me what I need.

Without waiting for her answer, he thrust two fingers into her vagina and started a quick, savage pump that had her quivering and bucking shamelessly. He finger fucked her with the deepest, longest strokes. Within seconds, a fireball slammed into her. She twisted harder and cried out as she writhed and gyrated upon his fingers.

Colorful lights flashed in her mind and shocking tremors shook her legs. Tears burned her eyes as spasms pounded through her. Thrashing her hips, she cried out as he worked her, his fingers plunging into her deeper and faster. Her vagina clenched and pleasure rode her body.

Her thighs trembled. Her tummy tightened. And she swore she lost her breath. Her mouth opened as she held tighter to his shoulders, digging her nails into him. The need, the craving, the desperation spiraling through her since she'd first seen him crashed together, making the wicked bursts of pleasure sharper and exquisitely painful... but so beautiful, too. She gyrated her hips with maddening speed, rocking into the explosion, and embraced the carnal shivers as they seared through her with perfection.

When he withdrew his fingers, she collapsed to her knees in front of him, gasping for air, her eyes shut so tightly she swore she would never be able to open them again. His hot mouth fused over hers, scattering all thoughts to the wind. Urges pounded her as his hands cupped her breasts, his fingers slipping through the nipple rings and tugging to this side of pain. He pulled the rings and kissed her harder, demanding she kiss him back. She returned his fire, melting her lips against his so intensely something deep inside of her—something pure and innocent and untouched—unraveled for him.

The trembling and spasms rocking her were so beautiful they pushed her right to the edge of control. His lips disappeared, his fingers left her rings. She wanted to open her eyes, to beg him not to stop, but the crackle of a zipper lowering had her breath quickening. A rustle of clothing followed. Her heart beat faster at foil ripping.

The condom.

Anticipation roared.

Oh man! He would take her now. It was going to be magnificent. She knew it. She would experience the most wonderful climax when he fucked her. Oh! She could barely wait.

Roughly, he grabbed her wrists and brought her to her feet. The cold, solid door slapped her ass and back as he pushed her against it.

His mouth slammed onto hers, taking her in a hot and fierce kiss, like a wild man conquering the mate he wanted. His hands sifted through her hair, holding her head, and she grabbed his naked waist to steady herself.

He impaled her. His thick, swollen cock penetrated her in one swift, brutal plunge, unraveling and melting her body until she became pressed around his hard curves.

Erotic anguish whipped through her as he withdrew and she whimpered as he thrust into her a second time, her body instantly tightening into a fierce pleasure ball. She exploded again. Violent tremors rocked her, making her cry out shamelessly as the desperate need for him to keep fucking her tore through her. She didn't care if the other men in the house heard her. Didn't care if Blade knew she wanted him so badly it hurt.

He buried himself deep and her vaginal muscles frantically stretched in order to accommodate him.

Perfect...like he belonged to her. He withdrew and quickly pumped back into her, firm and furious, unleashing the pent-up arousal keeping her hostage.

Pleasure pounded hotly through her veins, making her shudder. Her vagina gripped his condom-sheathed cock and milked him. Carnal need shattered her. She quaked violently within a mindless wild storm. She surrendered to him and he thrust harder and faster. She let out another tortured cry as tension snapped through her body, making her shudder and writhe in a dance of erotic gyrations.

God! Was this possible? Having climax upon climax?

Exploding on a guttural moan, she swiveled madly against his hips, grinding and riding the wicked tremors. She held tight to his shoulders as pleasure continued to pummel her. Within seconds, he too was crying out with a guttural groan of release.

For a few sweet moments he held her until her orgasm ebbed. His lips brushed over hers so tenderly, she swore she could fall in love with this man. As she began freefalling into that beautiful abyss again, he stopped kissing her, breaking the magnetic connection. With a tender caress of his hand against her right cheek, he smiled warmly.

"It can never be," he whispered.

Before she could mount a protest to tell him anything was possible, he withdrew from her. She almost collapsed as he moved away, his heavy breath ricocheting through the air with hers.

Disappointment that he wouldn't take her to his bed rankled her. He'd fucked her hard and fast and in those bursts of bliss, he'd given her something she'd hungered for—caring.

She wanted more.

By the time Reena regained her strength, he'd donned his jeans and opened the bedroom door.

He left without looking back.

* * * * *

Three months later...

Blade's finger tightened on the rifle trigger when he caught the petite red-haired woman in the scope. Red was flanked by two people. A man and woman who were friends of Blade's.

Pull the fucking trigger. That's why you're here, dammit! Kill her!

Try as he might, though, he couldn't bring himself to shoot the redhead. It should have been easy. He'd killed people before. He'd obeyed orders. Killed men and women who were trouble for the U.S. Government. But he'd never killed a woman he'd had sex with before.

Unfortunately, SKULL considered this woman a military object of elimination. He didn't agree. She was more of a...nuisance to the government. A woman heading a resistance in order to get all rights back for women shouldn't be hunted down like a dog. It was wrong.

Three months ago, she'd been the best fuck of his life. Now he'd been ordered to kill her. He'd no idea the woman SKULL had rescued from a pleasure house had actually been the leader of the U.S. Resistance Movement. He'd had no clue he'd fucked someone so goddamned important.

Dammit! Hell of a time to sprout a conscience.

Maybe he could wait until she was alone? Kill her then?

Blade frowned. The finger on the trigger eased as guilt slammed into him.

You're stalling, Blade. Take her down in front of witnesses. Follow your orders or there will be hell to pay.

This was the perfect opportunity. The two witnesses would report back to the Resistance that their leader was dead. The cause would collapse. Or so the government hoped.

Personally, he believed killing her would only make the Resistance stronger. Besides, he hated doing this right in front of people he knew. They were good people. Tyler Outlaw and his woman Laura had some rough years apart, but now they were back together. He didn't want to cause trouble for them.

They would just have to deal with this assassination. Just as he would have to deal with it.

Once again his finger tightened on the trigger, but he quickly eased off as cold metal kissed his temple.

"I don't think you want to do that, do you, Blade." He knew that deadly calm voice. Cade Outlaw, the brother of his ex-SKULL partner, Colter Outlaw.

"This isn't your concern, Outlaw," Blade warned coolly.

"You're on Outlaw land. It is my business. Drop the gun."

The icy threat sent shivers up his back. Blade hesitated.

"I know we're friends, Will, and I hope you won't hold it against me if I blow a hole in your head, but I will unless you drop the rifle."

And he probably would, too. Cade was just as much a killing machine as Blade. If not more. Especially if those rumors about him being a torturer during the Terrorist Wars were true. A man had to have a strong stomach to do that sort of work.

Blade sighed and dropped the gun. From the other side of the bushes laughter erupted. The two women hugged. They were saying their goodbyes. His gut twisted as the best opportunity for carrying out his job slipped through his fingers.

"She's your SKULL assignment, isn't she?" Cade asked.

Blade said nothing.

"You've been sent to kill her. Kill the leader of the Resistance. As if that will stop women from fighting to regain their freedom."

"She's a marked woman. If I fail, someone else won't," he replied.

"You've failed, Will. Tell your boss the leader of the Resistance is under Outlaw protection now. Anyone who tries to go after her will have us to answer to. Got it?"

"Got it," Blade replied, knowing full well the six Outlaw brothers were no match for the U.S. dictatorship that ran the country with an iron fist.

"Good."

The two of them stood in silence as the Resistance leader waved goodbye to her friends before she sprinted across the yard and into the meadow. A moment later, an entourage of her supporters came out of the trees edging the field. As the entire group vanished into the neighboring woods, the success of his mission disappeared and, strangely enough, relief poured through him.

Sure, he'd lost an opportunity to kill her. And yes, there would be hell to pay when he reported his failed mission. But at least he could live with himself tomorrow. That is, if Cade didn't kill him.

"The highway is about twenty miles to the east. Drop the keys to your vehicle and start walking, Will. Rest assured if you'd been anyone else, you would be dead. Consider this a favor. You owe me one. Big time. Just remember what I said. If I ever see you near her again, I will kill you and your body will be buried somewhere on Outlaw land where no one can find it. Buried with the others who crossed us. You know very well I speak the truth."

Blade was a smart man. He knew there were dead bodies buried on Outlaw land. Hell, he'd helped kill those men and buried some of them himself. This was the time to clear out.

He nodded and slowly unclasped the key chain he wore at his belt. He pulled his keys from his pocket and let them go. They fell with a jingle into the tall grass.

"I'll remember that," he said to Cade.

"You do that. Now go before I change my mind and kill you."

The area between his shoulder blades prickled as he started off toward the east. He half-expected Cade to shoot him in the back. He certainly deserved it for getting this close to almost killing a leader who represented freedom to all women.

The same woman he'd once helped rescue from the Pleasure Palace when he'd been on assignment with Cade's brother, Colter. A woman who hadn't been able to keep her hands off his men after they'd taken her to a safe house. Hell, she'd been pumped so full of sex drugs, she'd been quite the hot fuck. He cursed at the memories of the heat. Of her red, tangled hair. Her cheeks flushed pink with excitement as he'd gotten out of bed and stood beside her in that bedroom. He'd enjoyed the teasing glint in her eyes as she'd cupped her breasts and practically dared him to make love to her.

He still couldn't get the sweet echoes of their slapping flesh out of his mind as he'd entered her tight vagina in one solid plunge. Her aroused cries lingered in his mind and the awesome way he'd convulsed inside of her had shaken him right down to the tips of his toes.

After fucking her, he'd gone outside, craving cold air to chill the fierce desire of wanting to take her again. But when he'd come back into the house with the full intention of bringing her into his bed for the night and fucking her until they were both senseless, she hadn't been in his bedroom. Hadn't been anywhere in the house. She'd vanished.

Fuck! At the time, they hadn't known she was a member of the Resistance, let alone the leader of an enemy of the government. But she'd been willing. Willing and wanting and orgasming all over the place with a group of men who'd been desperate for a female.

The Pleasure Palace had done a number on her, that's for sure. It was a wonder she'd pulled herself together and returned to the Resistance. Most females, once on sex drugs, couldn't get off them. They were highly addictive. They'd been designed that way. To hook and keep the females as virtual slaves in the pleasure houses. If a woman escaped, she would crave the drugs to the point of near death and return to the place that supplied her, looking for more, plus the sex.

Apparently Reena had beaten those seductive drugs. She was tough, sexy and totally out of his league. Besides, she was damaged goods. She would need a man or men who were caring and patient with her and who would accept her desire for freedom for all women.

He could never be that man. As a SKULL assassin, he had too much blood on his hands. He didn't deserve happiness.

When he cleared the nearby tree line, he sighed in both frustration and relief. Relief because he'd been stopped from making a moral mistake. Frustration for the leader of the Resistance, because her troubles were only beginning.

* * * * *

Blade slipped away into the horizon and Cade sighed in relief. Blade wouldn't be back. At least not any time soon. He was a smart man and understood that what Cade said, he meant. Cade would have killed Blade if he hadn't dropped the gun, despite their friendship. It would have sent a strong message to SKULL to back off the leader.

Unfortunately for the Resistance, Cade was on a similar mission. Only Cade's orders didn't come from SKULL.

His mission—capture the leader of the Resistance, the woman they called Red, and bring her into the government safe and sound. Too bad Blade being here had screwed up his plan of capturing her. He wouldn't be able to catch the woman today. She'd have disappeared without a trace by now.

Tomorrow.

Tomorrow he would attempt to pick up the trail and start the hunt again. He'd capture the red-haired beauty and bring her in. He'd been told there was a deal on the table for members of the Resistance who came in peacefully. In the meantime, he'd make a large bounty for doing his job.

He just wished he could trust the government when they assured him her freedom was guaranteed, even if she didn't take the deal. Cade frowned and shoved his gun back into the ankle holster, then headed back to the Outlaw farm.

Chapter Two

Six weeks later...

Reena "Red" Wilde topped the tree-enshrouded embankment of the winding creek she'd been following for the last half an hour. She tried hard not to shiver as sheets of frigid air blasted against her jean-clad legs and her face. The cold mid-November wind had picked up and she was grateful she'd had the forethought to slip into her late grandfather's green camouflage hunting jacket before leaving the cabin. Thankfully she'd also donned an extra pair of wool socks before opting to put on her winter boots despite no snow on the ground—although from the looks of the sky that would change soon.

She focused her attention on the dark-gray clouds rolling above the gnarled branches of the hardwood forest prevalent in the southern half of the state of Maine. She should have taken the weather forecast more seriously when she'd listened to her portable satellite radio this morning at the cabin.

In her desire to reconnect with nature, she'd spent hours walking through the woods. The small, picturesque frozen ponds in the valley behind her grandfather's hunting cabin made her breath catch at their beauty. She had admired the birds, deer and other wildlife she encountered. But in doing so, she'd ventured too far.

She probably had another hour or more of walking before she could get back and warm herself by the wood stove. Maybe she could avoid getting caught in the snowstorm that was sure to drop a good load before nightfall.

As if the angry-looking sky ignored her wishful thinking, a defiant snowflake twirled a taunting dance past the white mist of her breath. Another snowflake landed in her eye and she quickly swiped it away with the back of her mittened hand. Any split second of blindness was dangerous.

Cursing the impending bad weather, she hoped her luck would hold out and the erotic throb of need wouldn't erupt between her thighs. She was overdue. The crushing craving for sex hit at the most inopportune times. Ever since being infected with the X-virus, her life was a chaotic rhythm of yearning for sex, masturbating and then having a few days to several weeks of peace before the overwhelming need to orgasm hit again.

The "big O" is what she needed when the cravings kicked in. A climax in order to keep from dying—literally.

She'd end up freezing to death out here if she didn't get her ass in gear and head back to the cabin. God, why had she let her good friend Maggie talk her into taking a couple of weeks away from her job, anyway?

Her job. She chuckled harshly beneath her breath as she continued to gaze at the desolate wilderness beauty. *Yeah right. Now that is an understatement, isn't it?* If life ever returned to a semblance of normalcy—which she highly doubted—what in the world could she write on her resume?

Job experience: Fugitive. Leader of the Resistance. Wanted dead or alive by every bounty hunter in the United States. Wanted dead by various government factions. Wanted alive by any group of men who could catch her and screw her brains out just so they could claim rights over her and call her their wife.

Crud.

Why hadn't she been smart enough to bring an entourage of her most trusted bodyguards into seclusion with her? Because Reena, or "Red" as the members of the Resistance had nicknamed her, was just plain stupid, that's why. Well okay, aside from being stupid, lately she'd been snapping everybody's head off due to the stress of being the Resistance leader.

Her need for alone time—the first alone time in years—had clouded her judgment. She'd been in seclusion only two days of her two-week hiatus and already she was climbing the walls. Hence, she'd disregarded the storm warning and did her five-mile run this morning, following up with a wilderness hike.

Reena sighed and stuck out her tongue, catching a couple of snowflakes. The wetness made her yearn for something to drink. Maybe some sparkling water drawn from the ice hole she'd augured in the lake in front of the cabin. Or better yet, some of that cool white wine she'd brought in via her very heavy food-laden knapsack after being dropped off by a male member of the Resistance about three miles from the cabin.

Women were forbidden to drive these days. There were checkpoints along most roads so it had been quite difficult to arrange her hiatus. But, in the end, everything had worked out and she'd finally gotten her much-needed solitude.

Perhaps she should have taken a man or two along too to keep from getting bored. Now that men were returning from the Terrorist Wars, many of them were joining the Resistance. Some were prominent doctors and lawyers, and others blue-collar factory workers from the cities or farmers from the countryside. If she got her way, they would amass a large enough group to overthrow the dictatorship that now controlled the U.S., then they could start getting things back to normal...if that were possible.

Once upon a time, she'd wanted to be a teacher, a wife and mother. But she wanted none of those things now. Even if she did get back to a somewhat ordinary existence, she didn't have the desire to get into that kind of life anymore.

Life now included extreme danger. Living on the edge. Not knowing one minute to the next if she'd end up with a bullet in her brain because of her vocal protests against the government, who—in an effort to quickly repopulate the country—had with the stroke of a pen removed all women's rights, forcing them to be nothing more than men's sexual possessions and baby-making machines.

She sighed again as more snowflakes drifted out of the sky and clung to her eyelashes. This would be the first snowfall of the season. In the past, before the Terrorist Wars, she'd loved the crisp cold air slapping against her face. Had enjoyed the fresh, virgin-white snow blanketing the ground and draping the trees. The snow always turned this area into a sparkling winter fairyland.

Not anymore. These days the presence of snow on the ground meant extreme danger. She, as well as all the women in hiding, could be easily tracked in the snow.

Besides, she'd been surrounded by so much activity over the last few years a constant state of adrenaline had her in automatic survival mode. That's why she'd let herself get talked into coming here. To help herself unwind. Unfortunately her hiatus wasn't working. Every noise alerted her to possible danger and, as she stood on the embankment overlooking the meandering creek that led back to the cabin, the silence almost overwhelmed her. It was so quiet the snowflakes splattered against the frozen ground. But something that didn't belong in these woods whispered along the soft, flowing wind.

She tensed as a warning seared through her like an explosion. Was that a footfall from somewhere nearby?

The hushed crunch came again.

Yes, footsteps. Light. Fast. One person.

Shit! Someone is following me!

She ran even before she could inhale her next breath. Zig-zagging around trees and boulders, her feet hit the ground with assurance and confidence. She'd been in situations like this before and had always escaped capture, except for the one time she purposely got caught for the pleasure house.

Involuntary shivers of angst zipped through her and, in an instant, she tamped down the anxiety, refocusing on running, praying and escaping.

Despite someone keeping pace with her, she concentrated on keeping her breathing even. Soon an odd, familiar calm melted over her. Quickening her pace, she smiled as the person chasing her cursed.

Figures. A man. Just as I suspected.

She picked up more speed. He cursed again. The son of a bitch was still keeping pace. Usually she had no problem outrunning someone. That's why she made a point to jog several miles every morning, to keep herself in shape just so she could elude potential captors. Perhaps this guy did the same thing?

Oh great.

He breathed loudly as he gained ground. Panic split into her like a sharp axe.

Dammit! Who was this guy?

Soon her lungs began to hurt as the icy-cold wind seeped deep inside her.

She should have been paying more attention to her surroundings. She should have known someone could be following her. Instead she'd been enjoying herself in the wilderness and now she'd pay for it.

No! She wouldn't pay! He would have to catch her first!

She breathed deeper and pumped her legs harder until pain sawed through her thighs and the frosty air burned her face. Still he drew closer.

Fuck! Who the hell is this guy? She wanted to look over her shoulder and see who had the same stamina, but her curiosity would waste precious seconds.

She cut sharply to the right, heading for what appeared to be a meadow or hopefully one of the many lakes in the area. If she could just get a clear run on an ice-covered lake, she would drop her pursuer like a stone. Her hopes soared as she focused on the escape route looming in front of her.

Yes! Past the branches of the trees she could make out a lake. A big one. And it appeared to be frozen solid. Or at least she hoped so.

Twenty feet to go. Ten feet.

She blasted onto the bare black ice, running wide open at a dangerous speed, hoping to heaven she wouldn't slip and tumble. Ice crackled beneath her feet. Heck, falling would be the least of her problems. Behind her, the man shouted something about her having a death wish. Yet he just kept coming.

Damn him!

The rustle of his clothing and the determined slap of his boots on the ice made her groan in frustration as he continued his pursuit. Snowflakes twirled wildly, screwing with her field of vision, and the cold wind swept against her cheeks like shards of ice. She kept running.

Hell! He had just as much of a death wish as she did, coming after her with all the ice cracking beneath them. A man with a death wish was deadly. It meant he was desperate and had nothing to lose.

The farther she ran, the more the ice shifted beneath her feet. Her gut twisted in anxiety. It was only a matter of time before she fell through.

If this guy was serious about catching her, he wouldn't give up his pursuit until one of them plunged into the icy water. Maybe that's what he hoped. It certainly would make his job easier than chasing her around. But damned if she would make his job easy.

Anger seared through her and she veered sharply to the right, heading back toward the shoreline. With her sudden turn, he followed and fell.

She decided to go for her gun. But he already had his weapon in hand and pointed at her. Unzipping her coat, she reached for her shoulder holster while keeping her stride. She grabbed her weapon and yanked it out, but her stupid knitted mittens prevented her from getting a finger on the trigger.

Behind her, he shouted something stupid like "stop or I'll shoot", but she figured if he wanted her dead, he would have shot her already. Hopefully he didn't mean he'd wing her and bring her down that way.

With him flat on his ass and thankfully not shooting, she gained a significant amount of distance. She dared hope that maybe, she just might get out of this situation. Once she hit land, she could get better bearings beneath her feet, ditch the mitts and blow this son of a bitch away if he came any closer.

The powers that be obviously had other plans. About three feet from the shoreline, her right foot caught on a rock and she sailed through the air.

The black ice rushed up at her with mind-numbing speed and she managed to protect her face by breaking the impact with her arms. Her elbows smashed into the ice, sending jarring pain up her arms and into her neck, making her gasp at the intensity of the collision. The gun careened from her grasp and frustration ripped through her as the weapon sailed along the ice out of reach. The rest of her body, stomach and legs, hit hard, sending the air whooshing out of her lungs as she landed squarely, belly first on the ice. For a horrible few seconds, pain slithered through her chest and she lost her breath. Another few precious seconds passed as she struggled to grab some air and finally sucked in a lungful, and then two lungfuls, before managing to get her feet beneath her again. As she stood, she went for the second gun she kept in a thigh holster, but then froze as the cold metal of a knife blade kissed the right side of her jugular.

Oh, she was so screwed.

"Make one move and I'll give you a red necklace to go with that red hair of yours."

She didn't recognize the voice, but his ice-cold tone informed her he was quite pissed off. Rage wafted off him as his powerful arm snuggled like a vise around her waist, holding her captive. The man held her close enough, the scent of soap wafted off his skin and into her nostrils. So close, his hot heavy breath caressed the chill from her cheeks. Although her brain screamed at her to fight and free herself and kill the bastard, her highly trained senses told her to do what the man instructed.

At least for the moment.

"What do you want?" she whispered as the prickly rasp of his five o'clock shadow rubbed her cheek.

"You," came his hot reply.

Damn!

Panic punched her stomach like a two-by-four and she tensed. She thought about stomping on his foot to get out of his tight grasp or going for the gun in her thigh holster again, but his light chuckle and the increased pressure of the blade on her jugular made her pause.

"Don't even think it, Red. Now I want you to spread your legs for me."

She couldn't help but inhale sharply at his command as panic threatened to burst through her like a bolt of lightning.

"I'm not joking, Red. Spread your legs. Now. I won't ask again."

Reluctantly, she spread her legs. The position would make it that much harder to take off at a full-speed run.

"That's a good girl," he breathed.

He withdrew the blade from her neck, but his strong arm continued to clutch her waist. She was trapped. Her panic notched up a few degrees. She steadied her breath.

"Now I want you to move slowly, Red. Lift your arms up to the back of your neck and clasp your fingers."

"I'm wearing mittens," she snapped.

"Take them off. Easy...no sudden moves..." The undertone in his otherwise soft voice was deadly serious.

She tugged off her white knitted mittens, probably not as slowly as he wanted, but she was ticked at being caught. Cold air splashed against her fingers as she dropped the mittens and did as he instructed, bringing her hands up and clasping her fingers behind her neck.

"You're considered armed and dangerous, so I can't see why you'd let me catch you so easily, Red. That is, unless you wanted to be caught?"

He said the last sentence in a low, sensual voice as he moved into view. Although they'd never formally met, she knew him—bounty hunter, Cade Outlaw.

He was her ex-boss's brother.

She relaxed and almost laughed at the irony. She'd worked with this man's brother overseas during the Terrorist Wars. She'd been his youngest brother's teaching assistant. Tyler Outlaw had joked on more than one occasion that she and his brother Cade would be a good match. Something to do with both of them having fiery tempers.

She had to admit, luscious heat did whip through her as she inspected the enemy. He was a good-looking man, in a rugged sort of way. His lips were perfectly shaped for kissing and, if his mouth hadn't been fashioned so sensually, she might have said his nose was too straight and gave him a hardened appearance.

He was tall. Very tall. Probably six-foot-three to her five-foot-four inches. He was big framed with wide shoulders. He had the appearance of a renegade Indian with his dark tan, probably due to his working the fields of the Outlaw farm with a couple of his brothers.

This Outlaw brother was considered lethal. During the Wars he'd been a professional torturer, carving up terrorists nice and slow. They said his cold heart allowed him to keep his captives alive for days until he'd extracted the information he needed from them. He might even have been hired to torture her so she shouldn't—in the least bit—be reacting to him.

But she was responding.

His shoulder-length dark-brown hair was windswept and messy, and his crisp blue eyes were full of smug appreciation. He was glad he'd finally caught her.

"I'm going to have to cuff you while I do a search." He spoke in a deep timbre, way too husky to be professional.

She couldn't help but blow out a steadying breath.

God! Did he know how dark his eyes went when he threatened her with handcuffs? Didn't he know how erotic those words were to her ears? She inhaled slowly and loved the delicate scent of spice wafting off his skin.

Reena blinked and tried to thrust away the carnal need sweeping through her as Outlaw lifted his coat, revealing two pairs of metal handcuffs hanging from his belt. She caught a glimpse of a holster as well and an empty knife scabbard.

Another round of warmth skipped through her as she spied the impressive bulge between his thighs. She really should make an escape attempt. Maybe take him down with a knee to that nice groin of his before he discovered her other weapons. But all she could think was Cade had to be harmless, despite what she'd heard about him. He must know she'd worked with his brother Tyler, and he wouldn't approve of Cade hurting her under any circumstances.

She bit her bottom lip as a sudden bout of nervousness ripped through her. Unless...Cade didn't know his brother was now a member of her Resistance?

"Easy, Red. I'm not going to hurt you."

To her shock, his calming voice reassured her and she relaxed again.

She wondered if he'd strip her naked in order to frisk her. Would he press his full lips against her mouth, push her up against one of the nearby trees on the shoreline and fuck her senseless?

Oh shit, don't start thinking that way. She cleared her throat, chastising herself for the string of wicked ideas rushing through her mind.

Control, Red. Self-control.

Her thoughts of having sex with him had everything to do with her being infected by the virus. She could handle this. She could handle him. She'd done it with other men when her symptoms kicked in. She could resist this man too.

As Cade stepped forward, she held her breath. She didn't need to inhale any more of his rugged masculine scent. If she did, she just might be in trouble.

Self-control.

Again she cleared her mind and her dry throat. He studied her as he circled to her right side. He probably expected her to bolt and she really should run. Ordinarily she would, but the heated way he gazed at her caressed her senses. Suddenly she didn't want to be anywhere but here.

"That's it. Hold nice and still," he ordered.

When the cold metal snapped around one wrist and then the other, the metallic clinks sent a shaft of unwanted excitement through her. Visions of her naked, the rough tree bark brushing erotically against her breasts and mons as he stretched her arms in front of her, pressing them around the tree as he cuffed her wrists, seeped into her consciousness.

He would kick her legs apart, hold her hips steady, and his engorged cock would plunge into her pussy from behind. His hard body would press along her backside and he'd kiss her shoulders, her neck and nibble on her ears, taunting her with teasing promises of luscious pleasure.

"In the way you're looking at me, I take it you know me," he stated coolly.

She melted beneath his firm, bold stare. She wanted his full, warm mouth claiming hers and she licked her lips with anticipation as need, fierce and hot, lashed her. She blinked the naughtiness away and focused on what he was saying.

"Then you know I'm very thorough when it comes to my job. Any weapons on you besides that gun in your thigh holster?" he asked as he unzipped her jacket.

She said nothing and his lips tilted upward as he retrieved the hidden gun.

"Okay, let's take this up against a tree," he ordered.

Reena's eyes widened in surprise at his instruction. Oh man! Were they on the same wavelength or what? She wasn't fast enough to follow his orders, so he roughly grabbed her cuffed hands and pulled her off the ice. He led her to a nearby tree where he gently pushed her left cheek up against the coarse bark and held her head in place. At least now she didn't have to look into his scorching blue eyes and she would be able to think clearly.

Or not.

A booted foot nudged the insides of her feet apart.

Damn him!

Reluctantly she obeyed and spread her legs, envisioning his hands sliding against the curves of her ass. He let go of her head and pressed a strong palm against the small of her back and held her firmly against the tree.

The hiss of the knife as he slid it into the scabbard at his waist didn't give her any relief. His body had been firm when he'd held her and, despite her best intentions not to think about how easily he'd overpowered her, she imagined Cade Outlaw thrusting into her with commanding strokes.

Dammit! Stop thinking. Stop reacting.

But this man was an Outlaw. She'd secretly fantasized about her boss Tyler when they'd worked together during the Wars. But his heart belonged to another woman, so she'd never physically pursued him. Ah, but mentally was another story. She'd fantasized about him. Oh boy. Had she ever.

She'd even lusted after his suggestion that when they got back to the States, he would introduce her to Cade. She'd imagined doing both brothers, but that, of course, had never happened.

Too many things had gone wrong during the Terrorist Wars. After Tyler had been taken captive, she'd been left wide open to the mandatory R & R. Servicing men. Many men.

The intimate way Cade touched her as he frisked her was nice. Her pussy creamed warmly as his hot fingers danced along one side of her neck then the other as he checked her thoroughly for weapons. Pleasure tingled over her skin wherever he touched, despite knowing he was simply doing a body search. She sensed he patted her down slowly on purpose. Stroked her tenderly, committing her curves to memory.

Oh stop it!

He was a man. A bounty hunter. Her enemy.

Despite the thickness of her grandfather's hunting ski jacket, the strength of Cade's fingers swept erotically over one shoulder before moving to her other one. She tensed as his fingers slid into her breast pocket and he withdrew her jackknife and cell phone.

"Not that your cell works out here, being out of range, but I'll confiscate it anyway."

A moment later, his hand dipped beneath her jacket. He danced his long fingers along the waistband of her jeans and she sighed in frustration when he discovered her homemade switchblades in each back pocket.

"You certainly do have as much of a fascination with knives as I do." He chuckled. Looking down at her with an amused smirk on his face, his left eyebrow quirked up in surprise. It was a cute gesture, that thing he did with his eyebrow.

She blinked aside the rogue thought and forced anger into her voice. "Didn't anyone teach you it isn't polite to put a knife to a lady's throat? Or touch her without her permission? It seems you've forgotten the manners your mother taught you."

He answered with a snort and continued frisking her. Her raspy breaths echoed in the air as his palms skimmed along the swell of her hips, then over her ass curves, before sliding intimately down the insides of her legs. Wherever he touched her, his body heat scorched her and she shuddered, biting back her moans.

God, she'd better escape soon or she'd beg him to fuck her, compliments of the X-virus. Not that having sex with him was a bad idea. Far from it. She hadn't been with a hottie, sex-on-a-stick in months. Since that night with the man they called Will Blade.

She groaned in frustration when Cade discovered the small gun she kept strapped to the inside of her left calf. He snorted, lifted her pant leg and unclasped the gun from her holster. His soft, amused laughter was a sensual sound that had her body humming despite her being pissed off at his discoveries. He stuffed the gun into another one of his endless coat pockets.

Tell him to fuck you!

Reena shook her head and fought the naughty idea until it faded into the background. Defiance splashed through her like a black wave.

"You've signed your death warrant, Outlaw. My people will hunt you down and take you out if you hand me over to whoever you're working for. You'll be a corpse within twenty-fours of my death."

"No one's going to die, Red," he said gruffly.

"I'm sure you'll reconsider that thought when you're six feet under."

"Quit with the dramatics, Red. You're tougher than this. At least that's what I've been told."

"Oh? And who told you about me? Your brother?"

"I'll tell you all about it once I have you shackled and near a nice warm fire. You seem to be trembling a little too much. Now come on. We're moving. I have a camp set up about half a mile due south."

With a firm hand to the scruff of her neck, he pulled her away from the tree and then angled her toward the south.

Shit! The last thing she needed was to spend a night in a camp with him. Especially when she might need to orgasm. But her being cuffed, shackled, naked...

The thoughts of him dominating her rolled over her in a sensual wave and she stifled a moan. Moving carefully forward, she made sure her thighs didn't rub together too hard or she'd be moaning out loud for sure. What things had he been told about her? Did he know she was infected? That she'd be begging him for sex pretty soon?

Up until now, she'd managed to keep her infection a secret. Only a handful of her bodyguards knew and a few other trustworthy souls. Hopefully Outlaw didn't know and she'd be able to escape before she resorted to shameless begging.

Chapter Three

Cade Outlaw wasn't one who gawked at a woman. He preferred to play it cool. Preferred not to let a woman know he was interested in her until he was *really* interested. But hell, these days there weren't many women around because of the virus. He'd trusted women once. Not anymore, compliments of a woman he'd known overseas.

He certainly didn't trust this one, although she did have all his senses firing up to full alert and his body primed and reacting. Especially when he'd frisked her.

Oh yeah, his male instincts kicked in big-time while patting her down for weapons. Her soft, seductive curves beneath his calloused fingertips as he brushed areas where she might conceal a weapon had him groaning to himself and his cock hardening in appreciation. Everything about her blew him away, and nothing ever blew him away. At least not since he'd been a teenager.

Whenever she spoke, her voice melted over him in delicious waves like the chocolate icing his brother's woman Laurie poured on the chocolate cake he and his brothers loved so much. Red sounded whispery, bedroom smoky, and she possessed a very strong, determined voice, but then she had to in order to be the leader of the Resistance.

He couldn't inhale her sweet, sexy female fragrance enough. Her scent was a combination of delicate flowers, soap and prime female. The sight of her flesh affected him, too. When he'd yanked up her jacket, her top had edged up, allowing him a visual of her creamy smooth flesh, not to mention her ringed bellybutton. That sight was the beginning of the end for him. He tensed in awareness every time she so much as shifted.

She sat on a downed log, staring angrily into the crackling fire, her wrists cuffed, ankles shackled, snowflakes lacing the sweet tumble of fluffy, shoulder-length, red hair that peeked from beneath a black wool toque.

This was the first time he'd gotten this close after months of tracking her. He was surprised she'd let him follow her so easily today. She seemed to not have a care in the world. He'd overheard Laurie whispering about Red to Tyler a few mornings ago. They thought Cade was still asleep, but he'd been awake, sneaking around and eavesdropping on their conversation, hoping to learn tidbits about Red. Laurie had said Red was taking a break and would probably end up going to her grandfather's cabin in the woods.

A few discreet inquiries regarding Reena Wilde, and he'd discovered the name of her late grandparents and where they had a cabin. Hell, if it been this easy for him to find her, he wouldn't be surprised if there were more bounty hunters on her ass. It was why he should be getting her to the government—pronto—instead of cozying up to her by a campfire in the middle of a snowstorm.

But he was bone weary after barely any sleep over the last few days—in anticipation of capturing her. He could have gone in and gotten her any time since discovering the cabin. But she could have had the place booby trapped or worse, so he'd waited patiently for her to come out into the open and far away from that cabin.

From the way she'd taken off, her reflexes were in top-notch working order and, thankfully, so were his.

Being this close to her had his hormones sizzling like a son of a bitch. Her pictures certainly didn't do her justice. She was pretty as hell in person, and thinking of wrapping his hands into that flaming red hair and kissing her luscious mouth made his cock scream with need. She had big hazel eyes framed by long lashes and a gentle spattering of freckles over high, rosy cheekbones. Yes, a looker, and past experience proved he needed to beware of these types as they were deceiving.

Instincts told him if he permitted his emotions—make that his hormones—to get the better of him and he let down his guard, she wouldn't hesitate killing him in order to escape. It had happened once before with another woman during the Terrorist Wars. He'd let down his guard and had the knife scars to prove it.

"The food will be done in a few minutes," he said. His gaze was jolted back to her when she licked her pouty lips while she stared at the frying bacon and eggs. He always celebrated a capture with bacon and eggs. Besides, he was starving.

"I'm not hungry." Her soft reply spiked his heart rate.

"That's fine. It'll leave more for me."

She grunted in annoyance. Even that sound was sexy.

After a moment of silence, she asked, "Who hired you?"

"I was wondering when curiosity would get the better of you." He chuckled and she threw him a fierce scowl. He laughed again, enjoying the sweet way his gut clenched as she scrunched her forehead in her pissed off state. Maybe he should let her suffer a little while longer with curiosity. Or maybe he should get this conversation rolling so he could lay all the cards on the table. He opted for the latter.

"I've been hired by the United States Government," he stated. He wasn't surprised when she laughed first then followed that by cursing him up one side of his body and down the other, telling him what a stupid idiot he was. When she finished cursing, she laughed again and he got the feeling she knew something he didn't.

"Obviously you find this amusing," he said as he turned the several strips of bacon with a fork. The bacon was done. Way over done, but with her reaction, he'd lost his appetite.

"I find *you* amusing. What do your brothers think about you working for the United States Government?" She spat the last three words at him as if they were dirt.

He certainly understood her hatred for the dictatorship, especially when they so actively endorsed removing women's rights, making rape legal. "My brothers don't have a problem with how money comes in to pay the bills."

"Blood money," she grumbled, her lips twisting in disgust.

"As I said earlier, no one's going to die."

She shook her head. "Do you think you can just walk me in without any blood being shed? I've got an entourage a mile long waiting to hear back from me, and if I don't check in by sundown they'll be on your ass so fast you'll wish you'd gone through that ice out there and drowned."

"And here I thought you liked me."

"You're an asshole." She rolled her man-killing eyes at him and set her jaw in a firm pout. He'd irritated her with his remark and she stared at him, either trying to gauge if her words had scared him or trying to figure out another avenue of attack.

"You don't scare easy, do you?" she finally said.

"Nothing to be scared about. Now have yourself some bacon and eggs."

He forked two strips of bacon and two eggs onto the small aluminum plate he carried with him whenever tracking a bounty.

He was surprised when she lifted her cuffed hands and accepted the plate. He was equally surprised when she turned it, allowing the bacon and eggs to slide off onto the ground between her shackled legs.

Okay, she was trying to irritate the shit out of him. And it was working. She'd wasted some damned good food.

"I said I'm not hungry." She grinned and then whipped the plate as if it were a Frisbee, off into the looming darkness.

He shrugged, pretending her ruining a perfectly good meal didn't rub him the wrong way. "Well don't come crying to me tonight when the wolves decide this place smells good and they drag you off into the woods and eat you."

Just like he wouldn't mind eating her.

He ripped a hunk of bread off the loaf Laurie had baked for him after learning he was heading out for a bounty. He hadn't told her he was going after her friend Reena or she would have laced the bread with rat poison.

Just thinking of Laurie had him smiling. She enjoyed playing mother hen to the four men currently living at the Outlaw farm. Aside from his brother Mac and himself, she also cooked for Tyler and his best friend Hunter—her two lovers.

He sighed at the memories of what happened when darkness descended over the Outlaw farm. That's when Laurie and Tyler and Hunter headed off to the bedroom the three of them shared. Their guttural moans and her whimpers would send him and Mac scurrying outside to get away from what was going on behind closed doors.

Cade knew something was going on between Hunter and Tyler, too. It was evident in the way the two men looked at each other—expressions filled with caring and need and love.

The two had suffered years of torture in a terrorist prison. They'd also shared a prison cell for several years before being rescued. After returning to the States, they'd seduced Laurie into their bed.

But he and Mac never complained about the erotic groans and moans coming from that bedroom at night, because they knew how lucky they were to have the youngest Outlaw brother back alive. Lucky, too, that Tyler had a strong woman like Laurie to accept him and his male lover.

Cade didn't know if he would be able to share a woman with another man. Some of his brothers had been able to share. But he wasn't sure he could do it with a woman he loved. These days, however, men had to adapt. There were so few women to go around. He'd finally come to the conclusion he may not end up with a wife in the traditional sense.

"What's got you all smiling? Are you picturing me getting ripped apart by wolves? I guess all you really would have to do is bring my head back to get your bounty," she said coolly from the other side of the fire.

"They want you alive. They just want to talk."

"See? That's why I find you amusing. With you being an Outlaw, I wouldn't have expected you to buy bullshit like that. The government needs me dead." She reached up with her cuffed wrists and brushed a stray strand of hair off her rosy cheek.

"Actually they want you to come in and negotiate a peace agreement. They're willing to talk."

"Over my dead body," she whispered.

She didn't believe the government. Hell, he hadn't believed them either. At first. But a close friend of his who worked inside the government, a man Cade trusted, had confirmed the request was legit.

"There's something you should know, Red. Your father is now working with the people you hate so much, and he's been able to convince the president that having you on their side would be more productive than having you dead and a martyr...or in prison. So they've asked me to bring you in so you and the president can come up with some compromise."

He'd expected her to be surprised at the news of her father being involved. Or at least doubtful. Instead she merely shook her head.

"My father is dead," she said softly.

"Well, he was very much alive when I left him several days ago. If something's happened in the meantime that I should know about—"

"He's dead to me," she clarified.

She raised her head and looked straight at him. The pain shining in her eyes unexpectedly rocked him.

Cade inhaled slowly, trying to settle his composure. He hadn't figured he would be in the middle of some family dispute. Whatever her father had done, she wasn't happy about it. Her father had reassured him that once she found out he was involved, she wouldn't be a problem. Looked like daddykins didn't know his daughter as well as he thought. Or maybe her father wanted her dead just like the others? No, the guy seemed sincere. His face had glowed with love and even remorse. His voice had filled with regret when he'd told Cade he'd been away from his daughter too long. His wife was dead and Reena was the only thing left in his life. Sincerity like that couldn't be faked.

"Okay, so you two had a falling out. He still wants to talk and I still need to bring you in."

She didn't say anything. She didn't have to. The woman remained totally pissed at him. He could tell by the way her mouth twisted tight and the muscles in her jaw twitched.

"We'll have to spend the night here."

Her head snapped up. Surprise and panic flared in her eyes. "Why can't we head back to my cabin? I'm sure I can find it in the dark."

He shook his head. Roaming around in the storm could prove fatal. They could get lost, one of them could trip and break a bone and, besides, he had no idea how many weapons she had in that cabin. She could have anticipated getting captured and set a trap.

Call him paranoid, but she was a resourceful woman and he wouldn't put anything past her. Even if they did make it to the cabin and he permitted her to call her Resistance friends as she'd said she needed to do, she could call at a predetermined time and give them some sort of code indicating trouble. Nope, it was better this way.

"We'll leave at first light. That's final."

"Oh, come on. It's cold out here."

"You've got me to keep you warm," he teased, but her cold glare had him dashing any such hopes of snuggling under the covers with her.

Sighing, he grabbed a tin cup from his packsack. He'd have to eat his supper out of the cup and retrieve his plate later. He doubted he could find it. There was already a thin layer of snow covering everything.

As he scooped his dinner into his cup, she merely rolled her eyes at him—indicating he was a hopeless case—shook her head and focused her attention back to the fire. Okay, so she was giving him the cold shoulder treatment. Figures. He'd finally caught himself an unattached and very attractive woman and she wouldn't give him the time of day. Man, sometimes he just had the most rotten luck.

While he ate in silence, she sat quietly, not saying a word, not taking her cold gaze from the fire, and he shivered involuntarily at her icy stare. When he finished, he unpacked the emergency plastic to place over the nearby lean-to he'd constructed last night. They would use this shelter tonight. Hopefully by morning she would be a little more receptive to a warm meal.

* * * * *

Since the night Will Blade had entertained that succulent red-haired woman, he hadn't been able to get her out of his mind. He'd tasted her that evening. She'd been as sweet as sin and sexy as hell. The erotic way she gazed at him when he'd kneeled between her naked thighs, her strawberry-red hair tumbling to just above her plump, pink nipples, her succulent lips parted as she panted and waited expectantly for him to take her pussy into his mouth had made him so damned aroused he hadn't been able to sleep for several nights after the encounter.

Heck, who was he kidding? He hadn't had a proper night sleep since seeing her that first time. Why he hadn't taken more time pleasuring her eluded him—fucking her up against the door, pumping fiercely into her, her cries of arousal undoing the cold tight lid on his emotions. He hadn't been able to tie up the fact he wanted to take her again and again. That's why he needed to kill her and get some peace.

He stood behind a tree, his finger on the trigger of his rifle, keeping an eye on Reena Wilde and Cade Outlaw as they spoke around a fire. His last encounter with Cade was still fresh in his mind, despite it being several weeks ago. Cade had made it clear he would kill Blade if he went near Red again. He might have to take out Cade as well tonight.

He'd been floored when his boss Bev White had given him the assassination assignment against Red. Not because he had to kill someone, but because Reena was Red, the notorious leader of the Resistance.

He'd known she was different. Her strength showed in the defiant way she'd carried herself when he'd first seen her at the Pleasure Palace, and then again when he'd met her at the safe house after she'd been rescued.

Blade shook his head and tried to remember back to a time before the Wars. To before the X-virus. When a normal evening meant taking a woman out to dinner and then to his bed. Where a regular work day meant performing pap smears, breast exams and informing a patient of her pregnancy, then moving to the adjoining examination room to tell another patient she had stage four ovarian cancer.

Fuck, his life had all been so normal. So routine he'd even pondered the idea of settling and marrying a sweet, quiet nurse he'd been dating. And then the X-virus had come along and screwed his world. Hell, it had screwed everyone's world.

Yet even in this crappy new States there were still jewels. Sexy women like his boss Bev and Tyler's woman Laura...and now Reena.

Reena. Or maybe he should call her Red. That had been his nickname for her. He'd never imagined the Resistance called her Red, too.

Red, with the flaming red hair and gorgeous hazel eyes. Red, who'd proudly worn gold rings on her large pink nipples and teased him with a bellybutton ring, and made his knees melt when he'd seen her labia rings.

She hadn't shied away from showing off those rings. Maybe she'd had them removed since their meeting? Or had she accepted them as part of her body?

The first time he'd entered the safe house where the SKULL men had taken her, his pulse had picked up speed as her moans echoed from one of the bedrooms. When he'd peeked into the open doorway and spied her lying spread-eagle on the bed, his body had tightened in awareness, his cock and balls tensing and swelling like a son of a bitch.

She'd been naked and moaning. Damned irresistible too with her tangled red hair billowing around her face while she thrashed beneath the mouths of two men—one tending her breasts and one lapping between her thighs. She'd begged them to fuck her.

Oh man, he'd wanted to undress. Wanted to take her. To claim her for his own.

But she was only pleading because of the drugs. He wanted more than just fucking a woman pumped full of sex drugs. He didn't know how long he'd watched those SKULL men fucking her. Could have been minutes. Could have been hours. But the imprint of her naked and writhing beneath the erotic handling of the men was forever etched into his mind.

Sexy woman.

And she would have to die.

Here. Now. Right in front of Cade Outlaw.

Lifting the assault rifle, he peered through the night-vision scope and took a bead on Red. She sat on a fallen log in front of a small fire that fully illuminated her. Vulnerability flickered across her face in the waves of yellow firelight.

One shot to the brain and she wouldn't feel a thing. His finger tightened on the trigger. He held his breath.

Hesitated.

Man. This was harder than the last time he'd tried to pull the trigger. Cold sweat popped out on his brow as he took aim. He hoped she would forgive him for this.

Many women preferred death as opposed to the virus they carried. Would she welcome death? Would she thank him for putting her out of her misery when they met in heaven or wherever people went after they died?

He continued to hesitate. Stiffened as a cold blade of death cut painfully into the skin of his neck.

"Déjà vu, dead man." The voice exploded through the stillness of the snowflake-drenched night air, much the same way it had several months earlier when Cade Outlaw had stopped Will from killing Red. Just as he planned tonight.

"This knight-in-shining-armor fetish you've got regarding saving this chick's ass is getting to be a real pain in *my* ass," Blade replied. He didn't ease up on the trigger.

If Cade followed through in killing him, Blade would make sure Red joined him in the afterlife. It almost seemed sweet and fitting. To die with the woman he'd been lusting after for months.

"I'm glad you still have your humor, Blade. I'm sure it'll keep you warm in your grave," Cade growled quietly.

"Just as Red will keep me warm in my grave when I pull the trigger," Blade warned.

The harsh press of the skinning knife against his neck loosened. A warm trickle of blood dripped along the side of his neck. The cut couldn't be deep or he'd be dead. It appeared Cade had other plans for him.

"I made myself clear what would happen if you came near Red again."

He sounded pissed. That was a good sign. It meant Cade had feelings for Red. Will would have to play those emotions to keep himself alive.

"I guess you should have killed me. Then and now. You're getting soft in your old age, Outlaw."

"The ladies don't think so," Cade retorted coolly.

Sex. Always on the mind of a man these days—especially with so few women around.

"Drop the rifle...nice and easy...and I'll let you live," Cade instructed.

"You already let me live, and because of it you're at a disadvantage." Blade slightly jerked his assault rifle up in acknowledgement. Tension zipped through the air from Cade.

"Or maybe that's an advantage, Outlaw. Depends on how you look at it. A group of hunters are tracking you...and the female. About four miles west. They've made camp for the night. You'll need an extra hand if you don't outrun them."

"I know. Now drop the rifle, Blade. Then drop any other weapons you have on you and we can join Red at camp."

It was the truth. There were several men following Cade's trail. Will just hoped Cade believed him. "I'm serious, Cade."

"I know, Will."

Okay, so the guy was keeping his enemy alive in case he needed help? Will had to give it to Cade, he was either an idiot or he had the balls to trust that Will would help when the chips fell. The trust probably came because Blade was Colter Outlaw's good friend.

Fuck. He should kill Cade and take Red for himself. He just might be sorry if he didn't.

Blade sighed. He surrendered his rifle and allowed Cade to search him for his other weapons.

* * * * *

The handcuffs that bit into Reena's wrists and the shackles lacing her ankles did nothing but cause sensual images of having sex with Cade to whirl around in her mind.

Men! She'd come out here alone for a reason. To de-stress. Instead she wasn't getting anything *but* stress. Where the hell was Outlaw, anyway?

Desperation shifted through her as she stared into the snow-swirling darkness. Nothing moved except snowflakes. They were coming down hard, spiraling out of the night like tiny demons and covering the ground in a white fluffy blanket.

It was getting colder, too. Crisp air chilled her cheeks and every time she breathed another plume of mist shot from her mouth, blinding her. Despite that, a fevered neediness raced through her.

Her pussy throbbed. Wetness had drenched the area between her thighs and her body had tightened with sexual tension when Cade had secured a plastic sheet over the small lean-to on the other side of the fire pit.

He hadn't spoken anything more while he'd set up the sleeping quarters, but she'd caught him casting her glances. Hungry and hot looks that made her very aware he hadn't been with a female in awhile.

Damn him! Where was he anyway? He'd taken off to search for the plate she'd whipped into the forest and to take a leak more than ten minutes ago. More than long enough. If she'd thought he would be gone this long, she could have masturbated, had an orgasm and been good to go. It would have been tough with her hands shackled, but the rough bark of the fallen tree she sat on would cause enough friction. Maybe she could start...

Footsteps echoed in the dark perimeter outside the warm glow of the firelight and her pulse pounded with alertness. Maybe Cade had been gone so long because someone had killed him? Her people? Or someone else?

Regret slithered through her like a snake. She didn't like the idea of Cade being dead. She liked his brother Tyler and didn't want harm to come to Cade, even if he was a lowly bounty hunter. Besides, her attraction for him when he'd first caught her on the ice wasn't totally the virus. It was feminine instinct. She sensed he wouldn't hurt her. No matter how bitter the Terrorist Wars had made him.

When he first caught her, she had been pissed, but there had also been an attraction similar to what she'd experienced with only one other man. The man she knew as Will Blade. He was raw lust and powerful arousal rolled into one hot explosion.

Just as she thought of Will, his image drifted out of the darkness like a ghost. For a moment, she could do nothing but blink in shock and wonder if perhaps she was experiencing a fantasy of him. But when he threw her an amused smirk, emotions sizzled inside her. Happiness, confusion, need, want. Arousal.

What in the world was he doing here?

Behind him, Cade appeared. Concern ripped through her over how Cade held a rifle pointed at Blade's back.

Cade's mouth was twisted in anger and his eyes were narrowed with suspicion. In contrast, Blade seemed calm as a cucumber. Except for the smirk on his face when he gazed at her, he appeared as cool as the night she'd approached him in his bedroom.

Immediately she knew why he was acting so composed. The attraction between them still existed. The need of wanting him hit her like a searing arrow the instant his familiar pine-and-mild-soap scent whispered against her nostrils.

A man wouldn't look at her coolly, dispassionately, yet his eyes so full of fire unless he was trying to run from his attraction to her. Or hide from it, which—on the surface—he appeared to do quite well. Yet beneath the surface, he was doing a piss-poor job. He held himself tensely, awareness flaring in his eyes as he studied her like she was the untamed mate that had gotten away.

"Sit down on that stump. I don't need you snapping her neck," Cade instructed.

Snap her neck? What in the world?

She drew her attention to Cade. His fierce gaze was fixed on Will as he sat down a good six feet away from her. Cade warily eyed Will as if he were her mortal enemy. Boy was he ever wrong.

Blade's scent increased in intensity as the wind whipped against her, making her body tighten in hyper awareness. Making her breasts ache with a need to be held in his large hands. To have both men licking her body. Touching her. Kissing her. Making love to her.

Reena tried hard not to moan at the sudden burst of submissive need welcoming her into its embrace. But she *did* moan. It was a sultry sexy sound that made Cade and Will Blade snap their gazes to her in full-awareness mode. Reena closed her eyes and broke the erotic-magnetic connection.

Both men remained silent, except for their breaths lashing the air.

Cade—harsh and erratic.

Blade—coolly even. Forced. Too even.

They were both fighting their reactions to her. Just as she was fighting them.

God only knew how long she could hold out.

* * * * *

Secrets. They zipped between Red and Blade like sparks of electricity. Cade saw their awareness of each other in the way their eyes sparkled with lust amidst the violent swirls of snowflakes. The storm was picking up intensity. Somewhere, far off in the distance, the wind roared. Once it hit them, it would be a damned cold night.

Unless...

He shook away the visions of naked feminine skin and concentrated on remaining professional.

"I can see SKULL wants Red dead," Cade said. He may as well let Red in on what was happening. That Blade was an assassin. Here to kill her.

Reena's sharp inhalation and Blade's eyes narrowing in anger encouraged Cade to continue. If there was something between these two, an erotic connection or whatever the hell it was, he'd squash it right now. No woman would want a man who had been sent to kill her.

"It beats what you seem intent on doing to her. Taking her back to them alive. They'll torture her until they get the information they want. And they will succeed. You should know that more than anyone, especially with your background."

Cade grimaced at the taunt about his past. He wasn't proud of what he'd done during the Wars, but his acts had been a necessary evil. He'd extracted plenty of good intelligence to help fight the terrorists.

"Besides," Blade said. "My way will save her a whole lot of unnecessary pain. Unless she's into pain," he whispered.

"You...you've been sent to kill me?" she asked, but the hostility and anger Cade wanted to see didn't accumulate in her eyes. She seemed stunned and maybe even a bit fascinated at having Blade here.

Blade nodded and she frowned in disappointment. Yes, something was going on between them. Hell, what had she expected with Blade showing up? That she would free him and then her and Blade could have a frolicking good time in the snowstorm? Streaks of jealousy and anger slammed through him like battering rams.

"Okay, so you two know each other. Maybe you should let me in on how well?" Cade snapped as he kept the rifle on Blade and tossed a piece of driftwood onto the fire. He wasn't worried about the sparks showering into the swirl of snow. The group of hunters Blade suggested were out there wouldn't see anything through the storm.

Neither of them answered, confirming his suspicions.

Fine, then. Whatever was going on had nothing to do with him. He was a bounty hunter not a jealous asshole. He stomped on his anger and focused his attention on what Blade had said earlier. "Those men following us. Any ideas who they are?"

"Men are following us?" Reena cried.

She sounded surprised not hopeful, though, which probably meant she really was out here all alone. How the Resistance would allow her to do something so stupid said plenty about this group she headed. They were idiotic and untrustworthy if they didn't even have protection for their leader.

Bounty hunters he could deal with. He probably knew them. He may be able to get them to back off, too. But if they were coming after him because of Red, then they needed to get moving out of the area and pronto.

"Hunters looking for females," Blade said coolly.

Cade stifled a curse. Men looking for a woman were desperate. They would kill both himself and Blade in order to get their hands on her. Somehow they'd discovered she was out here.

Cade turned to her and inhaled sharply. Wisps of hair caressed her red cheeks, making her look gorgeous. Her sultry lips were parted and had him thinking of oral sex. Suddenly she tugged off her hat and her fluffy hair blew wildly in the wind. He'd love to thrust his fingers into those silky strands and hold her head while he fucked her mouth.

Cade blinked in stunned amazement at the direction his thoughts were heading. He didn't know what was going on. Usually he was professional as hell, but the smoldering whimper that escaped her mouth moments earlier when Blade had appeared, and now the heated flush in her cheeks and sparks in her eyes, screamed sex. He struggled to regain his composure.

"You probably have a leak in your organization. Too many people know your whereabouts," Cade said, his voice way too thick with arousal for his own comfort.

She didn't answer. Her lips parted more, as if she were about to speak, but she remained silent. He'd seen a similar look on a few other women's faces before. During the Wars' mandatory R & R sessions the soldiers were ordered to participate in. He'd only lain with women who were volunteers. And some of them had looked at him the same way as Reena.

Hot. Needy. Submissive.

Uneasiness zipped through him. Mentally he went over the notes the government had supplied him regarding Reena "Red" Wilde. There had been no mention of the X-virus. He'd assumed she'd been one of the lucky ones and was unaffected.

Was she infected? A stab of bitter disappointment shifted through him, but it was quickly followed by denial. No, a beautiful, sexy, vibrant woman like her couldn't be infected.

Could she?

Chapter Four

Secret eye signals were snapping between Blade and Reena again and it was pissing Cade off. Suddenly she closed her eyes and nodded in surrender.

"So you want *me* to tell him?" Blade growled. He seemed totally ticked yet something else laced his voice. Excitement? Maybe. Whatever it was, Cade sensed something wild racing through his own veins. Something at the back of his brain warned him if she was infected with the X-virus, she may have one of those versions that would make her needy. Wanting sex. Wanting him. Just as Tyler's woman wanted Tyler and Hunter pretty much every night because of those erotic fantasies she got compliments of the virus.

Man, he was fucking shallow and desperate, wasn't he? To wish Reena would want sex with him simply because she was infected and needy...instead of out of love and caring.

No, she couldn't be infected. There had been no information about her having the X-virus when he'd been hired to hunt her down. Unless they'd left it off or they didn't know...or they hadn't wanted *him* to know.

She shook her head as she caught his gaze. Her cheeks were flushed with embarrassment.

Oh hell.

"She's infected," came Blade's reply.

"Which version?" Cade asked as disappointment and disbelief rocked him. His voice was thick and strangled and distant, as if someone else asked the question.

"The O version," she whispered. Her reply punched him in the gut.

"O" meaning she would need sex. Eventually. She would need to orgasm. At the very least, she would have to masturbate.

The O version was one of the worst mutations a woman could get. With that particular version, a female's brain and reproductive hormones were targeted by the virus, twisting them into a cycle similar to that of cats in heat. Once in the heat phase, she would exhibit a sexually receptive behavior.

Was she entering that phase now? Is that why she appeared so...bedroomy sensual?

The erotic way the pink tip of her tongue wet her full lips made his breath hitch. Her condition must have been one hell of a secret if the government didn't know about it. But it couldn't have been that big a secret if Blade knew.

Cade noticed both of them watching him closely. Most likely waiting for his reaction.

"How often do you need to..." He wanted to ask how often she needed to orgasm, but he couldn't seem to bring himself to say the word.

"I'm fine," she snapped.

"Maybe for now," Blade interjected quickly. "Answer his question."

"I can take care of it myself when the time comes. Now back off. Both of you," she retorted and swung her gaze to the fire.

"And here I thought we could revisit that one night together," Blade remarked and winked at her. Rage splashed through Cade. Why the hell Blade would dangle a night together in her face, in front of him...it was just plain ungentlemanly.

Cade raised Blade's gun and aimed it at his midsection.

"Watch your mouth," he growled, making it quite clear he didn't approve of the way Blade was talking to Red.

Blade glared at him and she said nothing, not that he was expecting her to. Okay, so maybe he was hoping she'd send him a look of thanks.

He shook his head at his puppy-dog thoughts. Man, he was pathetic, wasn't he? Looking for appreciation from her.

"The storm is going to be nasty." Blade's comment ripped Cade back to reality.

He was right. The wind had picked up, driving a thick sheet of ice cold flakes against them. Reena had lifted her cuffed wrists and was rubbing her hands near the fire.

Shit. He'd forgotten he'd made her drop her mittens back on the lake. Her hands would be on the icy side.

"Stand up, Red. Time to tuck you in," Cade instructed.

Her head snapped up and she glared at him with pure hatred.

"I'm not going anywhere," she snarled and returned her attention to the fire.

"The lean-to is a hell of a lot warmer. Out here you'll freeze to death."

"Out here she's got me to keep her warm." Blade chuckled.

Cade grinned as Red cursed a blue streak at Blade. She grabbed her hat from the ground, shook off the snow and slipped the hat onto her head. She stood.

"You're colder than an iceberg," she retorted to Blade, then calmly waited for Cade to unlock the chain that secured her ankles to the downed log she'd been sitting on.

"Stand right there," Cade ordered and quickly unlocked the chain from her ankle cuffs.

To his surprise, she did as he asked and her heavy-lidded eyes had him swallowing at his dry throat as his cock tightened painfully.

Keeping an eye on both of them, he quickly removed his last pair of handcuffs from his belt and tossed them onto Blade's lap. Cade jerked his gun toward the chain from which he'd just released Red. "You know what to do."

Blade frowned and shook his head. "You're making a mistake—"

"Just do it!" His patience was running thin, especially with Reena standing so close and her seductive sweet scent sailing on the wind, teasing his nostrils until he could barely think straight.

Blade shrugged, leaned over and grabbed the chain. He secured one of the cuffs to the end of the chain and the other to his left wrist. The clicks of the cuffs snapping home shot through the air, making Cade sigh in relief. Blade was now locked up tight.

"After you," Cade instructed Red and swung the rifle toward the lean-to.

She moved into the makeshift shelter where he'd laid out one bear fur as a bed and another as a blanket. It hadn't been easy carrying all that around in his backpack, but it sure beat freezing while tracking Red.

She slipped off her boots, crawled over the bear rug and covered herself with the second skin.

"Would you at least unshackle my legs? The metal is making me cold," she said softly, keeping her voice low so only he could hear. She stuck her socked feet out from beneath the fur and Cade caved with compassion. The foot-long length of chain between her legs did look uncomfortable, and so did the cuffs around her ankles.

Damn her. She sure did know how to push his buttons, didn't she? He never let a bounty go without shackles. It's why he was always known for catching his man or—in this case—his woman. Hell, he didn't want her to think he was an iceberg like Blade. He could cuff her to himself tonight, preventing her from escaping. That wouldn't go over well, though. He may need to move fast in case of company from those hunters or if Blade tried anything.

In his thoughts he was saying no to her, but the rest of him was doing her bidding. Reaching for the keys at his waist, he removed the one for the shackles.

"Maybe you aren't as stupid as I thought you were, Outlaw. There's hope for you yet," she said. To his surprise, she smiled at him, the curves of her luscious lips tilting sweetly upward into what he could only call a sunbeam that wrapped him in warmth.

Oh man, he could drown in that sweet smile.

"Thanks, I appreciate it," she said in that soft, intriguing voice he loved. He tried not to notice how feminine and clean she appeared as she stuffed her feet beneath the bear skin. Tried to ignore the flare of heat shifting low in his belly and into his balls and cock as she peered up at him with her fuck-me eyes.

Okay man, chill. She had the virus and that's all he was reading in her eyes. Just the virus.

"I'll be back soon. I have to get Blade ready for the night."

She said nothing and snuggled under the fur. He waited until she closed her eyes before he grabbed the ankle restraints and left.

"Are you sure she isn't going to run?" Blade asked a couple of moments later when Cade joined him by the fire. Obviously he'd seen Cade remove her shackles.

"She's smart. She won't run without her boots." He held them up, and then placed them near the fire sideways with the openings facing the heat.

"She's domesticated you already." Blade chuckled as he nodded at the way Cade had set up her boots.

Irritation slammed through Cade. He knew he shouldn't offer Blade any explanations, but he did anyway. Then maybe Blade would keep his mouth shut.

"They're damp. She'll need them dry in the morning."

"And what about her? You gonna have her nice and dry by morning?"

Cade ignored the sexual innuendo and tossed a couple more pieces of wood on the fire. The son of a bitch was only trying to irritate the shit out of him. It was working.

"You won't be dry because you'll be sleeping out here tonight. Make sure you keep that fire going nice and strong or you'll be doing me a favor when I find you frozen to death."

Blade chuckled lightly and held up his cuffed wrist.

"Can't very well keep the fire going with my not being able to move more than a few feet."

"That's your problem, isn't it?" Cade snapped.

"It'll be your problem when those hunters catch up to us. And if they've sniffed out the woman, you can bet they're going to be up before the crack of dawn and will continue through the snowstorm, and then they'll see the fire."

"Then do us all a favor and stay awake and keep the fire small," Cade growled. He would be staying awake to make damn sure Red didn't make a run for it. He headed into the darkness to rip some more bark and branches from a nearby dead tree, as well as collect several armloads of wood.

He placed them within Blade's reach, but Blade's gaze was fixated on the opening of the lean-to. Another bolt of irritation slammed into him and he returned to the mouth of the shelter. Ensuring Blade couldn't see the woman, he propped himself on the cold ground right in the doorway, turned his back toward Red and faced the heat of the crackling fire.

If he were smart, he'd shackle her legs again. But when it came to women, he'd never been smart. Why start now?

* * * * *

Reena snuggled deeper under the bear skins, pulling her hat down around her ears, and told herself her trembling had everything to do with the freezing air breathing against her face and nothing to do with the two men sitting just outside the makeshift shelter.

She wasn't pissed off at being captured, at least not anymore. Not since she'd been able to wiggle her wrists out of the handcuffs beneath the camouflage of the bear skin. Hell, she was an expert at escape, especially getting out of handcuffs. Her wrists were unusually tiny and most handcuffs were designed for men's wrists. She'd expected better from an Outlaw. It appeared Cade wasn't as swift as his youngest brother Tyler.

On the other hand, she hadn't missed that he'd taken her boots. Even if he had left them, she wouldn't be going anywhere. Not in this storm. She wasn't stupid. Unlike Will "Blade" Smith who'd been caught.

She'd known Will was an assassin. All the people who worked for SKULL were assassins. She just hadn't expected Will to actually come here to try to kill her. Especially not after the hot sexcapade they'd shared that one evening.

She'd tried to show Cade she didn't care if Will wanted her dead, but she did care...and it hurt. Bad. Will came here to assassinate her and that meant she owed Cade for saving her life.

She hated being in debt to anyone. When she got the chance, she wouldn't be able to kill Cade. Plus, he was Tyler's brother and she couldn't do that to Tyler.

Will, on the other hand, was another story. She just might have to take him out. He was her biggest threat. Both men were threats. She'd seen the erotic gazes on their faces when Will revealed she had the virus.

The heat in their eyes was unmistakable. Men were so predictable, but she'd be lying if she said she hadn't reacted to those scorching looks.

Arousal shifted through her as she drifted, thinking about the two of them. Of the things they would do to her.

If she let them...

~ ~ ~ ~ ~

She was tense. Needy. Breathing roughly. Her senses alert. Her body on fire.

Just watching the two men, inhaling the powerful pine, delicate soap and male sweat, made arousal sweep through her so strongly she moaned at its intensity.

Blade crawled into the small lean-to first, crouching beside her, his hot fingers scorching her skin as he slipped the bear rug from her body and helped her sit up.

"I have to orgasm," she panted as intense need writhed through her like a coiled snake.

"I know. Cade and I will help you. Let's get your coat off."

Heat wafted off him in waves. She couldn't wait to taste him. To touch his hard body. Take his cock into her mouth. Into her pussy. Into her ass.

Then there was Cade. She wanted him in a different way than she yearned for Blade. Where she was attracted to Will's mask of coldness, she was just as intrigued by Cade's warmth.

Cade smelled like fresh outdoors and freedom. An intoxicatingly delicious combination. He might even be a man she could settle down with.

Reena tried to push away that last idea. She wanted to be the one in charge when it came to Cade. She didn't know why she wanted to resist him. Resist the strong, overwhelming desires lashing her like a tidal wave. The scorching way he studied her, as if seeking permission to gaze upon her naked flesh, both irritated and aroused her at the same time.

She sensed Cade understood she wanted both of them. She held her breath as his gaze dropped to her naked breasts. He groaned softly and a burn of arousal shifted through her.

He began to undress and it seemed as if she'd waited a lifetime for this moment when they'd only truly met today.

Cade pulled off his jacket, bunched it and laid it down on the bear blanket, meaning for her to use it as her pillow when the time came. Such a chivalrous man. Would he be the same during sex? Just thinking of the hot sex, of having both men wanting her, fucking her, had her creaming with anticipation.

For years she'd cursed the X-virus. Cursed the need for orgasming when the craving became unbearable. But right now, at this moment, she loved the arousal shifting like spears of lightning through her. If she didn't have the virus, she wouldn't be able to drop her inhibitions to a man or, in this case, men.

At the soft rustle of clothing being removed, her mind became intensely heavy with lust. Her body twisted tight with desire and she melted into the pulsing throb of arousal. She wanted this. She needed this.

A hot hand touched her shoulder and she hissed at the wicked flame of Cade's flesh.

She sat on the warm fur in the pale light. Cade and Blade crouched before her. Both were naked, primed and ready to take her, their long, thick erections spearing out from between their thighs, their swollen sacs beneath.

In a split second, she became lost in the dark dance of desire. Reaching out, she curled a hand around each of their cocks. Both men groaned as she gently pulled them toward her.

"Closer," she moaned, wanting to take both of their cocks into her mouth at the same time, knowing it was impossible. They were too big together. Their hot flesh throbbed in her palms. Their heated lengths pulsed against her fingers. Cade was just a bit thicker than Will. Will just a bit longer than Cade, but Cade was catching up fast as his shaft continued to harden and lengthen.

Truthfully, she had never expected to see Will again. Had never expected an Outlaw to capture her.

Yet a small section of her heart sang with joy at these two men being here. A joy she didn't quite understand since they were both a danger to her.

Nonetheless, instinctively she knew if these two men had been anyone other than Cade and Will, she wouldn't be bursting with joy.

No, they wouldn't hurt her. Not physically. Sexually, though. Yes, sexually they would hurt her nicely. She would welcome the pleasure-pain because with two big cocks like these, there was going to be both.

She decided to take Cade first. It would melt the guilt she'd seen earlier flashing on his face. Guilt that he wasn't sure he was doing the right thing by fucking her this way despite wanting her.

She pulled on Cade's cock some more, urging him forward. Opening her mouth, she covered his flared cock head with her lips.

He groaned. The erotic sound smoothed over her senses. She took him deeper, his hard, velvet cock filling her mouth.

God, she should be embarrassed or nervous, shouldn't she? Taking a man she'd only just met into her mouth? But she was neither. She wanted him. Wanted both of them. This was the stuff of her fantasies. And she needed an orgasm tonight. Needed it bad.

Strong masculine fingers pried her grasp free from Blade's cock. Disappointment zipped through her at the loss. She quickly recovered as Blade's hot hands curled over her bare shoulders, urging her to lean back against the fallen log Cade had used to build the lean-to.

Cade moved with her, his cock impaling her mouth as he placed his feet on both sides of her hips. Looking up at him, her pulse thundered as he gazed down at her. Lust sparkled brilliantly in his eyes. She could imagine how she appeared to him. A naked woman, sitting on a bear skin, her back pressed against a log with his cock stuffed nicely between her lips.

Her tummy tightened erotically. She liked how she appeared to him.

"Reena, keep sucking," he whispered, his voice urgent.

Lifting her hands, she curled them around his backside and grabbed his ass cheeks. They were rock-hard muscle and molten hot. Holding tight, she sucked his shaft. He growled his appreciation and thrust his fingers through her hair, holding her head steady.

She licked the head of his cock and prodded the slit and, from her crazy angle between his legs, she saw his eyes darken. As he moaned, she answered with a groan of her own, imagining his cock sliding into her vagina.

He jerked his hips, bringing his cock deeper into her mouth. Her lips stretched over his hot flesh and his penis throbbed against her tongue. She sucked again and his ragged breath hitched and released.

He liked this.

His eyes fluttered closed. While she rubbed her tongue back and forth in a leisurely pattern under his cock head, his breath grew harder and raspier. In her momentary concentration on Cade, she'd forgotten about Blade. That is, until his hot fingers curled around her ankles and he spread her legs.

God! She shivered with excitement, thinking about the night he'd dropped onto his knees between her thighs and taken her pussy into his mouth. The fierce arousal in his eyes when she'd come had made her believe he could give her so much more. She wondered if tonight he possessed that same look. Wondered if he would leave her wanting again.

She almost came just thinking about him gazing between her thighs. She jolted as Blade's fingers slid between her labia. Her mouth tightened around Cade's flesh as Blade's shoulders widened her legs and he wiggled between them. She whimpered when he began an erotic massage on her clit. His thumb leisurely, seductively killed her with sweet, brutal pleasure.

Cade's hands tightened their hold in her hair and pleasure-pain zipped along her scalp, making her focus her attention back on him. The velvety smoothness of his shaft and elevated veins pressed past her lips. His flesh was heavy in her mouth. Heavy and swollen and hard. And so wonderfully hot.

He began a steady, magnificent plunging with determined, powerful thrusts.

Between her legs, Blade's mouth replaced his fingers. His tongue licked and circled the drenched opening of her vagina. When she tried to clasp her legs around his head to increase the friction, Blade's grip on her thighs tightened, preventing her from doing what she wanted.

She whimpered in protest. Her breasts were throbbing. Her nipples ached. Yet no one touched her there.

Her pussy steamed with a need to orgasm. A need to be penetrated. And with Cade's cock in her mouth, his sensual thrusts and sexy moans of arousal just about drove her insane.

When Blade's warm, firm lips melted over her pussy, shock and pleasure released the wildness within. She didn't expect the fierceness of the orgasm that cascaded through her. It swept the breath from her lungs and all she could do was buck her hips and allow the exquisite explosions to slam into her.

Quickly, he removed his mouth and thrust a couple of fingers into her.

Carnal urges smashed her mind and pleasure racked her. Colors melted with emotions. The climax streamed endlessly, leaving her panting and weak and utterly satisfied.

She'd never experienced such jolts of pleasure. Never knew something so exquisite existed. As she lay gasping around Cade's cock, her pussy spasming with moistness, delightful tingles shivered through her over the sensual rhythm of Cade's thrusts and Will's erotic plunging. The combination swept her into another orgasm.

She tasted pre-come. Dark and delicious. And then Cade's straining flesh tightened and jerked. His hands held the sides of her head and then promptly loosened. To her disappointment, he let go, his cock slipping from her eager lips.

She cried out in protest. Tried to open her eyes, but couldn't. Her eyelids were too heavy.

"Turn her on her side. We'll take her that way."

That was Blade speaking. Calm and authoritative. Hands smoothed over her waist, lifted her and brought her onto her side. She whimpered as the cravings for more sex pulsed through her like a drug.

"She knows what's happening, doesn't she?" Cade's voice. Troubled. Concerned. Aroused.

"She knows."

Cade swore softly. She wondered if he would still want her after she'd had sex with both of them at the same time. The look in his eyes when he'd frisked her, before he'd discovered she had the virus, had been clear. He'd wanted her then. She'd wanted him.

Oh God! Was she crazy? There was no such thing as a traditional husband and wife relationship anymore. One man and one woman was illegal. Besides, she didn't even know Cade or Will. She had to stop thinking this emotional bullshit! Yes, emotions. That's all they were. Emotions and dreams of a young woman who'd once fantasized about Cade Outlaw, a man she'd never met. Until now.

Their breaths were heavy in the air as they lay beside her, one in front, the other behind. Again, she tried to open her eyes, but she couldn't lift her heavy lids. She wondered if the virus was dragging her under. Or the intense pleasure. Or both.

The hand holding her knee lifted her leg high and she cried out as something smooth and wet worked its way into her rear end.

A cock. Lubed.

Oh yes! Anal. She hadn't had anal since... No, she wouldn't go there. Wouldn't ruin this with thoughts of the past.

"She's tight!" Blade groaned.

That meant Cade was in front.

Anticipation pounded through her. She gasped as a warm mouth swept over her left nipple. Cade sucked her tender flesh, the hot pressure almost violent but oh so good. Boy, he knew how to make love to a nipple.

Her body tightened as Blade's cock impaled her ass. Hard and deep. So perfect.

Cade latched onto her nipple with searing fingers, tugging and squeezing. His mouth sucked, his teeth biting softly. It went on forever.

Dark pleasure-pain tingled in her ass as Blade entered and withdrew. Cade's hot body pressed against hers. Reaching down, she blindly grabbed his cock. He was so hard and his erection burned with heat.

"Inside me. Now," she managed to gasp as she fought for breath.

"Demanding little bitch, aren't you?" Cade chuckled around her nipple, his breath caressing her sensitive flesh. The deep timbre of his voice turned her on even more.

"Hurry...just hurry." Desperation played hell with her morals as arousal zinged along her nerves. Blade withdrew and Cade moved quickly. Lying on the rug in front of her, he slipped his cock into her vagina.

She was so wet and on edge, the instant Cade entered her, she exploded. The searing spasms pummeled her. Heat and pleasure and tightness melded into one. Perspiration dotted her skin and every snowflake that swirled onto her flesh made her skin sizzle. With every hard jerk of their hips, the men filled her as she'd never been filled before.

Uncontrollable reactions sliced into her. Laughter. Loving this. Going mad. The orgasm claimed her and tremors powered through her. The male groans were an added aphrodisiac to her pleasure. Soon all three of them were gasping, shuddering and clenching their teeth. Holding each other. Needing each other.

Oh yes, she was going mad...

~ ~ ~ ~ ~

Reena awoke with a start, knowing instantly she'd orgasmed while dreaming of an exquisite ménage with Blade and Cade. Her pussy was sopping wet and soft spasms whispered along her vagina. Her heart pounded against her chest and a thin sheen of perspiration chilled her body.

Wow! That had been one hell of a fantasy!

She struggled to slow her breathing as crisp snow peppered the plastic over the shelter and soft snoring came from somewhere nearby.

Moving her hand upward, she found the edge of the bear rug covering her face and pulled it down just enough to see the sky was getting light. Despite what may have been only five or so hours of sleep, a surprising freshness breathed through her. Time to escape.

If she played her cards right, she'd be back at the cabin within an hour and on her satellite phone, calling in reinforcements. Her hideout had been compromised. Vacation over. Why she thought she could get any peace out here was beyond her. It seemed as if she was destined to look over her shoulder for the rest of her life. She may as well get back to work. That is, if she could get away from here.

Moving as slowly and quietly as possible, she sat up and cursed inwardly at the man hunkered down in the doorway of the shelter. Cade Outlaw lay with his broad back toward her, barring her escape. He was the one who snored softly. Beyond him, snow swirled through the air. The storm was still active.

She shivered as cold air blasted against her damp forehead. Pulling down her hat, she climbed out from beneath the bear rug and crouched. From her perch, she peeked out the opening to see if she could spot her boots and was surprised to find them beside the fire. Blade sat on the ground, his back against the fallen log she'd sat on last night in front of the fire. His gloved hands were cuffed. His head down, he'd tucked his chin against his chest and the lapels of his coat had been tugged up around his ears. He appeared asleep. But experience told her looks could be deceiving.

Nonetheless, she had no choice but to try to get her boots and get the hell out of here. Holding her breath, she crawled toward Cade. As if sensing her nearness, he stirred. She froze, fully expecting him to open his eyes and grab her.

Instead he mumbled something in his sleep and she relaxed. A little.

She inspected his body for weapons and saw a gun in his gloved hand. She dared not try to pry it from him. He'd wake for sure. He probably had her weapons stashed in his pockets, but damned if she'd go through them.

She spied the end of his scabbard protruding from the base of his coat. She'd need to lift the bottom edge to get the knife. That might wake him.

Shit.

She'd have to chance stepping over him in order to get her boots. And walking through the snow would not be good for her socks. Soundlessly she pulled off her socks and thrust them into her pocket. Moving slowly, she held her breath as she stepped over Cade. She tried not to grimace as the wet snow enveloped first one and then the other foot.

She shivered as chills sliced through her. Damn, it was colder than cold!

Thankfully the snow was nice and fluffy and she didn't make a sound as she gritted her teeth and tiptoed through the icy snow toward the smokeless, tiny fire.

Grabbing her boots, Reena dared another glance at Blade who snored softly. She couldn't help but smile at her luck.

Cripes, what a couple of nimrods, falling asleep on the job. She didn't bother to survey Blade for weapons. Cade would have taken care of them. She should search Cade's knapsack, though, but it was too close to him for comfort. She debated whether sitting on the log beside a sleeping Blade in order to put her boots on was a good idea. With her luck, he'd wake and break her neck. She wished she could hang around and ask him if he really would have killed her, but hey, she had better things to do with her time.

She held her boots and crept silently through the snow and away from camp. Behind some nearby bushes, she put on her socks and boots and ignored the shivers racing up her spine. Then she started walking again.

About a hundred yards away, Reena broke into an awkward run through the snow drifts. She covered the rugged terrain at mind-boggling speed despite the deep snow tangling her feet and threatening to trip her. She stumbled over hidden rocks and stumps and wove a serpentine path around gullies.

The whole time she ran, she imagined Cade and Blade waking up any second and giving chase. Her arms prickled as she fantasized being grabbed by one of them and tackled to the ground.

She ran faster.

Her breaths sawed in and out in painful gasps as the icy air burned deep into her lungs. Even though she knew better than to panic, she couldn't stop the claws of fear from grabbing hold. With every step, her feet continued to get colder and her teeth just kept on chattering.

Suddenly, she wished for the scrunch of footsteps chomping through the snow behind her. Wished Cade and Blade were following her. They would warm her up.

Oh God, what the hell was she thinking? She shouldn't expect a rescue from them. They wouldn't follow her in this nasty weather. The snowflakes swirled so thickly, she couldn't see her hand in front of her face. The storm had intensified and she didn't recognize any of the landmarks. In her panic, she must have gone the wrong way.

Frig! They'd find her frozen stiff. A corpse. Cold forever!

Oh God! Get a grip!

But how could she stay calm? She didn't have the foggiest idea where she was heading. Despite spending her teenage years exploring these woods, nothing seemed familiar. Back then she'd loved the silence. Enjoyed the magnificent scenery—the snow-drenched trees, the tart bite of winter air splashing against her cheeks. But now the crisp air clawed past her clothing and bit into her skin like sharp teeth, making her shiver even harder.

Was she at death's door? Her hopes and dreams of freeing all women began to slip away. She'd wanted to give back what had been too easily taken. Return the freedom their forefathers had fought so hard for. Everything would be lost if she didn't find her way out of these godforsaken woods.

The snow flurries began to ease and a couple of feet ahead of her the landscape became visible. As she stumbled through the drifts, she thought the slight echo of men's voices brushed against the trees. But that was ridiculous. If Cade and Blade were stupid and came out in this nightmare weather, they would hunt her in silence. They would sneak up on her.

She had to be hallucinating or dreaming. Or hoping too much for rescue. Or...

Icy shivers skewered her. Blade had mentioned hunters.

A big shadow appeared out of the swirling snow and the instant a face materialized through the storm terror twisted like a knife in her belly. This person wasn't Cade or Blade. Or anyone she knew.

Oh God. No.

"Well, well, well. A woman. A fucking woman," the man growled.

His face was concealed in hair, the whiskers tinged with frost. His hat and shoulders were covered in snow. He leered at her in a very ungentlemanly manner that made Reena's stomach roll with sickness.

"Over here! I've found one! Over here!" he shouted.

Oh sweet Lord.

Renewed strength zapped into her limbs. Limbs she'd thought would never work again.

Spinning around, she struggled through the heavy snow, following her previous footsteps. With every step, she picked up speed, and then she ran.

Suddenly a burst of pain exploded in the back of her head. Everything went black.

Chapter Five

Reena didn't know how long she'd been out, but an agonized moan ripped her from the dark world of hibernation. The pathetic sound had come from her.

Pain throbbed through her temples and her entire body was sore. A chill of foreboding swept through her. Had the man raped her? She took a mental inventory and aside from muscle aches, hurting cold feet and a really bad headache, there didn't appear to be anything wrong. But that didn't mean...

Icy goose bumps shivered through her and slammed into her empty belly as she tried to move. The unmistakable sting of a rope bit into her already raw wrists, compliments of Cade's cuffs. Her ankles were bound and she couldn't move her legs.

Thankfully she was fully clothed and lay beneath a thick pelt of blankets. The blankets stank of pee and sweat, but were warm. Drifting all around her was the raspy breathing of men, the snap and crackle of burning wood, the tart scent of wood smoke and foul body odor.

The clatter and clank of metal against metal split the air. They were eating, and the unmistakable odor of salsa had her mouth watering despite her fear. Not that it mattered. She doubted she could keep anything down. They wouldn't give her food anyway. Starvation was one of the torture techniques men used against a captive woman to get her to submit to them.

Okay she wouldn't go there either. She needed to escape. And fast.

She forced her eyelids open. For a split second, sheer terror slammed into her as she encountered complete darkness, but a slight turn of her head let in some cold air. They'd covered her head with the blankets.

She'd best not move. If the pain pounding in her temples was any indication she'd taken a bad hit.

Okay so escape wasn't exactly an option at the moment. She needed to get out of these ropes first. Cripes! How come she kept getting into these situations?

"You sure you didn't kill her when you bonked her on the head? She should have come to by now." A gruff male voice with a slight southern accent shot through the air, too close for comfort. The guy was sitting right beside her.

Reena froze.

"Don't worry. She's just playing dead." Another man chuckled.

She didn't recognize either of the voices as the guy who'd knocked her out. That meant there were three of them. At least.

Her heart lurched in her chest. How could she escape three of them?

Shit. These men would be on edge. Desperate for female companionship. They'd most likely been without a woman for years. Once they got started with her, they would continue for days…

A burst of panic made her catch her breath. Her inhalation sounded like a bullet slicing through the air. She cried out in shock as the blankets were ripped off and cold air slammed into her bare hands and feet. The bastards had removed her socks and boots!

"You're awake, pretty thing."

He was the man who'd caught her. He leered down at her and the sight of him brought a roll of nausea to her gut. Grabbing her by the knotted rope around her wrists, he dragged her to her feet as easily as if she were a rag doll.

Her toes sank into the snow beside the blankets and the icy shock made her grimace.

"Hold her still, Bud, while I untie her ankles. Then we party!"

A round of hoots and hollers ripped through the air, making her tense. She wanted to run, to get away from their leers, but she forced herself to remain still. She wouldn't be able to get far in bare feet. There were eight of them. All sizing her up as if she were a prized possession.

Another man stood and held the rope around her wrists. He seemed around forty-five or fifty. Pockmarked face. Rotten teeth. Bad breath.

"What's your name, miss?" he asked as he stared at her. She recognized the hunger in his eyes. The need for release. It made her ill.

"None of your fucking business, asshole."

She'd learned long ago being nice to these types of men got her nowhere. They should know right away she wouldn't be pushed or taken easily. The man's smile dropped into a cold hard glare.

"Didn't anyone tell you it's impolite for a lady to swear?" he growled and yanked on the rope, pulling her closer. Close enough for her breasts to touch his chest. She tried to wiggle away, but he held her fast.

"Didn't anyone tell you it isn't polite being rough with a lady?" Reena snapped back.

The other men who sat around the campfire hooted and hollered again. The rope around her ankles gave way and she held her ground as the man holding her wrists came in for a kiss. At the last minute, she turned her head and he kissed her hair.

"Fucking bitch!" he complained and grabbed for her chin. She wrenched her head away and he missed. Another violent curse followed. More laughter from the others.

Oh shit. Here we go.

She would go down fighting like a wild cat. She knew as the bite of panic began to burn through her.

She'd go down fighting.

* * * * *

A high-pitched female scream sliced through Cade Outlaw like a knife sinking into his gut. It was followed by silence. Thick. Oppressive. Horrible silence.

"At least she's still alive." Blade's cool voice came from immediately in front of him.

Yeah but for how long?

Cade's throat grew dry and his palms began to sweat in his gloves as he imagined why Reena would scream like that.

"Hurry up, would you?" he prodded as a sense of urgency overrode his common sense to remain cautious.

They'd been following her trail for the better part of a day. The trek hadn't been easy. Far from it. Most of her footprints had been covered by the snow storm. Luckily though, here and there, in places where the wind hadn't been able to reach, they found her tracks.

About two hours ago, his blood had run cold when Blade pointed out her tracks had met up with another set, which had mingled with several more. He'd been hoping against hope she'd come into contact with other members of the Resistance. Prayed she'd be safe and sound. But the scream had shattered his illusions.

Deep down in his gut, he'd sensed trouble. Blade knew it too. Upon seeing the merging trails, he hadn't suggested stopping for a meal.

Cade should have killed Blade back at camp. That would have been the best way to protect Red from the assassin. But he might need the man if Reena was in trouble. If anything, Blade was known for his excellent tracking abilities, and Cade had to admit, it would have taken him a lot longer to find clues as to where Reena had gone.

Sex-crazed men could do a lot of nasty things to a woman. Spiritually, physically and emotionally. He'd seen a lot of men behaving ungentlemanly during the Wars. By the haunted way Reena had sometimes peered at him across the fire they'd shared yesterday evening, she'd experienced something bad too. Hell, he didn't want any more bad things to happen to her.

"If I'm going to help get her out of this mess she's gotten herself into, I'm going to need my weapons back," Blade tossed over his shoulder.

Cade ignored his request. "Keep going. When the time comes to decide if you need a weapon, I'll make my decision then."

Blade grunted his dissatisfaction and continued trudging ahead through the snow. But by the way he held his shoulders tense and his gloved hands clenched, the guy was angry. Bloody pissed off.

Good. That made two of them.

* * * * *

If ever there was a time Will Blade was grateful for his ability to keep calm under extreme pressure, this was it. Sure, Red's scream shot mega jolts of adrenaline through his system, but rushing blindly into the hunters' camp was suicide. There were eight men. Big burly men dressed in heavy coats. Hunters, just like he thought. And they certainly had their prey.

The men laughed while they roughly pushed Red from one man to the next. A ploy used to keep their victims off balance and to prevent them from running.

It was working.

Red stumbled and fell several times before being hauled to her feet and pushed toward the next man. He shuddered at their crudeness, having her feet bare. Out in this cold weather, her feet sinking into the icy cold snow would be brutal. Bastards. He'd enjoy killing them.

He tried to ignore the cold sweat running down his back while he studied each man. He committed their movements and features to memory, trying like hell to ignore Red's tired pants as she fought the laughing men.

Shit! Didn't she know not to breathe through her mouth when stressed?

Okay focus, Blade. Focus on how to get her out.

Beside him, Cade shifted uneasily. His anger sparked through the air between them as he readied himself to pounce blindly into the fray.

"You go in there without a plan and we're both dead," Blade warned as Cade shifted again.

Muscles spasmed and jerked in Cade's cheek.

Blade held his breath as one of the men back-handed Red across the face. The smack of flesh hitting flesh ripped through him like a cleaver. He fought the impulse to shout at them to stop.

He expected Cade to rush out and was surprised when he stood his ground. Hell, they might survive this after all if the guy kept his temper.

Not good odds if Red was fast enough to help. Crap odds if she hadn't sunk deep into herself in order to protect her mind.

"I'll take the four on the left," Blade said.

"Just make sure you don't hit her. If you do, I'll kill you," Cade warned.

Unfortunately when the shooting started, Red would be in the crossfire. Chances were likely she would get hit and, although Blade had been about to shoot her yesterday, he couldn't stomach killing her today, especially with his protective instincts clouding his judgment. He was in one hell of a situation, wasn't he?

Another sharp slap of flesh hitting flesh jolted him and the familiar burn of anger raged through him. He used it to stoke his adrenaline.

"Give me my fucking—"

His gun appeared in front of his face.

Hell, truth was all three of them probably wouldn't make it out alive. He really had nothing to lose if he accidentally shot Red. Maybe that's why Cade had finally given him a weapon.

Either way, it was a really bad day to die.

* * * * *

One minute Reena was being shoved to the next leering man and the next she fell over his prone body, her bare hands plunging into red snow.

She blinked at the color in confusion. Okay, so she'd lost her mind?

Gunshots split the air and she screamed in surprise. All around her, the hunters were grabbing their pistols and returning fire. For the longest time, she lay on top of the dead man, fearing any movement would bring a bullet into her head.

Paralyzing terror gripped her as the gunshots continued. She struggled to get her bearings and finally managed to snap out of her stupor and quickly searched the dead body for a weapon.

Whoever was shooting at them was either a friend or foe of hers. If they were friends...well...too bad. If they got in her way while she was taking out the hunters, she'd deal with the guilt afterward. But if only she could find this guy's damned gun!

Frigid air sawed into her lungs like fire. Ice-cold sweat pooled at the base of her neck and she continued to search the lifeless body, hoping to hell the other men were too busy firing their guns to pay her any mind. Acrid gunpowder smoke slammed into her nostrils, making her gag, and her ears rang from the zings of shots spiraling around her. She'd just about given up finding a weapon when she touched smooth cold metal at the small of his back.

Yes!

Self-control whipped through her like an explosion as she palmed the weapon. She rolled off the man and onto her tummy. Releasing the safety, she used the lifeless body as a shield, took aim and prayed the gun was loaded. She fired at the first man, the son of a bitch who'd conked her on the head. He cried out, dropped into the snow and lay still.

More gunshots rang out. She took aim at another man who turned toward her and pulled the trigger of his gun. The bullet slammed into the dead man's back. She plugged the asshole two times for good measure. He clutched his chest, dropped and remained motionless.

She fired at another figure hunched down behind a fallen log. Shards of snow flew up in the air like a white tornado. She'd missed.

Thankfully he didn't return fire and it was then she figured the guy was dead.

Great! Shooting blindly. Wasted bullets. She needed to chill and get her head into focus mode!

Her breath caught as another bullet tore through the upper back of the dead man she lay behind. A nauseating wave of lightheadedness almost toppled her as another man, his face bloody, took aim at her. He was the guy she'd shot earlier. The one who'd conked her over the head.

He stood about twenty feet away. Wobbly, but standing nonetheless, he aimed right at her head.

Oh God!

Frantically she tried to ignore the image of the bullet tearing into her brains as his finger tightened on the trigger. She held her breath as he stepped forward.

If she lifted her gun and aimed at him, he'd plug her dead. But she really didn't have much choice. He would kill her either way.

He took another step forward, a horribly smug sneer on his face.

She'd have to raise her gun. At least then he would kill her before he raped her. She blinked wildly as he dropped to his knees, fell face first into the snow and lay deathly still.

A huge knife protruded from the man's back. Cade stumbled toward her. Falling. Clutching his right arm.

Her tummy hollowed out. He was injured and he'd come to her rescue. Again.

She rolled onto her knees, wanting to put as much distance between all the dead men and herself as possible. Wanting to help Cade.

But as she got to her feet, dizziness swept through her and she dropped on her butt into the cold, puffy snow. There were bodies everywhere. They littered the red snow.

Sickness churned in the pit of her belly. Her side hurt like a bitch and her feet and hands were so cold and red she swore they would have to be amputated. An unexpected, sharp bite of tears stung her eyes and a dam of despair threatened to spill from her, but all that disappeared when she detected movement from one of the fallen men on her left, outside the fray of the campsite.

Sweet Jesus. No. She couldn't handle putting a bullet through another guy's head. Not now. The scent of death was too overwhelming.

But she recognized the man's coat and his light-blond hair.

Damn! Blade had come for her too?

She swallowed an anguished cry as she swept her gaze to Cade's motionless figure and then to Blade's slightly moving one.

They had both come for her? Saved her from these horrible men?

And gotten shot for their troubles.

Nausea rolled through her as she finally managed to climb to her feet. Feet that hurt so bad they were on fire. But the hurt was better than being numb and useless. She needed to find her boots.

Surveying the disarray in the camp, she wanted to run from the bloodied bodies crumpled here and there and get far away from this evil. She clamped down on the urge to flee and focused on locating her boots. They lay near the smoldering fireplace. Her gut twisted at the sickening scent of burnt flesh as she spied a man's arm that had flopped into the fire when he'd fallen after being shot.

She bit back the sour bile rising in her throat and struggled into her socks and boots. Inhaling at the fiery pain burning in her side, she swung her gaze back to the scene strewn with lifeless bodies. She could no longer hold back her anguish at what had almost happened to her.

She screamed. And screamed.

* * * * *

Reena's gut-wrenching shrieks rocked Cade right to his core. He lay in the snow, on his back, his breath shooting like white flares into the cold air. Through the haze of excruciating pain, he saw Reena sitting on a log, her eyes squeezed shut tight, her hands stuffed beneath her armpits as she rocked back and forth, screaming.

He wanted to get up out of the cold snow and wrap his arms around her. Wanted to reassure her she was safe. Unfortunately every time he so much as moved a muscle, powerful jolts of pain rocked into his right shoulder and chest, making him inhale sharply, which in turn made his head spin.

Warm blood flowed out of him, lacing his flesh, sticky and wet, and his body chilled as he readied himself to meet his maker.

Fuck, he was in bad shape. He opted to just lie there and listen to Reena's screams, knowing instinctively she was releasing her fear. Physically she seemed to be out of harm's way and it appeared the men were dead. At least he hoped they were after seeing them drop one by one, compliments of Blade and their surprise attack on the camp.

Icy snowflakes caressed his hot face. Yep, no use in moving, he'd only pass out. For all he knew, he was already dead. Blade was probably dead, too. Cade had seen him go down. At least with Blade out of the way she'd have a fighting chance to reach safety.

He wrapped himself in the comforting knowledge of meeting up with those bastards who'd just hurt her. In heaven or hell, wherever God saw fit to put them, he'd make sure every one of them—whoever had hurt Reena—would pay.

* * * * *

Blade drifted in swirls of searing pain. His left chest area hurt. Every time he inhaled, fire lanced through him. So he tried not to inhale. Tried not to breathe. But no breathing meant death. If he died, he'd never have another night like the one he'd had with Reena all those months ago, and he really would enjoy fucking her again.

Oh man, just thinking of her brought a lash of confused emotions. Up until last night, he'd been able to keep a tight lid on his attraction toward her and concentrate on following through on his kill orders.

But seeing her wrists cuffed, her ankles restrained, the need for protection shining in her vulnerable eyes—he'd caved like a sixteen-year-old school boy raging with hormones.

Yeah, he'd like to have her again, but that would mean he'd have to get up. Breathe. Endure more pain.

Suddenly, he became aware of noise. It grew louder and louder until it mixed with his red-hot pain. An engine? But that couldn't be. They were in the middle of nowhere. No roads. Just trees and snow. He tried to open his eyes. Couldn't.

He was cold. Icy waves speared right down into his bones like a poison, anesthetizing his mind and chilling his brain. Numbing his senses and crippling his well-honed reflexes. To his surprise, the ground moved beneath him. No, not possible. The ground couldn't move like this. Or maybe he *was* moving?

His temples throbbed with an excruciating headache. The roar of the engine broke into his mind again, followed by the strong scent of gas. The motion continued and so did the racket.

He drifted off and slept. For how long, he had no idea. A sound...maybe a door closing? Whatever it was woke him. He tried to open his eyelids again. It was hard. But he managed and winced at the blinding glare of the setting sun. No, not the sun. A light? Yes, a porch light. It glowed, stabbing like daggers into his head, thrusting his vision into a world of pain.

He closed his eyes again, welcomed the relief. Waited a few seconds and then opened his eyes, this time squinting and wishing he had a pair of sunglasses.

Behind the painful glare, he made out a building. A big one. A log cabin. One story. A roof covered in snow and lots of snow-drenched pine trees towering behind the building.

He recognized it. Had come across it while tracking Red. This was where she'd been living. He'd gone into the cabin after finding the door wide open. Someone had busted in and vandalized the place.

Despite the mess, he'd found the place rustic. Bookshelves had lined the living room. An old cast-iron potbelly stove was warm to the touch and coals glowed in a nearby fireplace. She'd left an erotic romance novel lying on the couch. A quick glance at the back cover blurb revealed the book contained lots of hot sex and a threesome. He could just imagine what the men who'd broken into the cabin thought about what she'd been reading.

He'd left the building in a hurry, following the tracks until he'd come upon the group of men who'd set up camp. In the nearby bushes, he'd listened to their conversations about tracking down the woman who was staying at that cabin. Blade would have opened fire on them, but there had been too many for him to shoot. He wouldn't have been able to get away without being trailed by survivors. The last thing he'd wanted was for them to know he was around. So he'd left and gone in search of Red himself. He'd found her and Cade and then the storm had hit.

Blade focused back on the present, to the square logs with cement caulking. Homemade job. With matching stone chimneys on each end. His gaze lifted toward the sky where a spiral of gray smoke puffed into the black night air. Chimneys meant fireplaces and that meant heat. Warmth cracked through the chill encasing his heart and, for a split second, he had the weird sense of "coming home".

He ripped himself free from that odd homey comfort when someone stepped down the rough-hewn wood-planked stairs. He wondered if the person was a hallucination, but the shadow seemed solid as it moved toward him. Red's face floated from beneath a black hat and scarf, and just like every time he saw her, his breath seemed to halt in his lungs.

She was a striking woman. Beautiful. A ripe, sensual mouth. Gorgeous eyes. A man could drown in her eyes. Her hair was loose and spilled from her black hat like wildfire to the tops of her shoulders. He didn't know how he could see her hair in all that dark shit she wore, but he could.

His gaze flew back to her face. Bruises and cuts lashed her high cheekbones where she'd been slapped. The cold deepened inside him and at that moment he wanted to once again kill those bastards who'd hurt her.

She squatted beside him and white puffs of mist escaped her mouth with her every breath. Her lips moved. She was talking. He must have blacked out because he'd missed what she said. Her lips moved again.

"Will? Can you hear me?"

Hell, he didn't remember giving her his first name. Warmth shot through him. Although he'd known it was the drugs urging her into his room that night, and he'd sworn he'd turn her down flat if she approached him, the instant she'd exposed herself to him—along with the tugging on all those rings—his self-control had vanished. He'd taken her up against the door and she'd been like a drug in his system, making him crave her again.

The erotic scent of her pleasure, her heat, her arousal, swept in around him and for a moment he was back in that room, kissing her pouty warm lips and licking her engorged clit while he held her ass cheeks. Her moans had been sweet and succulent.

"Will? Will? Can you hear me?" Her insistent voice snapped through his memory.

"I need you to wake up, Blade. Or you're going to end up freezing your ass off out here on my grandparents' snowmobile. So come on! Do me a favor and wake up!"

Snowmobile?

A sharp pain snapped against his frozen right cheek and damned if the reflexes he thought dead didn't come to life. With lightning speed, he grabbed her by the wrist and held tight. Her surprised gasp made his cock tighten in awareness.

Well, what do you know? He wasn't in such bad shape, after all.

"You'd better make sure I can't catch you the next time you do that," he croaked. Her cheeks darkened more than they already had from the cold.

Shit. She was blushing. Maybe she wasn't as damaged as he'd originally thought.

He drifted again. Drifted into the memories. Of warmth. Of Red. Kissing her. Her hot, eager lips melting over his. Her mouth swollen and moist, opening to him, his tongue invading her sweet cavern.

Oh man, he could just about drown in these memories. She tasted so succulent...

* * * * *

He held her wrist so tight she couldn't escape even if she'd wanted to. And she really didn't want to because the sexual darkness in his eyes, his exquisite warning about her slapping him—as well as her need to wake him any way she could—had her lowering her head until their lips met.

Scorching tingles shot through her mouth and mind as her lips melted over his. She'd expected the kiss to be as weak as he appeared. It wasn't. It was potent. Powerful and needy.

Just as needy as the sexual desire pounding through her. The heat of his kiss pushed aside everything else. Suddenly it was just the two of them. Just as it had been the one other time in that bedroom.

She fought to breathe as a rush of want raced through her. Lust, hot and heavy. Thick and powerful. It swept through her entire being like a firestorm, lashing her senses and sparking in her brain.

She wanted Blade. Wanted him like in her fantasy last night. Like she'd had him at the safe house. The kiss deepened and she inhaled him deep inside her lungs.

He was male. Raw and primal. Dominating. His scent powered through her and sailed deep into her bloodstream. Her body tightened with arousal, her pussy clenched. Hot moisture splayed against her panties. The driving hunger for him to fuck her took hold.

His tongue mated with hers. Erotic tingles swept through her and, with the growing heat, she unzipped her coat and cupped her breast.

Jolting at the realization she was getting carried away, Reena moaned with regret and broke the kiss. Blade groaned. His eyes were open and he seemed lucid.

"Need to get inside," he panted. She wondered if he meant inside the cabin or inside of her. In the lamplight, his dark eyes glittered with pain and he inhaled sharply as she helped him off the snowmobile. Standing, he swayed like a drunkard but thankfully didn't fall over.

Her legs went weak with relief as he stumbled forward. With her help, he managed the stairs, lurched across the planked porch and yanked open the screen door.

Within minutes, she had him sitting on a cot set up beside the woodstove. Heat blasted him in waves and Blade wished to hell his limbs would continue to co-operate, but it was as if his body knew it would be better if Red undressed him.

And she did. He was weak as a kitten and barely able to enjoy the show as she unzipped his jacket. Pain burst through his chest and he gasped as she tried to maneuver his jacket off his shoulders.

"Sorry," she soothed.

When she had his shirt off, concern flushed her face. Concern for him. He spied the blood streaking his upper body and the puckered hole in his shoulder. With every breath, the pain slicing through him grew more intense.

He wondered about Cade. Had he fared any better? He had been shot and went down about the same time Blade had been hit himself.

Was Cade dead? A spear of bitter disappointment grabbed him. Cade's five brothers would hurt with the loss, and Blade might have made a good solid friend in the guy if they both hadn't been after Red.

Through the pounding pain knocking through his brain, he wanted to ask her about Cade, but a motionless figure lay on another cot directly on the other side of the potbelly woodstove. Relief whispered through him.

Outlaw was pale. Like death warmed over.

"Cade?" he muttered.

"He took a couple of bullets. One in his right shoulder, the other in his upper chest. You've got a head wound besides this one." She nodded to his blood-soaked upper torso. "Cade is alive. For now."

For now. The two words echoed through his splitting skull like a death chant.

By the time Red had him naked, he was quite aware of his swollen erection and the erotic way she licked her lips. Licking lips was a sure sign she wanted to have his cock thrusting into her mouth.

She lifted his legs and maneuvered him onto the bed. His arousal was quickly forgotten as he lay down and a wave of dizziness swept through him. He sank onto the warm, cozy mattress, his vision swimming. Despite the pain, he managed to free himself from it to whip her a teasing grin.

"I guess I'm at your mercy this time around, eh, Red?"

"You better keep that in mind and behave, Will. Because there really is no reason for me to keep you alive, is there?"

Her words penetrated his foggy brain with an icy fierceness that made him realize he just might not get out of this alive. With that knowledge taking hold inside him, her face floated away, fading into the dark pain until nothing else existed but blackness.

Chapter Six

It was way too warm in the cabin, but she'd forced herself to eat. Her throbbing headache and the nausea clutching at her belly went away and, as she resettled the gauze over the tender-looking bullet slash on Will's right temple, she said another prayer of thanks. One of many prayers tonight as she'd patched up the two men.

The wounds on Will weren't too bad. The one on his temple wasn't deep. Just a flesh wound, but he'd still bled like a stuck pig. She considered him lucky. Extremely lucky.

His chest wound had been more serious. She'd dug out a bullet, but it hadn't penetrated more than an inch. Hadn't hit anything vital. On his chest, she'd placed a poultice with some herbs she carried with her—herbs that should attack any infection that might follow her digging around.

She was glad she'd made alternative medicine a part of mandatory first-aid training for all Resistance members. Not only did alternative medicines work, they were easier to obtain than traditional antibiotics. And in many cases, members were able to grow their own herbs in the meadows around the areas where they hid.

The sharp snap and crackle of wood brought her attention back to the high temperature. She couldn't be sure if the heat was due to the X-virus kicking in and her need to orgasm or because she'd been stoking too much wood into the woodstove and the living room fireplace. Or if it was due to the fact she had two naked men lying on the cots she'd set up on each side of the stove.

Reena sighed and checked Cade's forehead again. Hot. He stirred beneath her touch, mumbled something about a beauty and then smiled in his sleep, sending a wild fluttering deep inside her heart. She answered his smile while surveying the damp hair sweeping over his forehead and the long, dark lashes framing his cheeks, flushed pink with fever.

Luckily she'd been able to get him to sip a few spoonfuls of a special blend of tea the Resistance's trusted doctor had given her before she left to come out here.

Medicine of any kind, whether naturopathic or synthetically produced, was extremely hard to acquire—not to mention expensive these days with the bad economy. But she'd vowed to the doctor she wouldn't take any unless absolutely necessary. Well, easing the men's discomfort seemed to be a necessity.

The tea was a potent drug. Only a few spoonfuls every four hours would help fight infection and a fever. Given in larger quantities, it also acted as a sedative, knocking out the recipients for hours and making them virtually helpless.

She yawned as she tucked the blankets back in around Cade's scar-riddled body. He'd been careless or taken too many risks during the Wars. He had several bullet scars and healed-over knife wounds where he'd been stabbed. He also had a bad habit of thrashing around when he slept, and she certainly didn't need any more glimpses of his long, thick shaft or those interesting-looking slash-like scars lacing his lower belly and onto his cock. She'd seen the scars when she'd gotten him out of his clothing and, oh boy, how her pussy had clenched at the sight of him. She'd longed to stroke his shaft and watch it come to life. To touch it. Feel it. Hold it. But she'd been in a hurry, cleaning his wounds, applying ointment and feeding him tea before getting back onto the snowmobile to rescue Will.

She'd also had to deal with Will's wounds. He'd remained semi-conscious as she'd undressed him. She hadn't been able to coax too much tea into him, but he'd taken enough to help with the fever starting inside him. And his cock...oh my. Just as big and a bit longer than Cade's.

She blew out a tense breath and came around the stove. Checking Will's forehead, she found him hot, but thankfully not as hot as Cade. A similar, wild stirring snapped through her lower belly—just as it had with Cade—when she gazed down at Will's body. His hair spilled over his damp forehead, giving him an innocent, boyish look. But she knew better.

He was no innocent and no boy.

Yep, definitely getting too hot in here.

Despite the horrors of what had happened today and her mind wanting to shut down, the X-virus wasn't going to give her body a break. She needed to orgasm and she needed to get outside and cool herself down. She headed over to the sofa bed, pulled it open and grabbed the thick vibrator wrapped in a clean towel she'd hidden under the blankets. The vandals hadn't discovered her vibe and she cursed the bastards as she walked past the damaged satellite radio they'd left strewn on the floor. Those hunters hadn't wanted her to call for help, but by tomorrow night the Resistance would know there was a problem because she'd have missed the scheduled check-in time. Unless, of course, they tried to contact her before then.

She doubted that scenario, though. Lately, from the way she'd been biting off people's heads and being such a bitch, they were probably glad to be rid of her.

Oh well, at least she had her vibe for companionship. It was the only toy she'd allowed herself to buy. Because sex toys were forbidden for women to use, she could only secure one through the black market. Talk about expensive. Guilt assailed her when she thought how the money could have been spent in better ways, like on medicine or milk for the few babies the Resistance now took care of. But she'd needed something powerful and safe to give her some relief and this handy, big gadget did the trick most of the time.

The vibe was lifelike and she couldn't wait to use it as she rushed toward the door. Molded in a black jelly with raised veins, it measured a good eight inches long with a two-inch girth and was the most powerful vibe on the market. Past experience taught her it would help bring the orgasm she needed so badly to survive.

An icy sweep of winter air greeted her as she stepped onto the screened porch. It had grown dark outside, but not dark enough she couldn't see the silhouette of the snowmobile and attached trailer she'd used to bring Cade and Blade here. Grandad had loved his snowmobile and it was the first thing Reena had thought about when she'd stopped screaming and pulled herself together in the hunters' camp. She really should get the machinery into the shed and out of the elements. But it was cold out and she just wanted to forget the awful day, do what needed doing and get some rest.

Ever since returning to the cabin with Cade and then Will, the insistent, warning throbs of craving an orgasm had plagued her. She needed release and she needed it bad.

She moaned as she pulled down her panties, turned on the vibe and began to massage her clit. The cock head pulsed and pounded and she moaned louder as the electric pleasure mounted. She moved the cock head between her labia and plunged into her creaming vagina, crying out as the orgasm quickly rocked through her.

She withdrew and thrust it in again, imagining the vibrator was Blade fucking her up against the door of that bedroom. Then, to her surprise, thoughts of Cade fucking her burst to the forefront.

Confusion pummeled her as her thoughts whipped back to Blade again. Then Cade.

Both men fucking her? The devilish idea made her explode on a strangled cry. The orgasm tore into her like a tornado and Reena went with it.

Breathing deeply and thrusting her vibe in and out, she bucked her hips and with her free hand tugged on her nipple rings. Quickly, she became lost inside the magnificent spasms as they rocked through her at lightning speed. Too soon the orgasm ebbed, leaving Reena unfulfilled, knowing the momentary fantasy of Cade and Will making love to her would never come true.

The idea was crazy. She'd only just met Cade and she'd only been with Will that one time, but that didn't stop her from smiling at the idea of having the Resistance keep the two men as captives purely to pleasure her.

Sighing, Reena withdrew her vibe, pulled up her panties, closed her eyes and rested. Her vaginal muscles spasmed softly and the blood pounded through her ears. Somewhere far off in the woods, an owl screeched, its echo sending chills down her spine. A moment later, its mate answered from close by.

Desolation crowded in around her. There were no neighbors to run to for help. She was alone and on her own to deal with what had happened to her.

After a few minutes of silence, the cold seeped into her. It didn't frighten her as it had when she'd been handed back and forth between those men. Here, she could step into a building to warm herself.

Her feet were almost back to normal, nestled in a couple of pairs of wool socks and dry shoes. Tenderness still lingered though, and if Cade and Blade hadn't shown up when they had, she wouldn't be walking. She would have been those hunters' slave.

Uneasiness zipped through her. She should have made sure all those men were dead. Some of them could still be alive, maybe even heading back here. Back to her.

She wished Granddad were here. Being with him and Grandmom had given her the safety and stability she'd always craved, even if it had only been for short bursts of time.

She'd loved her stays here.

Granddad had even shown her how to take his snowmobile in and out of storage. That's how the vehicle had been in working condition, because she'd known exactly what to do to get it started.

Reena bit back a swell of nostalgia as she visualized her grandfather out in front of the cabin, sitting on the snowmobile, revving it up, waving to her and shouting for her to get a move on if she wanted to go out for a midnight run across the frozen lake.

Oh man! The icy wind blowing against her face as they raced the snowmobile back and forth across the flat of the lake had exhilarated her. The unleashed speed created a freedom that melted right into her soul. Grandpa had been such a sweet old man and her heart broke when she got the call from Grandmom, saying he'd died in his sleep up here in the cabin not too long before the X-virus had taken hold around the world.

Her grandmother died only weeks later after she herself had succumbed to the virus. Her mother had died shortly after that, leaving Reena with her cold, emotionless father. She tossed aside the sadness of her past and gazed around the picturesque scenery, smiling at the quietness. Yeah, this is why she'd come here alone in the first place. To get some solitude and figure out which direction she wanted to take the Resistance. She truly had no idea.

Wiping away a stray tear, she inhaled a cold breath as she tried to collect her jumbled emotions. It might have been easier to leave the two men back there to die. That would have solved her problem of taking care of them. But hell, she'd never been a woman who took the easy way out. And they'd saved her life so she owed them big-time.

While they were here, she'd have to make the best of the situation. Forcing away the memories of the violence she'd experienced earlier in the day, she inhaled and exhaled slowly until a peaceful calm entered her system. After a long while, she headed back inside.

~ ~ ~ ~ ~

"Now you know how it feels, don't you, torturer?" the woman whispered in a low, deadly voice. Cade clenched his teeth and pulled at his binds as she sliced into his flesh. Pain burned unlike anything he'd ever experienced before.

This cut was the deepest and too damned low on his belly. If she kept going in the general direction she was headed...

Cade breathed deep and fought the urge to scream as she cut again into his flesh. This time way too close to his cock.

"I have no wish to kill you, torturer," she taunted.

He tensed as she lapped at the blood that spilled from the latest slash. Her long black hair tickled his left hip and made him cringe. He didn't like any part of her touching him. At least not anymore.

Lifting her head, she gazed at him and he jolted at the sight of his blood dripping from her lips and down her chin. There was a mad glaze in her eyes. One he'd never noticed before, not even while he'd carved into her over the past several days. Was his torture of her responsible for that look? Or had she always been mad and just waiting for the right time to strike?

She held the knife close to her mouth. The blade gleamed beneath the light, flashing off the lone bare bulb hanging from the prison interrogation room ceiling. She licked the blood-soaked blade and he swallowed the sickness gushing up the back of his throat.

Jesus. He must have driven her insane. But he'd gone easy on her the last few days—after he'd developed feelings for her. Caring for a "client" was something he'd never done before.

It hadn't been the first time he'd driven one of them off the deep end with his handy knife. Until this woman he'd enjoyed his job, carving into a terrorist's flesh carefully and slowly, relishing his or her screams and begging. Appreciating their confessions as they spilled secrets the US Army wanted to know.

He tortured them because of what had happened to his sister. These sons of bitches had killed her by unleashing the X-virus, and he would continue to make them pay for as long as the Terrorist Wars continued. But with this prisoner, the process had been different right from the start.

She was a Saudi. A beautiful woman who, according to the reports of why she'd been captured, knew the whereabouts of three of the top ten terrorists on the US Most Wanted List.

But her beauty had blinded him. He could see that now. It had unleashed his long-suppressed lust for a woman and brought out his buried protective instincts. He should have known the moment he'd accepted her offer to open her legs for him. Should have walked away right then. Should have called in someone else to torture her.

Fuck! He'd ignored the number-one rule of a torturer. Never experience empathy for the "client". But he'd folded. Accepted her propositions. Had come to her prison cell and, instead of torturing her, instead of permanently marring her soft velvety skin, he'd fucked her and enjoyed the way her beautiful face twisted with the pleasure he gave her. But he'd also cut her flawless flesh after each visit. Not too deep. Just enough to avoid suspicion until he could find a way to break her out of here.

How the hell had he been so naïve in thinking he was in love with this viper? He'd been used. Plain and simple. She'd been acting. She'd conned him as if he were a teenage boy high on hormones. He'd been eager to make love to her.

Yesterday, he'd told her he would figure out a way to help her escape. He'd meant it. By God, he had truly meant it.

"You are the best lover I've ever had, Cade. Even better than the Immudin brothers and there are three of them. When they find out you had me, they'll want you dead. I need to get back to them. I hope you understand?"

The crazy gleam in her dark-brown—almost black—eyes intensified. But he met her gaze and held it. Defiance burned through him as she lowered the blade again.

He wanted to tell her she didn't have to go back to them. She was an object to them. A sex slave. They would probably kill her when she went back.

"Before I go. I need to leave you a little reminder of our time together. I want you to remember me."

The knife sliced into his skin. Pain blistered across his flesh and he ground back his moans of anguish.

She cannot break me. She will not break me.

"How does it feel? Huh?" Haylah asked in her sexy Saudi accent, then giggled and carved another deep gash just above his cock and balls.

It hurt like a son of a bitch. He should scream, but the gag he'd woken up with after she'd knocked him out prevented him from making too much noise. Through the searing pain he wondered not for the first time where she could have gotten the gag. Had one of the guards come in? Used it on her? Is that why she was doing this to him?

Rage splintered his pain. Had Haylah been raped in here? But wasn't that what he'd been doing? Raping her? She'd been under duress, begging him to stop torturing her and make love to her instead. He'd taken advantage of her. He couldn't hide behind the excuse that she'd begged him to sleep with her. She'd said she needed human companionship. Needed a man to protect her. She'd been so convincing. Saying she wanted him. He'd been so desperate to make love, to fall in love, he hadn't thought of anything else.

He'd heard of this happening to a few of the other torturers, but he'd never expected it to happen to him.

She cut efficiently into his flesh, so fucking slowly every excruciating slice brought extreme pain shooting through him. She carved lower with every strike. His body jerked with awareness and he strained against the binds. The same binds he'd used on her when he'd first started torturing her.

"I want you, Cade." The Saudi's voice swept through the fog of pain. "I want you to make love to me while I carve into your flesh."

She wrapped a hand around the base of his cock, squeezed and twisted his shaft until he was panting with pleasure. But with her other hand, she kept cutting.

Ice-cold sweat drenched his body. Ran in rivulets off his face. He was inside a fire and an iceberg at the same time. Burning. Freezing. Dying.

Pain ripped his body apart, shredded his mind, and when she cut into the base of his cock, she shattered the pleasure she'd created.

Oh shit! Not there. Not there! Fucking bitch!

She giggled as she sliced into him. Her laughter was a crazy cackle he would remember for as long as he lived. That is, if she let him live.

She lifted the blade and, for a moment, relief whipped through him. It was short-lived as she lowered the blood-soaked blade yet again.

Bitch! If he hadn't been bound, he might have killed her right then and there. Anything to stop the anguish of betrayal and the bite of searing pain as she cut into him again.

And again.

~ ~ ~ ~ ~

Cade jerked awake, his body drenched in cold sweat and his heart slamming against his chest with explosive speed.

He ached. Boy, did he ever ache. Especially the right side of his chest and his shoulder. Fiery pain throbbed as if someone was knifing him over and over again.

He groaned.

Panic pummeled him at the soft rustle of clothing from somewhere nearby. For a split second, he believed he was back in that cell. Was she coming back to slice into him again? A woman hovered into view. A woman with flaming-red hair.

Reena?

He blinked in confusion as he recalled capturing Reena, Blade showing up and then Reena escaping.

Concern for her safety snapped through him like a live wire.

"Are they all dead?" he managed to croak.

The concern knitting her perfect eyebrows vanished and relief etched her eyes. She nodded. "I think so. I didn't hang around long enough to find out, but I think so."

"Are you okay?" His voice grew a bit stronger.

She smiled and his gut did the most fantastic flip and he knew she would be okay.

"Blade?" he asked with hesitation. He wasn't sure he wanted to hear the news that Blade hadn't made it out alive.

She barked a short burst of laughter, her eyes twinkling with happiness. "I don't know about you two guys. I got the feeling you wouldn't have had a problem killing each other, yet your concern for each other is killing me. I take it you two have a history?"

Cade couldn't stop himself from smiling at the memory of him, Blade and his brother Colter making love to Ashley the sex slave. Colter had fallen in "love at first sight" with her during the Terrorist Wars. Thinking of Ashley made him think about how long it had been since he'd had sex with a woman.

Too. Damn. Long.

Had he died of his injuries, he would have died without making love to Reena. Yeah, he was crazy for thinking this way about a woman he barely knew.

Curiosity washed over her pretty face, yet a little tinge of pink crept into her cheeks.

"What? Why are you looking at me like that?" she asked, her voice a soft ribbon of caresses, melting over his senses.

Cade closed his eyes. Damned if he was going to share the memory of having sex with another woman while entertaining the thought of doing the same with this one. Reena was different than most women he'd known. He liked her defiance. Loved the fact that she'd saved his life and it seemed, based on her comment about Blade's concern for him, she'd saved Blade's life too. She was too caring for her own good.

"Can you sip some more of this tea for me? It's medicine. It'll help with the fever."

She smiled again and his insides twisted in a really nice way. He'd do anything for her. He would have told her as much, but weariness threatened to pull him into sleep land. She pressed a spoon to his lips and he opened his mouth, accepting the foul stench of her tea. To his surprise, a sweet, warm liquid splashed over his taste buds. He was thirsty and eagerly accepted more spoonfuls. His eyelids grew heavier with every sip and finally, he closed his eyes. If he died, she would be the last thing he remembered. For now, that's all that mattered.

* * * * *

Red sat on the edge of Cade's bed, spooning something into his mouth while talking to him in low whispers. At one point, she laughed. It was music to Blade's ears and instantly reminded him of another woman he'd once known...

~ ~ ~ ~ ~

"Excuse me?" Will couldn't believe what SKULL Chief and Commander Bev White had just said. The US Government had recruited him for some top-secret special ops program? Him? A gynecologist? Were they fucking insane?

The woman didn't look like a chief, a commander or a soldier when she'd entered the tent he'd been instructed to wait in just outside what the US Army called Soul City, Afghanistan. Well yeah, she'd flashed him an authentic-looking ID badge and she wore green fatigues and black combat boots, but she was a hot chick with cropped spiky blonde hair and melt-me dark-chocolate-brown eyes. Yet she told him he would be trained for some newly formed assassination team called SKULL and she was his new boss?

Uh uh. He didn't think so.

"I'm sorry, lady, but I'm a doctor, not an assassin." He figured his firm refusal would take care of it. She'd send him on his merry way back to the disgusting hospital tent crawling with rats and cockroaches. Then he could continue treating the scores of raped women and girls that streamed in looking for help from his small team of grossly overworked doctors and nurses.

"Sir," she stated, a stern smile on her plump pink lips as she rounded the only desk in the tent and sat down.

He waited for her to continue, but then quickly realized she expected him to address *her* as "sir". Fuck her. When he didn't speak, those luscious lips of hers tightened in annoyance.

"You'll address me as 'sir', soldier."

"I'm not on board..." *Bitch*, he added silently.

"You don't have a choice in the matter. The government says jump and you ask how high. Do I make myself clear?"

Her confidence spoke volumes. She was in charge whether he liked it or not. He stood with the full intention of leaving.

"You walk out that door and you'll spend the rest of the Wars in the brig and your staff won't get the meds and extra help they need," she chirped.

Okay, so the brig meant he couldn't help anyone and then his people would be effectively screwed. He hadn't realized he'd stopped walking toward the door until she ordered him to sit down.

Fuck. He hated the Wars. He hated her.

He sat down. Her eyes sparkled and a smile curved her lips and, to his shock, her expression warmed his soul. Unfortunately, her smile only lasted a couple of seconds before she returned to her cool, commanding manner.

"Make a wish list of what your people need. I'll make sure they get everything."

Anger flared through Blade as he read between the lines. He would not be going back to his team. "How will I know they'll get what I asked for?"

Her eyes twinkled merrily. She enjoyed teasing him. "You won't."

"Then show me to the brig." He stood again and, to his astonishment, she did too. He was halfway to the door when she grabbed him by the elbow. The power in her grip amazed him.

"You walk out that door, soldier, and there is no more mandatory weekly R & R."

"I masturbate quite nicely," he answered truthfully. "I'll survive."

Her grip on his elbow tightened. He almost yanked his arm free in a sudden burst of anger, but the sweet touch of her silky warm fingers brushing against the nape of his neck gave him pause.

"You will be having sex with me," she whispered in a hot, saucy voice that had him swallowing at his dry throat.

"I want reassurances my staff will be well taken care of," he demanded.

Her sultry mint-scented breath caressed the side of his face and almost had him forgetting he should be putting up a hell of a bigger fight.

"The mandatory R & R starts now, soldier."

Oh. Damn.

"Reassurances, first," he stipulated and held back a groan as her hand slipped to the front of his neck. He sighed, melting into the softness of her caress.

In the rapid manner she breathed and the sensual way her eyes sparkled, he knew he'd won. A sharp tug on his shirt sent several buttons flying.

"As you wish, soldier." Her voice was breathy. "Just give me the list after we're finished here. I'll guarantee you an inspection of your hospital in one week's time. It should take about that long to get things in order."

Blade smiled inwardly. *Yes!*

"Condoms," he stated and turned around to face her.

She was about one head shorter than him and a whole hell of a lot of feminine. Her gaze was cool and businesslike as she loosened her belt and unzipped her green pants. His cock hardened in anticipation as she slid her pants and underwear over her hips. He cursed softly as he noted her nude pussy, her inner thighs glistening with wetness.

"You turn me on, soldier," she whispered.

Hell, they'd just met and she turned *him* on...big-time. She hoisted her naked ass onto her desk and unbuttoned her green shirt.

"Missionary position for me only," she stated coolly. "No kissing on the mouth. Feel free to go down on me or take my nipples into your mouth. I'll reciprocate."

Her voice was still cool and businesslike, but he detected a cute little tremble.

"Condoms are right here." She reached for what he'd assumed was a stone paperweight on the edge of her desk, but when she opened it, he spied several condoms inside.

"I've been told by some of the females you're bigger than most. I assume the condom size I picked will fit."

"I hope you haven't picked me just for my size, *sir*." He stressed the last word sharply as he reached for a package.

"Don't flatter yourself, Blade. I'm not the one who picked you. My superiors do their research and apparently it's who *you* know that got you into SKULL."

He wondered whom he knew.

This chick was an attractive fuck and he couldn't wait to pleasure her. He ripped open the package and removed the condom, placing it on the desk within easy reach for when he needed it.

"So who do I know?" he asked. Damned if he could think of anyone important enough they would want him to assassinate. She shook her head, her gaze firm as she whipped open the edges of her shirt to reveal a nice pair of curvy, tanned breasts.

His cock twitched and throbbed.

"Fuck me, soldier," she whispered softly. Her fingers curled tightly along the edges of the desk as if she were holding on for dear life. Or maybe she just didn't want to touch him?

That last thought vanished as the tip of her pink tongue peeked hungrily from between her luscious lips.

No kissing. Okay, he would deal with her rules...for now. He did have to follow orders.

Her breaths grew louder as he undid his pants and quickly produced his raging erection. Her eyes widened in surprise as his thigh slipped between her knees and he opened her legs. He let his pants drop to the floor, reached for the condom and sheathed his swollen shaft.

"Since you're already wet for me, sir, I'll skip the foreplay."

She hissed as he impaled her in one quick thrust. The warmth of her ultra-tight pussy grabbed hold of his engorged shaft like a vise, making him groan at the wicked pleasure jolting through him.

Cripes, if someone had told him early this morning he was going to be inducted into some black ops assassin group and taking his boss on her desk within minutes of meeting her, he would've said they were crazy.

He withdrew and thrust into her again, loving the meek little hiss of pleasure she made as he impaled her to the hilt. Her velvety heat snapped around his cock like blades of lightning.

He withdrew and thrust harder, watching those curled fingers tighten even more over the edge of her desk. Her eyes closed and she whimpered as her vaginal muscles spasmed like crazy around his erection.

Oh man. He couldn't breathe. Couldn't so much as think as pleasure wrapped around him. He exploded on a gut-wrenching shout and awoke with his body twisting in both pain and pleasure.

~ ~ ~ ~ ~

It took him several precious seconds to orient himself. To rip himself free from the cobwebs of the past. For a split second, sadness wrapped around him. Bev was dead now. Blown up in an explosion a few weeks ago. Yeah, he had regrets. He'd never told her he'd grown to care for her.

Suddenly, a unique pressure wrapped around his cock. The pleasure seemed to be alive, following him out of his dream.

He blinked in disbelief and through heavy-lidded eyes stared down to find Red sitting on the side of his bed. Her gaze was fixed on his midsection where her hands were wrapped snugly around his swollen erection.

She lapped at his cock head, the bristle of her tongue sending shivers of ecstasy shooting into his solid shaft.

He had to be dreaming. He had to be.

His balls tightened and his cock head disappeared into her mouth.

Oh yeah. Hot heaven.

He stifled a groan, knowing instinctively she would stop if she discovered he was awake and watching. She pulled her head back, cutting his cock loose, and then wrapped her luscious mouth around his throbbing flesh again.

Oh man. Why was she doing this? He'd been sent to kill her yet she'd saved his life and was pleasuring him? He must have done something right in his life to deserve this slice of heaven.

He lay quietly, damned hard under the circumstances. His teeth clenched as she increased her sucking on his cock. When he swore he couldn't take the pain of his hardness anymore, she stopped playing with him.

Foil ripped.

Condom?

Oh man.

Between slitted eyes, he saw her lift off her top and toss it to the ground. Yeah, he remembered how perfectly her breasts had fit into his hands. He ached to palm them and have her silky skin press against his fingers.

She climbed onto the bed. Climbed onto *him*.

Wow! Some magnificent dream!

No, not a dream. Reality.

He gritted his teeth to keep from crying out as she impaled herself on him. Her snug vagina clenched his throbbing, overheated flesh, sucking him into her.

His hands tangled in the sheets beneath the blankets. He kept his eyes scrunched closed while he rode the waves of pleasure her sweet gyrations created. Her tight muscles milked his cock. Magnificent spasms powered around his erection, gripping him so tightly euphoria slammed into him.

Within seconds, he exploded on a strangled groan. Her body tensed and she climaxed right along with him. Her soft, barely controlled cries whispered through the quiet air. The violence of his orgasm was just as strong as his first time with her—if not stronger.

All too quickly, the pleasure faded and she climbed off him. The blankets were tucked in and around his naked body as she whispered goodnight. Then she was gone.

Blade sighed with immense frustration as his wounds began to throb. Damn her. Why was she reminding him of how great sex could be between them? Why hadn't he just reached out, grabbed her by the waist, rolled them over and started taking her again? But he was so tired. He couldn't move a muscle. It felt so good lying here and enjoying the sex and just being alive.

Blade sighed deeply and drifted off into peaceful sleep.

* * * * *

Oh wow.

What she'd done with an unconscious Blade had been intense. Guilt was the least of her emotions, though. Exhilaration, satisfaction and happiness wafted through her in waves as she tenderly washed her sensitive pussy, taking care not to pull on her labia rings.

How in the world could she live with herself? Fucking an unconscious man wasn't something she did every day. She prided herself in pursuing the rights of other people and she'd infringed on his right to consensual sex. She'd taken away his decision by feeding him some extra medicine, knowing its sedative effects would make him defenseless against her.

But she'd needed to come so badly. Masturbating outside with her vibrator had worked late last night, but this morning she awoke with the familiar craving for sex. The insane need to orgasm.

She'd tried to masturbate, but the pleasure hadn't appeared. That had never happened to her before. Frustration plagued her all day as she tended to the two unconscious men, and then finally late this afternoon, she'd given into doing what she'd done to Will.

She gazed over at him. He lay quietly, his chest rising and falling slowly. He was still fast asleep. Thankfully he wouldn't know she'd taken advantage of him. She would never tell him how deceitful she had been.

An icy blast of air slapped against her near-nude body as she opened the cabin door and ducked into the wind. She tossed the used wash water over the railing and gazed off into the late afternoon sunshine.

Nearby, the pine branches creaked beneath the heavy weight of snow and it was beginning to snow again. She'd hoped the storm was over. A couple of hours ago the sun had come out, bright and cheerful, its warm yellow glow dancing off the snowdrifts. Unfortunately, large, lacy snowflakes began drifting lazily from dark, heavy clouds that had quickly chased away the sunshine. She estimated about two feet of snow had fallen last night and today.

Shoot! Additional snow would only make it that much harder for her to get out of here...or for people to get to her. She was surprised some of her crew hadn't come to her rescue already. Due to the satellite phone being damaged, she'd passed the allotted time she should have called the Resistance last night.

Maybe they weren't coming. Maybe her bitchiness had encouraged them to vote in a new leader during her absence. She'd be left out here in this desolation to fuck her brains out with two sleeping men.

Reena smiled as she dashed back into the warm cabin. Fucking them wasn't a bad idea, actually. But what would happen when the medicine ran out and they woke? She shivered. She'd have two virile men on her hands. That's what would happen.

And then her troubles would really start.

Chapter Seven

Cade was floating in a dark place. He didn't like it. Evil lurked here. Evil and emotional devastation. A sob bubbled up from somewhere deep inside him and he tried to stop it, but it came up and wrapped itself around him like a blanket of depression. He knew the feeling well.

He'd lived with it for many years, honing the raw emotion until it was razor sharp, just like the knives he carried to torture terrorists or those people he suspected of harboring them.

He remembered when the dark, evil depression had started, along with the scorching need for revenge. The day had begun innocently, the cheerful early-morning sunshine streaming through his bedroom windows at his parents' farmhouse. It heated his skin, baking him, but he didn't toss aside the warm comforters. He just lay there, cherishing this time of the morning.

His parents spoke in hushed voices in the kitchen down the hall. They did that every morning, talked intimately about their kids, their plans and what they were going to do that day. Then they roused their six sons and one daughter and got on with their chores.

He didn't think it the least bit funny that he, a twenty-five-year-old man, still lived with his parents. He had a girlfriend he fully intended on marrying. He slept over at her place a lot. They had magnificent sex. But for now, he was perfectly content helping his dad out on the farm and saving money for the land he planned on buying so he could farm too.

He and his sister Melanie were the only ones staying here at the moment. Their brothers were either in college, university or living at their own places.

Just thinking about his only sister made him smile. She was the youngest of the Outlaws. Being Tyler's twin she'd been born five minutes later. After the twins, his parents had two more daughters but they'd both been stillborn.

Needless to say, Melanie was the most precious Outlaw of them all. And she certainly used her leverage to the full extent. Wrapping them all around her little finger, getting anything she wanted. All the brothers caved when she asked them for a favor. Whether it was getting them to try out her latest cooking creations for the catering business she ran or setting them up on a blind date. That's how Cade had met Sue. Melanie had set them up and he'd fallen for Sue's gentle ways hook, line and sinker.

He held so much love for his sister and mother it had been perfectly natural for his feelings to overflow toward Sue. With her, though, he experienced a different kind of love...but it was just as fierce.

Strong, tart-scented coffee made him gaze at the clock. Time to get his ass in gear, shower, grab breakfast and head out to the fields with dad. He was just about ready when a light rap came at his door. Before waiting for an answer, which everyone did out of respect for one another's privacy, the door was flung inward.

His sister stood in the doorway in her nightgown. She was beautiful. Too pretty and nice for that preacher's son who'd come sniffing around lately. Anger burst inside of him. He didn't like Rafe. The kid was too polite. He was only after one thing—getting Melanie into bed with him. Cade's anger vanished when he saw his sister's fever-bright eyes.

He knew that look. His world collapsed and so did Melanie. Right on his bedroom floor. The X-virus had come calling.

They spent the next couple of days trying to save her life. The brothers all came home and tried to keep Mom away from Mel, but she wouldn't hear of it. Then his mother fell ill. Then he got word Sue was gravely ill too.

Fuck! People always said things happened in threes and they surely did. The three women he loved died within hours of one another.

The brothers buried them all on the same day. The coldness in his heart as the three caskets were lowered into their respective graves, one by one, had made him numb. None of the brothers had gone to the viewing. Not that anyone had shown up. Except Luke's wife Callie, the woman he and his brothers had years later Claimed after her request to make the union legal in the eyes of the law so she couldn't be touched by strange men.

Callie, who'd taken care of the women while they lay dying. Callie, bless her, hadn't been touched by the virus.

But virtually every other woman he knew had either died or survived the X-virus. Survivors were left with various side effects and many times he gave thanks the three most important women in his life had died because the world, as it was now, sucked.

Ah shit, this depression was threatening to take a firm hold. He didn't want that to happen. It was a frightening place, a desolation where he couldn't control his emotions and his mind threatened to drown him in the same despair he'd lived through immediately following their deaths. He concentrated on shrugging it off by thinking about Reena and, to his amazement, the crappiness hugging him vanished.

Thankfully despair hadn't been present when he'd sniffed around Reena. Despite not wanting to put his heart out there again, he'd physically fallen for her. The instant he frisked her warm, curvy body, ran his fingers through that gorgeous cloud of red hair and saw defiance in her eyes, he'd been hooked.

Despite the cold darkness, the snow flailing around them, he'd been on fire for her. It had been a long time since he'd been with a woman—Callie being the last. But she'd moved with his brother to Monaco where the Claiming Law didn't exist.

"Hey. How do you feel, Cade?"

Reena's feminine voice curled out of the evil darkness and she leaned over him. He caught her fresh gentle-soap scent which twisted through him like a teasing ribbon of lust.

He loved her delicate features. High cheekbones, skin that flushed so easily when a sexual remark was mentioned. Her cute button nose. Sparkling eyes framed by long, black lashes. Yet it was her dewy mouth that drew his attention.

Warmly curved, her lips would be full, cushiony and so sweet wrapped around his cock.

"Cade? Can you hear me?" she asked. Concern flooded her features and a cool hand whispered across his hot forehead. This was nice.

"You still have a fever. But it hasn't gotten worse."

"Hot," he muttered as the heat of pain rushed up and wrapped itself firmly around him.

"Yes, that's right. Because of the fever."

What he actually meant to say was she looked hot. Fantastic. Sexy. Beautiful.

The tinkle of falling water split the air and then a cool, wet cloth danced over his fevered chest, just around the area where the pain throbbed. It hurt with such magnificence he wondered if something vital had been pierced by the bullet. He'd had his share of bullet holes, knife slashes and bayonet stabs, along with being tortured. He'd experienced various levels of pain with each wound. This was one of the worst. Right up there with his own knife being carved into him.

Through the haze of pain, he determined he was in a room. Dark-brown stained board and batten-style wood flanked the walls, and thin strips of pine board made up the ceiling. The walls and ceiling were clearly handmade, but very good craftsmanship. Whoever built this place had known what they were doing.

Beside him, about four feet away, the silhouette of a potbelly cast-iron stove stood in the middle of the room. Shoved against a far wall was a couch draped with blankets.

He inhaled her enticing scent as she caressed his chest with the cool, wet cloth.

"We'll have you feeling better soon. I have medicine," she said. Tenderness laced the pretty features of her face and her soft words spread wonderful warmth into him, pushing aside the fever.

He sighed in relief. After all these years, the scorching warmth for a woman was back and the cold anger he'd been harboring was gone.

"I love you," he said. His voice sounded strangled, unused. He hadn't said those three words in one hell of a long time and it just seemed appropriate he should say them now. To her. Before he died.

"I know," she said. She may have figured what he said had something to do with the fever. Well, it probably did.

Just before he drifted away again, he vowed he would show her how much he truly did love her. He closed his eyes and slept.

* * * * *

Cade had been watching Red for hours. At least, it seemed like hours. He awoke to find her feeding the woodstove. Then, while humming a soft tune he didn't recognize, she prepared a meal in the adjoining kitchen. She cooked something on a portable camping stove and, every once in a while, the rich scent of frying beef—the kind in those store-bought cans—taunted his nostrils. His stomach growled in appreciation.

He hoped she didn't hear. He didn't want her to know he was awake and spying on her. He enjoyed watching her. She seemed so free. Like a graceful butterfly, flitting from the camp stove set on the table to the kitchen sink to wash something in a bucket, and then back to the kitchen table to cut vegetables before returning to the camp stove.

She lifted the pot and headed toward the potbelly stove beside him. He closed his eyes and feigned sleep. A couple of unidentifiable clanks split the air. His curiosity got the better of him and, through lowered lashes, he dared a peek.

The pot sat on the woodstove but Reena was nowhere in sight. Disappointment spilled through him. The soft hiss of the glowing gas lamp on the kitchen table was his only companion.

Where had she gone?

He tried hard to push back a surge of panic. Had she left the pot of food on the stove because she had every intention of clearing out and leaving Blade and him to fend for themselves? But then she coughed and the rustle of clothing followed. She was undressing.

His cock reacted, pulsed and began to tremble. He envisioned her creamy, full breasts pillowed in his palms. Nipples engorged and red from his sucks, her face flushed as she erotically gasped.

Cade inhaled and tried to shift his body as his cock continued to harden and his balls swelled in a burst of arousal. In order to focus on something other than his discomfort, he thought of Blade.

Just before losing consciousness in that camp, he had seen Blade take down the man who'd shot him. And for his troubles, Blade had taken a bullet from another man who'd been covering the guy who'd shot Cade.

He owed Blade for saving his life. He owed him big-time.

An odd clank made him peer to his right. Reena was shoving more wood into the potbelly stove. He lowered his lids to half-mast so she hopefully wouldn't see he was awake and watching her. She'd changed out of her day clothes and wore a loose-fitting, white, very short t-shirt. The sensual curves of her breasts were outlined beneath the shirt, her nipples stabbing boldly at the material. Gold glinted in the lamplight, illuminating a belly ring, and when she moved past the potbellied stove, the luscious round curves of her bottom came into view.

Oh shit.

No pants. No panties. Just the prettiest, curviest ass he'd ever seen. He almost groaned out loud at the sexy sight, but managed to catch himself as she lifted her top and tossed it to the floor.

What the hell was she doing?

Oh man. Oh man. Was he dreaming?

Cade clenched his fists in frustration as she quietly climbed onto Blade's cot.

No fucking way.

She had long legs for a petite woman. Nice wide hips. She swung a leg over Blade's body and a glimpse of gold gleamed on her pussy lips. Labia rings.

Nice.

She crouched over Blade's lower belly. In the lamplight, wetness shimmered between her thighs.

Wake up, man! Wake up and see the present she's giving you!

Blade didn't wake. Didn't so much as flinch or groan as she sheathed herself on him.

Good Lord! The man must be dead not to realize what she was doing. Cade forced his breathing to slow.

Strangely enough, jealousy or possessiveness didn't entertain his thoughts as Reena played with her breasts, tugged her nipple rings and gyrated upon Blade. Her pretty lips parted as she cried out quietly.

Cade tensed at her strangled outburst, his cock and balls swelling like a son of a bitch. Gritting his teeth against the awesome pressure, he continued to lie perfectly still. Man! This was hard.

He didn't want her to know he was watching. Didn't want her to know he was aroused while she pleasured herself with Blade. She seemed pretty confident Blade wouldn't wake up as she let out another cry, this time a little louder. She wiggled her hips faster, grinding into Blade's prone figure.

Cade almost swore out loud at the realization that Blade must have been drugged. He couldn't be that far into a fever he didn't know a woman was riding him. Reena was fucking Blade while he was unconscious. Was she drugging him as well?

Shortly after drinking the tea she continued pouring into him, an odd dopiness would hit. His gut twisted with awareness. She must be putting something in the drink. That would explain Blade lying there and her confidence in using his body for her sexual satisfaction.

Cade held back a moan as Reena gyrated harder and faster. Suddenly she stopped and her mouth went slack, the tension eased from her body. Slowly, she climbed off Blade. Cade didn't miss Blade's swollen shaft, hard as a pole and glistening with her juices as she wiped him with a cloth.

Afterward, she grabbed her top, her perky breasts jiggling as she padded over to the gas lamp on the table. She turned off the lamp and the room plunged into darkness. A couple of moments later, his eyes adjusted to the new lighting as the moon's glow drifted against the curtained windows.

Movement at Blade's cot had Cade's breath backing up in his lungs.

"Little bitch," Cade said softly as he kept his eyes glued in Blade's direction, cursing the bastard for being asleep through the whole thing.

A strangled gasp erupted from Blade.

Son of a bitch. He *had* been awake while Reena rode him and now he was masturbating.

Cade grinned. He wrapped his good hand around his shaft and began stroking himself, moaning softly as pleasure quickly curled through him. He'd have to figure out how to make sure she didn't get any more drugs into his system. He'd have to keep an eye on her every move. And he would, of course, have to plot the perfect sexual punishment for her.

He could hardly wait.

* * * * *

It was so quiet in the cabin. Reena surveyed the several pairs of panties and one bra she'd washed and hung on a string she'd suspended across the hot area above the woodstove. She tossed another log into the fireplace and shoved yet another into the potbelly stove before dropping some pills into her palm. These meds were meant to prevent infection. So far they were working. But she would have to stop drugging the men soon with her special tea. If they lay in bed for too long, they would have health issues like blood clots or pneumonia from lack of movement.

Maybe one more night. They should be strong enough by tomorrow to fend for themselves. There was enough food here to feed them until she could send in some members of the Resistance to rescue them. And then what?

Try to talk some sense into them? Try to get them to join the Cause?

Yeah, right. Cade's brother Tyler would spring Cade and Will the instant he found out her group had them, and then Will would come after her and maybe kill her, and Cade would try to recapture her and bring her in so he could collect his bounty to pay his bills. Well, let them try. That's what she had bodyguards for.

Reena sighed. She really should leave now. Tonight. She could use her old snowshoes to get out of this valley and head up to the main road where there was a cell signal.

Her momentary hope deflated. That is, if she had her cell phone. Cade had taken it when he'd captured her. She'd gone through his jacket after she'd rescued him and her cell and weapons hadn't been there. He'd probably put them in his knapsack back at his camp—the pack now buried under a heap of snow and her phone so frozen it wouldn't work anymore.

No, she would need to rest here tonight and decide what to do in the morning. An uneasy jittering still haunted her over what had happened with those hunters. Oddly enough, a sense of security flooded through her at having Will and Cade here, even if they were unconscious.

Her defenses were down. Despite being out of harm's way, there was a vulnerable and naughty side to her, wanting both of these men making love to her at the same time. This was so not good.

She grabbed a glass of water and headed to Blade. He appeared to still be out of it. Good. She'd forgo his tea tonight and coax him into taking a traditional antibiotic pill.

She'd have sex with Cade tonight. She'd be careful not to open his wounds. The anticipation of orgasming with Cade shot quivers of excitement through her. She blew out a breath and trailed her fingertips along Will's jawline. He moaned softly and her lower abdomen fluttered. She loved that sound.

Primal. Sex-on-a-stick. Man.

Touching the edge of his lips, she spoke softly, asking him to open his mouth. Thankfully he did.

"Stick out your tongue. I have some more antibiotics for you," she said.

His mouth opened partially and he stuck his tongue out. Reena couldn't hold back the shiver of heat zipping through her at the memory of his luscious tongue dabbing into her vagina.

Okay, Reena. Chill.

Her breathing grew faster and raspier and it took her a moment to steady her breath. She placed the pill on his tongue and he took it in, his Adam's apple bobbing as he swallowed.

Huh, no need for water tonight. That was easy. He must be getting better.

She checked the new poultice she'd placed on his chest and the wound appeared to be healing quite nicely. No sign of infection. The pill would keep him doped up and drowsy so she could have her way with Cade.

Reluctantly she left Will and moved around the woodstove to Cade's cot. His blankets were bunched up low on his abdomen, giving her a nice view of his tanned muscles and the steady rise and fall of his chest. He was sleeping.

Good.

Licking her dry lips, she gently tugged the blankets down past his waist, revealing a hard, juicy cock standing at half-mast. Oh boy, he had to be dreaming about some red-hot sex to be up like that tonight. Well, she'd get him a little harder in no time flat. She began touching him, the powerful throb of his penis beneath her fingers making her cream.

He groaned softly, animalistic and primal. Rena stopped, her tummy hollowing out with anxiety. She snapped her gaze to his face, but his eyes were closed. She breathed in relief.

Asleep. Perhaps she hadn't given him enough tea earlier to put him fully under? Maybe she should give him some more, just to make sure he didn't catch her. For a few seconds indecision raged, but the solid heat seeping into her fingers from his long, swollen cock encouraged her to continue with her agenda.

"You are so nice and big," she whispered, excitement and need firing through her bloodstream.

Gently, she twisted her hands around his scarred shaft. He grew bigger, his cock slowly turning an angry, demanding red.

"Almost, there," she said quietly as he blossomed bigger and bigger. "Nice and big and juicy for me."

Lust and curiosity at having him in her mouth wrapped around her. Holding his shaft steady at the base with one hand, she reached down with the other and stroked her sensitive pussy. Lowering her head toward his hard shaft, she moaned into the pleasure from her massages upon her clit.

Just one taste of him, that's all she craved. Just one taste while she stoked her fires and then she'd mount him. Licking her lips, she opened her mouth. As she sucked his big cock head, her lips stretched until they burned in a nice way. The velvety hard bulge of him in her mouth had her vagina clenching as she imagined him slipping into her pussy. She tightened her lips around his cock head, stopping when he groaned.

Oh shit.

Her eyes snapped back to his face. His lids remained closed.

But what else did she expect? She was arousing him. He was a man with sexual needs and he would react—even if he was asleep. He would think the pleasure was coming from a dream...that she was a dream. At least, she hoped that's what he would think.

She really should stop. This was a dangerous game. At least Blade quietly endured her needs while he slept and there weren't any sexy, aroused groans like from Cade.

Oh hell! Fire licked through her with an intensity she couldn't push away. She needed to satiate herself on him...tonight. Just him.

Using her tongue, she slurped around his big cock head, exploring the curves and ridges and the pulsing, elevated veins. She loved the bigness of him, the heat and the potential risk of him waking up while she was licking his shaft.

The thought of him fighting the sedative effects of the tea, of overpowering her, tying her down to the bed and fucking her senseless for hours, had her whimpering with need.

She released his cock.

Quietly and quickly, she sheathed his erect cock with a condom. Panting with impatience, she climbed over him. Squatting, she sucked in a hot breath as his wet cock head slipped between her labia and into her cunt. He slid into her, deep and powerful. Her sensitized vaginal muscles quickly accepted him, clenching his massive shaft, sucking and spasming. She rocked her hips, melted against him and rode him, all the while watching his face.

He was breathing harshly but his eyes remained closed. If he hadn't woken up by now, he would just think of this as a dream. But gosh, his lips looked so yummy. They were curled upward slightly at the edges, as if he were secretly smiling. Yes, he was in dreamland.

One kiss wouldn't hurt, would it?

Leaning over, she touched her lips to his and reveled in the soft push of her mouth against hers. Surprise zipped through her as he parted his lips, his tongue pressing into her mouth, mating with her tongue.

He was demanding, his tongue stroking hers, pistoning inside her like a miniature cock. Pleasure splashed around her and she moaned as she climaxed. The orgasm rocked her right down to her toes and she struggled for breath as tremors embraced her straining body. She ground herself senselessly against his strong body, her mouth fused against his.

Vibrations whipped against her, over her, all around her. She cried into his succulent mouth as the pleasure sent her into a mindless vortex where nothing existed except stars, streaks of color and helpless excitement. She could barely catch her breath as the orgasm ebbed and she awkwardly climbed off Cade. Wiping her fingers over her sensitized lips, she gazed down at his sweat-sheened body.

If she didn't know any better, she'd swear he was awake. How else could she explain the raw and desperate way he'd kissed her back?

And how did she explain her reaction to him? Like a wild, out-of-control animal high on lust, that's how.

Sweet heavens. Had her X-virus mutated to another, wilder level? All she wanted to do was rub herself, like a cat in heat, all over these two men. Her fingers trembled as she slipped the condom from Cade's semi-erect cock. Tying off the condom, she tossed it into the wastebasket in the kitchen. After making sure his wounds hadn't reopened, she hurriedly mixed a fresh poultice. Relief splashed through her after packing his wounds.

Rest. She needed rest. But first she had to wash the insides of her thighs.

A few minutes later, a wonderful freshness clung to her skin as she climbed beneath the blankets on the couch. Boy, she was tired from all that gyrating on Cade. She should have been more careful with him, but she had lost control.

Reena closed her eyes and blew out a breath. Boy, had she ever lost control.

Hopefully the snow would stop by morning and she could get out of here. Hopefully...

She slept.

* * * * *

"Was it as good as it sounded?" Blade's chuckle snapped through Cade, making him jolt from where he stood at the front porch railing. He'd waited until Reena fell asleep before getting out of bed.

To his surprise, he wasn't that tired or wobbly. His chest and shoulder barely hurt, compliments of her good nursing skills. Except his wounds got quite sore when he moved his right arm, so he kept his motions to a minimum and used his left. He'd tiptoed around the kitchen, grabbed some bread and cheese and gulped it down while finding the matches she used to light the camp stove as well as some candles on a kitchen shelf.

Via candlelight, he'd quietly grabbed the weapons and stashed them in a back room out of sight, because when Reena discovered they were awake and not drugged anymore, she just might decide to do something stupid...like shoot them. He'd found his pants and cleaned shirt and sweater, the bullet holes sewn up quite professionally.

Donning his jacket and boots, he'd come outside to grab some fresh air.

Blade had also waited to make sure Reena was asleep before getting out of bed. The man grinned happily as he tossed a pill out into the snow. He'd apparently discovered his cleaned clothing as well and, aside from a few little grimaces as he slipped into his coat—also cleaned of blood—he appeared pale but strong.

It seemed not only was Reena a good Florence Nightingale, she was also a good laundress and seamstress.

"Better than good," Cade admitted, trying not to act surprised that Blade had witnessed Reena ride him into orgasm. All her gyrating had made him hotter than hell and he was thankful the cold winter air was doing a good job of cooling him down.

"So, what's on our agenda?" Will asked. "Not that I'm complaining. I rather enjoyed it, but she needs some kind of punishment for drugging us and taking advantage of us like she did." Humor laced Blade's voice.

Amusement sifted through Cade at the thought of getting back at her and giving her a taste of her own medicine. It would be more than enjoyable. He hadn't been this keyed up in one hell of a long time.

Snowflakes swirled out of the dark night sky and, having lived on a farm since he was born, he was a pretty good reader of the weather...and the sky was spelling trouble.

"Looks like another blizzard." Cade nodded at the sky. "We won't be going anywhere at least for a couple of days. I, for one, don't expect to be lying around anymore pretending I'm sick."

"I'll second that," Blade agreed. "I take it you've got something in mind?"

"Damn right I do," Cade admitted.

The camaraderie with Blade was rare. They'd worked together before, along with his brothers, in serious situations. And teaching Reena a lesson was a serious situation as far as he was concerned.

"So do I," Blade said. "How about we put our two ideas together and see what we come up with? I mean, I can't very well kill a woman who saved my life. How about a truce?"

Cade blinked in stunned disbelief as Blade stretched out his hand. After a slight hesitation, he shook hands with the man who—had Cade not stopped him—would have killed Reena twice by now. Now that he knew Reena and Blade shared a past, Cade's defenses dissolved. Blade was a man of his word. If he wanted a truce, then he would stick to it. Cade had no doubt about that.

"Truce," he agreed.

"One problem," Blade moaned.

"What?"

"Condoms."

Cade grinned. "I just happen to know where she keeps them."

"Fuck, yeah!"

Cade grimaced when Blade slapped him hard on the back.

They turned and hurried back inside.

* * * * *

Reena dreamed of happier times. Life before the Wars, before the X-virus. Life being a free woman who could do whatever she wanted, when she wanted and with whom she wanted. She'd had no plans except for becoming a teacher, getting married and having kids. In that order. But one thing she'd known for sure, she didn't want to end up like her parents. Miserable.

She'd been raised by a mother and father who fought all the time. That is, when her father was at home. Her dad was a five-star general and away a lot. "Home" had been military bases all over the world.

When she was a kid, she swore she'd never travel again. Never have anything to do with the military again. But the X-virus had changed all that.

The day had started out simple enough. She'd been in her third month as a substitute teacher at an all-boy's private school in Boston, and the X-virus was just starting to make headlines. Rumor had it some terrorist organization had unleashed it at an international women's conference. By the time the women had returned to their respective countries, they were in full-submission mode.

Her father, "Sir General" as she referred to him when she was pissed off at him—which had been often—had called and told her to return home immediately. Home at that particular time was on a German military base. She defied him. She was, after all, on her very first full-time teaching position, and wasn't about to run home because the general said so.

Besides, she had told him, she *was* home. She had a quaint little apartment that overlooked Boston harbor and was in no mood to return to the middle of her parents' in-fighting. She hung up, pretending the call had been disconnected, and hadn't picked up the phone when it rang again during her two-week Christmas hiatus.

Screw them.

She did, however, keep an eye on the news. Yes, it frightened her that women were becoming submissive, but the news also said medical authorities had the virus under control and there was no need to panic. Various countries were putting any woman with symptoms under quarantine. So she had no reason to worry, right?

In the meantime, she had her eye on a cute, hunky art teacher named Brian Thompson. Too bad he'd gone home to his parents for the holidays or she would have made her move.

She would ask him out when he returned to school. If she played her cards right, they'd start dating and maybe she'd even have sex with him. Back then, she'd taken her freedom for granted. She could go anywhere she wanted, any time, without asking for permission. So she'd travelled to New York City over the holidays and ended right smack-dab in the middle of a hot zone.

She hadn't known it at the time. The X-virus was just spreading outside the quarantine zone in New York City. New York...another first for her.

The wild stampede of pedestrians, the endless stream of yellow taxis...and Ground Zero. Now *that* visit had chilled her. She was exposed to so many people. Hadn't a clue her life would change so dramatically the day after she returned to her apartment.

Sickness and extreme tiredness had knocked her off her feet. Not only had the illness affected her physically, but emotionally and mentally as well. It sapped so much strength out of her she could barely stay awake longer than half an hour. Fear had encouraged her to call her parents and her dad had a military escort at her door within an hour.

Two men in uniform had never looked so hot as she lay in the backseat of their car. Despite the sickness clawing through her, she wanted to have sex with them. She craved to have them fuck her. Needed it so badly her entire body ached. It was then she realized she'd contracted the dreaded X-virus.

And when those two men asked things such as "please step out of the car" or "please follow us" she'd obeyed without question, relishing the wonderful high that accompanied following their orders.

Her father's fast thinking and getting her to the closest state-of-the-art military hospital had saved her life. The doctors immediately ordered blood tests. Within fifteen minutes, they confirmed her suspicions. She had a version of the X-virus. The O version. A nurse was called in and, to Reena's horror and utmost embarrassment, the nurse sexually stimulated Reena until she'd orgasmed. Relief had pulsed through her and she thought she'd been cured.

But the relief wouldn't last long, the doctors warned. She would need to orgasm when the symptoms came. Orgasms released certain hormones, temporarily subduing the X-virus and keeping her sexual urges under control.

What a nightmare!

Her father arrived a day later. He didn't so much as flinch when the doctor told him what she had. He'd just kept that stern, emotionless face and whisked her away to their country home in England—the one they rarely used but paid through the nose for. He sequestered her there with a full-time staff. She learned to masturbate on a daily basis. Learned to keep her illness a secret. Soon the staff, mostly women, became ill. One by one they died.

Word came her grandfather had passed. Then her grandmother. Her mother, too, quickly succumbed to the virus, leaving Reena disoriented, panicked and abandoned.

Then the Terrorist Wars hit and the threat of the Claiming Law. Her father got her into the Teachers Without Borders program and she was shuttled off to Afghanistan where she assisted a very nice male teacher—Tyler Outlaw, Cade Outlaw's youngest brother.

It hadn't been easy keeping her secret from Tyler, but when the pangs of submissiveness began sweeping over her, she made her excuses, did the deed, felt better and returned to the classroom.

Even now, in her sleep, the sultry shudders of lust and pleasure threatened to pull her out of her dream. Her awareness of Blade and Cade in the same room was so strong, she could smell them.

Cade's clean, soapy scent, very near. Dark and dangerous. It mingled with Blade's spicy-pine smell, powerful and dominating. The combination of both men was lethal. It made her do things she normally wouldn't comprehend doing—like drugging and fucking them.

Their fingers wrapped like handcuffs around her wrists as they lifted her arms over her head and tied them to the headboard. They'd restrained her legs already, spreading them wide, her ankles tied with silken scarves to each foot post.

She struggled in her sleep, but the binds kept her in place. She couldn't get away. Wouldn't, even if she could.

She inhaled as their mouths latched onto each nipple. Oh God, how their moist, hot mouths burned her alive as they sucked furiously, the bite of pleasure and pain knifing through her...

Reena came awake on a strangled gasp and discovered a set of eager lips attached to each of her nipples. Blade and Cade. Shock snapped through her. Sweet heavens! Was she awake?

Chapter Eight

Was her fantasy of Cade and Blade really happening? Or was it just that—a fantasy?

Carnal pleasure raged through her and she twisted against the restraints, moaning at the tremors embracing her. She'd heard some females had several different mutated versions of the X-virus. Until now, she'd thought she only had the O version. Had her version mutated into the F-Fantasy version as well?

She stared down in stunned fascination as their tongues lashed her engorged, ringed nipples, making her writhe beneath the pleasure. The bindings on her wrists tightened painfully and she jolted with awareness.

Oh, goodness! This *wasn't* a dream.

Just go with it. Enjoy what they're offering. Enjoy this punishment for using them without their permission.

"This isn't happening," she blurted, trying to gather her self-control.

Both men stopped what they were doing and lifted their heads from her breasts to stare at her.

Reena inhaled sharply at the dewy redness of their lips. How long had they been sucking on her nipples, anyway?

"We thought you'd never wake up, baby," Cade murmured.

"W...what are you doing?" Dumb question. They had her tied to the bed! It didn't take a brain surgeon to figure it out. They wanted her. She could read the lust in their eyes and a sultry hum of arousal shifted through her every fiber.

"Tell us if you don't want this, Red, and we'll stop," Blade said. His voice was thick, drenched with desire.

"Why?" she replied and wrenched at her bonds. She should be embarrassed, lying here, her breasts bared and only her panties between two men and her pussy. She wasn't, though.

It was insane!

"We're returning the favor," Cade replied. "Did you think we didn't know what you were doing to us?"

Her cheeks burned. Cade knew what she'd been doing? Did Blade know too? But her embarrassment at getting caught was quickly pushed aside as concern for their health gripped her.

"But your wounds will reopen."

Blade shook his head and pointed to the white linen bandages wrapped tightly around their upper chests. The two of them had been busy, ensuring their wounds wouldn't open while they plotted their revenge on her.

"We figured you'd rather have both of us attending to your needs while we are here. Any opening wounds can be handled," Blade replied. "And you don't need to fear for your life. I've decided pleasuring you is a hell of a lot better than killing you."

"And I've decided the government can do without you. I need you more. Sorry if it sounds selfish."

Cade parted his lips and sucked her left nipple ring into his mouth. He smiled, showing her his even, white teeth and the gold ring. He tugged gently.

"Harder," Blade instructed, keeping his intense gaze on her face. "She likes it hard, don't you, Red. And I'm glad you decided to keep these rings. They look great on you."

She trembled as Blade's hand slipped between her thighs and beneath her panties. A hot finger pressed and twisted and rubbed against her tender clit, wrenching some awesome quivering from deep inside her.

"Just say no and we'll stop, Red," Blade whispered.

Stop? Her head whirled at that one word. For a second, she didn't even understand what it meant. Stop what she'd been fantasizing about for the past couple of days? How could she deny her fantasy?

Excitement at what they offered surged through her bloodstream at lightning speed.

"Consider it a sweet punishment," Blade continued.

She cried out as Cade tugged harder on her nipple ring.

"A simple nod of your head will suffice," Blade breathed as his finger continued its sensual assault on her tender pussy. She whimpered and jerkily nodded. Blade grinned and Cade's eyes glazed with appreciation.

"Let the punishments begin," Blade said softly.

Punishments?

She yelped as Blade let go of her pussy. Quickly, he slipped his fingers beneath the waistband of her panties and with one fast tug, ripped them in half.

"I hope they weren't your favorite pair," he said as he lifted the fragments aside, allowing warm air to brush against her.

Her breath caught as he came up over her and nestled himself between her spread legs, his wide shoulders pushing seductively against the insides of her thighs. She whimpered with anticipation as his head dropped. His hot breath seared her pussy.

"Don't think I haven't thought about having your sweet pussy in my mouth, Red," Blade murmured.

She didn't miss Cade's curious grin at Blade's comment. He certainly seemed eager to know more about her past with Blade.

"Rest assured, Cade," Blade winked at the other man, "one taste of her and you'll be hooked just like I am."

"I can hardly wait," Cade said, letting go of her nipple ring. His intense gaze had her trembling with need.

"She's got rings down here, too," Blade purred.

Sweet lightning lanced her labia as he took the rings into his mouth and tugged none too gently. She creamed and he lapped at her opening, slurping her arousal into his mouth.

An animalistic groan from Cade had her tensing harder. His eyes blazed with hunger. He lowered his head toward her other breast, his hand cupping her. He held tight while he sucked her nipple into his mouth. Pleasure snapped through her as both men orally tended to her. The exquisite vibrations rocked her and she couldn't stop from crying out and rising against her bonds as a body-wrenching orgasm whipped her into submission.

* * * * *

"Trade places, Cade," Blade gasped from between Red's thighs. "I need to feel her lips wrapped around my cock."

Cade didn't stir and annoyance whipped through Blade. Cade appeared to be so into sucking Red's nipple, he was oblivious to Blade's desperate request. Frustration smacked through him and he growled.

Cade moved quickly, releasing her nipple with a pop. He jerked his chin for Blade to untie one of her bound wrists while Cade did the same, fumbling while using his left hand.

"Get her to the edge of the bed." Cade indicated the foot of the pullout bed where Reena had made her sleeping quarters.

Blade untied her wrist on his side. His gut clenched fiercely at the scorching heat shining in her eyes. He couldn't wait to have her lips wrapped around his shaft. Couldn't wait to fuck her.

Once her wrists were free, he strolled down to the foot of the bed where he and Cade grabbed her ankles and tugged her to the edge. They positioned her on her back, legs bent, knees in the air, her feet planted firmly on the mattress.

They brought her arms up over her head and, after lengthening the ropes, they bound her wrists again.

Stroking his engorged cock, Blade moaned as sultry quivers snapped around his shaft. Cade put his hands on her knees, bringing those trembling legs gently apart, allowing the two of them to gaze at her intimate parts while they quickly donned condoms.

Her pussy looked so beautiful. Her labia lips were swollen and pink from when he had just taken her into his mouth, and the rings glistened a breathtaking gold against her flushed flesh. He lifted his gaze to her face and his gut jolted at the erotic desire flaring in her eyes and the lusty rose blush of her cheeks—a color that almost matched the red of her hair.

She shuddered and moaned softly as Cade climbed onto the bed, came down between her legs and slid his condom-sheathed cock into her wet vagina. Blade let out a slow, deep breath at the carnal sight and fought for control of his senses. He wanted to take her. Bad. But he also wanted to watch her getting fucked by another man.

Her hands curled into tight fists and she arched her lower back as she accepted Cade. Blade's cock jerked at her sexy whimper as Cade pulled out and thrust into her again.

With every stroke, her breaths grew heavier and faster. The succulent slurps of wet sex vibrated through the air along with Cade's groans and Red's sultry moans. When Blade could no longer hold the need to take her, he quickly crawled onto the bed, maneuvered his way past Cade and got into position with his knees straddling her shoulders, his hips over her face.

He stared down at her. "Open your eyes, Red," he urged softly, very impatient to come.

Her eyes fluttered open and she seemed surprised to find him peering down at her from overhead. She smiled quickly and opened her mouth. He slid in and her velvety lips snapped like a vise around his highly sensitized cock. He gritted his teeth against the succulent pressure. Her mouth tightened and he sensed her nearing climax. He wanted to come with her.

Keeping a tight restraint on his need for release, he moved his hips slowly, sliding in and out of her mouth in a steady rhythm. Her guttural moans grew deeper and more strangled as he picked up his pace.

Movement to his left had him turning to find their reflection in the glass panes of one of the living room windows. The threesome looked awesome. Cade stood at the edge of the bed, his hands on her outstretched knees while he fucked her. Part of Blade's engorged cock disappeared into her mouth. But he couldn't watch long, because her sultry breaths quickened and her mouth tightened, alerting him she was about to orgasm.

He slid in and out of her mouth, matching Cade's thrusts, pushing her body closer to the headboard every time he entered her. If he didn't come soon, he would lose his mind from this awesome killing need.

* * * * *

Cade swore he was dying and going to heaven every time he entered her tight, wet vagina. Her muscles gripped his cock in a warm, wicked welcome. Blade was right. The harder he thrust, the sultrier her moans, the more she enjoyed the sex.

Those intoxicating mews of hers were like heat-seeking pleasure missiles bombarding his body. The erotic way her muscles in her abdomen tightened, the sweetness of how her body jerked and wrenched with his every sensual thrust had him ready to explode. Have mercy, he was going to burst the minute she came.

* * * * *

Whatever they were doing to her, the exquisite pleasure had Reena's senses soaring onto a plane she'd never encountered before. Having a man fucking her mouth at the same time another fucked her pussy had her jerking toward a climax she sensed would be the ultimate experience.

Blade's swollen erection plunging in and out of her, making love to her tongue, her teeth, her lips, had her straining toward an exquisite fire uncurling deep inside her core. Cade plunging hard and fast had her heady with excitement and wicked need. The harder Cade fucked her, the deeper she wanted him, the more she needed from him. It was crazy. It was beautiful.

Her vaginal muscles burned for release and her mind fragmented as she tried to comprehend the exhilaration of having these two dangerous men fucking her. They played her body as if it were a musical instrument. Their thrusts and groans touched emotional and physical cords at every level of her being.

In her past, she'd been with several men at the same time. But Will and Cade impaling her, stretching her, drawing her toward her own pleasure, pushing their own needs aside as they awaited her orgasm, was something she'd never experienced before with a man. Or in other men.

They put her needs first. Their concern for her pleasure was such a sensual act she swore it turned her on even more. She began to cry out their names as they kept fucking her, drawing her closer to those lusty flames, their hard, driving strokes so sensual, powerful, perfect.

Her muscles clenched and spasmed around their plunging members and the orgasm snapped into her with such gut-wrenching, exquisite speed, every part of her danced and convulsed in unison. Vibrations rocked her and sultry flames embraced her, hugged her and loved her. From somewhere far away, grunts and groans echoed in her ears as they dove into the inferno of pleasure, losing themselves right along with her.

* * * * *

The wind and icy snow snapped against the cabin's old window panes with such fierce intensity, Reena feared the windows would cave inward, shattering the old, brittle glass into a million tiny pieces. But as the night hours ripped by and nothing happened to the windows, a serene quiet sifted through her.

She lay peacefully between the two big naked men as they slept soundly and snored. Sometime during the night, they'd untied her bonds. When she awoke to find herself free, she'd immediately thought of escape. The survival instincts she'd honed over the years were certainly alive and well and, for a few brief, intense moments, she decided it best to sneak out and just leave them here. But if these two brutes had meant to hurt her, they could have easily done so by now.

Especially Blade. He'd been sent to kill her and somehow that mission had changed for him. She was still alive. Besides, if she were to die, she'd rather it be by his hands than a stranger's.

Stuck in a desolate cabin without electricity, in the middle of yet another blizzard, with two guys who'd gotten shot in their efforts to rescue her, was the safest place for her to be. She could trust them. Reliance was in such short supply these days.

They'd been exquisite lovers and she swore she'd never been so wonderfully sore, or so satisfied and lusciously loved.

Those were crazy thoughts because she barely knew these men. Maybe that was for the best. Maybe if she knew more about them, she would be scared and fear for her life once again. Right now, though, she didn't want to be afraid. She just wanted to live in this afterglow lullaby. These two men were her knights in shining armor. They'd saved her life and, despite her saving their lives, she still owed them because they never would have been hurt in the first place if she hadn't wandered away in a blizzard.

She could also argue that if Cade hadn't caught her, then none of this would have happened. However that didn't sound romantic, and right now, fantasizing about these guys really caring about her, enough to save her life, was what she wanted.

Another blast of wind rattled the window panes and she burrowed deeper beneath the thick blankets, snuggling closer to both sleeping men. Their sexy scents teased her nostrils and their strong body heat wrapped her in a protective barrier. This was the only place in the world she wanted to be. This safety was good. Just like...home.

* * * * *

Icy pellets stung Will's face and he quickly jammed his freezing hands into his coat pockets. He ducked back around the side of the cabin to retrieve another armload of split firewood from the nearby lean-to. His shoulder pained him like a bitch, but at least he could move it.

Last night's sexual escapades with Red and Cade had tired him out so much he'd slept like a log late into the morning. He awoke to a stiff, aching shoulder, a damned cold cabin and Red fast asleep, snuggled up beside him, her warm face burrowed right against his neck. Damned if she'd been using his wounded chest as her pillow.

To say "ouch" was an understatement. Despite the throbbing pain of his injuries, he'd experienced an overwhelming urge to continue lying beneath the warm comforters and simply enjoy the array of enticing scents wafting from the petite woman.

Soap, flowers and a unique freshness teased his nostrils and had him hard as a rock and longer than a pole. She'd sponge bathed while he and Cade had slept. Hell, she could have easily escaped during the night and taken off into the storm. But she hadn't. She'd stayed and climbed back into bed with them.

Blade grimaced as pain danced through his chest and he used his left arm to hoist some more firewood onto his right. He trudged through the knee-deep drifts, stomped up the stairs and dumped the firewood onto a dry area of the porch, adding them to the other armloads he'd already collected.

Having the firewood close at hand would be nice. He wasn't one for wandering outside into the freezing cold if he didn't have to. He preferred a nice warm cabin and a certain succulent redhead.

Blade frowned as his cock decided to twitch and press boldly against his pants. Man, every time he thought about her he got one hell of a hard-on. It had been a struggle walking over the past few months, his cock and balls so hard whenever his thoughts became focused on her. Now that he'd had her again, he hoped he'd fucked her out of his system. No such luck. He couldn't wait to get back inside the cabin and into her.

Turning into the storm again, Blade cursed as another volley of ice pellets peppered his cold, sensitive face. Frosty fingers of wind slipped through his clothes, making him shiver. When he got back inside, he was going to take her again. It would be the best and fastest way to warm himself.

Giving her some hot and heavy pleasure first thing after waking her would put them all in a really good mood and, based on the dark skies, they would need to stay in a good mood...because it didn't look as if the storm was going to let up anytime soon.

* * * * *

Reena awoke with a start as a loud crash came from somewhere outside.

"Easy. It's just Blade piling up the firewood," Cade said from beside her.

At least she thought he was lying beside her, naked, his hot flesh pressed against her body.

Intense need zinged through her. She couldn't stop the anguished moan from escaping her lips upon discovering he lay fully clothed on top of the blankets. Her arms were once again outstretched and her wrists bound. Her neediness fizzled flat, instantly replaced by a surge of red-hot anger.

"I thought we'd moved into the trust range, Outlaw," she snapped.

He gazed down at her, momentary confusion flaring in his eyes. When she pulled against the restraints, he grinned.

Oh! What an irritating man!

"You look too sexy to not be bound and at our mercy whenever we want to take you," he said.

Oh my God!

"Don't look so shocked, Reena. Did you think we wouldn't want more of the awesome pleasure you gave us? That we wouldn't realize you wanted more?"

Of course she wanted more. But she wasn't about to tell *him* that.

"I want out of these bindings, Cade. I'm serious." She tried to inject seriousness into her voice, but she only sounded breathy. Gosh, she was all hot and bothered and ready for some more heavy-duty *bedroom* action. From both of them.

"You're nice and quiet, all of a sudden. Thinking about last night?" he asked.

Her cheeks grew hot, giving her away. "When are you going to release me?"

His eyebrows rose in question. "Why?"

"Because...I'm hungry."

That awesome gut-twisting grin of his whispered across his lips again. Gosh, she wished he wouldn't smile. He seemed way too nice a guy when he smiled. It chased away all the hardness lurking in the planes of his face.

"Actually, I'm way ahead of you on that. I've got food."

He reached down to his other side and, to her surprise, lifted a clump of red globe grapes. She'd brought them along with her and hadn't gotten around to eating them. Her mouth watered at the sight. Grapes were a delicacy these days and the only expensive food treat she allowed herself.

She held her breath as he plucked one juicy globe from the vine, raised it to his mouth and bit it in half. Juice dribbled down his chin and damned if she didn't want to lick it off.

"Delicious," he whispered as he chewed.

His eyes darkened and his gaze lowered to her mouth. He moved the half-eaten grape along her lower lip and she lapped at the sweetness it left behind.

"That's it, Red. Tastes good, doesn't it? You looked really hot last night, doing that licking thing with your tongue before Blade put his cock inside your mouth. I can't wait until your mouth takes me."

Reena trembled at the lashes of excitement racing through her. She would like to experience going down on Cade, but she was pissed off at him for tying her up again.

He fed her the half-eaten grape and she ate it quickly, savoring the wet, sweet juices teasing her taste buds. He fed her several more globes, his gaze intense as he watched her eat.

Without warning, his head lowered. When he brushed his lips against hers with a teasing featherlight brush her senses snapped into awareness mode. Her world tilted wonderfully and she swore she fell headlong into a fire pit of longing to have this man fucking her senseless...just like last night. She wanted to curl her arms around his neck, draw him closer, but the restraints prevented her from moving. Frustration snapped through her as he pulled away from her. That sexy half grin of his made her insides boil with need.

"You taste good," he whispered in a throaty voice.

They both jumped as the door burst open and Will stalked inside, his jacket and hat covered in snow. A whirlwind of snowflakes followed him and he quickly shut the door. As he turned around and spied Cade lying beside her on the bed, he froze.

His eyes darkened fiercely. She wasn't sure if he was jealous or aroused...or both. A muscle spasmed in his left cheek as he stared at the two of them.

"Am I interrupting something?" he finally asked.

"If you were, I'd be asking you to join us," Cade replied casually.

To her surprise, Blade grinned. His smile melted her insides just as fiercely as Cade's had done moments earlier.

Oh boy, she was in trouble.

"The snow isn't going to let up any time soon. It's too deep for the snowmobile and almost zero visibility, so we'd get into trouble if we left. Best to stay here. You may as well let her loose. She won't be going anywhere. She'll be too busy with the both of us."

He winked at her and she swore her world rocked.

Oh. My. God.

* * * * *

Cade cast sidelong glances at Reena as she washed the dishes. He stood beside her at the kitchen counter, drying the cutlery and placing it in the dish tray. Dainty. That's how he would phrase the way she handled the cutlery. Dainty and sexy. Yeah, very sexy. And this petite woman was the leader of the Resistance?

"Your brother mentioned you during the Wars," she said and he stiffened in surprise.

Over a dinner of canned meat, vegetables and potatoes, she'd been very quiet. He'd hoped what he and Will had done to punish her hadn't backfired on them. But that couldn't be the case. Not if the heated way she'd looked at him after he'd feather-kissed her on the bed was any indication. She was hot for him. And for Blade.

She shot quick glances to Blade every now and then when he wasn't watching. She shot Cade quick looks too. The fire in her eyes was unmistakable. She wanted more of what they had given her last night. Talk about a hell of a good way to break the ice between the three of them.

"Nothing better to do than to discuss me?" he asked.

He wondered exactly how much his brother Tyler had told this woman about him. They'd had plenty of chances to talk during the time Reena and Tyler had taught together overseas, and then recently rekindling their friendship after Tyler's return several months ago.

"He said we would make a good match."

"He did, did he? What do you think, Blade? Was Tyler right? Do Red and I make a good match?"

Blade gazed up from several pieces of the satellite radio he'd laid out and was inspecting on the floor by the potbelly stove. "I think the three of us make a good match."

Blade's answer surprised Cade. At first he thought Blade was kidding, but as Cade looked into the other man's dead-serious brown eyes, his resistance to the old ways of one man and one woman in a relationship began to dissolve. Some of his brothers had been in ménages with the women they loved. Their relationships were still strong. But was Blade nuts? Or Cade for that matter? Blade was an assassin. He'd been sent here to kill Red. How could Cade even entertain the idea of a possible relationship between the three of them?

They'd spent only one night pleasuring Reena. Yeah sure, it had been fantastic, and today had passed pleasantly enough—Cade and Blade bringing in armfuls of wood to pile beside the woodstove and fireplace and Rena doing the cooking. She was a good cook, or maybe he'd just been starving after their sex workout last night.

"No one is matching up with anyone," Reena said and he refocused his attention on her. Her shoulders were tense and her eyes blazed with anger.

"I am the leader of the Resistance or have you forgotten that fact? The leader is free to pick and choose what man or what men, for that matter, she wants in her bed. As all women should be allowed to do," she snapped.

Oh yeah, Cade liked the fire flaring in her eyes and his gut clenched really nice.

Will stared back at her, not saying anything. His intense gaze silenced her. She tightened her mouth, returning to washing the dishes.

Cade sent Will a warning scowl intended to tell him to back off, but Will just shrugged, shook his head casually and focused on the shattered satellite radio.

"No one is going to Claim me," she muttered. She spoke so low he suspected her words weren't meant for him to hear. But he did, and the isolation and heavy weight she carried with her sank deep into his very soul.

Reena was wanted by the law as well as any group of men who could catch and Claim her. The odds that she would stay free or alive were pretty slim, even if she were surrounded by an entourage of bodyguards. Which she wasn't. That fact made him believe she had no sensible protection or she wouldn't be wandering around alone out here.

She smiled weakly and handed him the last plate, which he dipped into the rinse bucket and then dried with a towel. A few minutes later, they joined Will, each of them pulling up a chair beside the woodstove. Heat blasted them and Cade leaned back against his chair as they all fell silent.

Outside, the storm continued to rage. Icy snow and blasts of wind pelted the quickly darkening windows and the fire in the stove crackled and snapped warmly.

"This place belonged to your grandparents," Blade said, breaking the quiet lull. Beside him, Reena stiffened. She'd been doing that a lot today whenever one of them suddenly spoke. He hoped it was a good sign. That maybe she was relaxed with them around—that is, until they reminded her they were here. Or maybe she thought Blade was still going to kill her.

"Until the X-virus came and screwed my life, I came here and spent two weeks with my grandparents every summer," Reena replied.

Pride and happiness flooded her voice. "It was our tradition. My grandmother and grandfather built this cabin shortly after they were married. They were young, but even back then they planned on spending their elderly years here. When he retired from his job as a butcher, they stayed here during the summer and fall and had a trailer in Florida where they stayed during spring and winter."

"Snowbirds." Cade grinned.

Reena nodded.

"That was a lot of people's perfect retirement plan," Blade said softly.

Then everyone got fucked, Cade added silently. He knew the others were thinking the same thing. He could see it in Reena's sad eyes and Will's thoughtful stare. These days there was no such thing as a retirement plan. Everyone worked until they dropped dead.

There weren't too many older people around. The feeble ones succumbed because there were no facilities to look after them. Loved ones died or did everything they could to survive on their own, leaving the elderly to fend for themselves.

"How did your grandparents meet?" Cade asked, wanting to know everything about her. This kind of curiosity had been inside him only one other time, about the woman he'd planned on marrying.

"My grandfather emigrated to New York when he was a teenager. His parents had died and he didn't want to impose on relatives. He was a very independent man. He became an apprentice for an elderly butcher he met on the boat ride over to the States. After he learned everything there was to learn, he opened his own shop. My grandmother was one of his first customers."

Reena got a really nice wistful smile on her face. "My grandmother was working as a housekeeper for some rich people and was only sixteen when he first saw her. He said she was the most beautiful woman with the reddest hair and greenest eyes he'd ever seen. He said he fell in love with her the instant he saw her. Grandmother said she didn't particularly care for my grandfather in the beginning because every time she came into the butcher shop he would stare at her and barely spoke, he was so tongue-tied."

Cade and Will laughed.

"She thought he was slow in his mind until one day he came to her rescue. As grandfather told it, even after months he still hadn't been able to utter a word to her and so badly wanted to get to know her. But for some unexplainable reason, he was shy around her.

"Anyway, one day he noticed two men passing the shop window immediately after she left. He got a really bad feeling because they looked unsavory. Leaving several customers stranded, he exited his shop with a cleaver in his hand and followed them. He quickly realized they were up to no good because when my grandmother took a shortcut through an alley, the two men cornered her. When my grandfather saw the two men were about to attack my grandmother, he showed the hooligans his meat cleaver and found his voice, ordering the men to leave my grandmother alone.

"Unfortunately the two men decided to gang up on my grandfather. When they attacked him, he chopped off the hand of one man and sliced off a good portion of the other man's forehead before they both ran away. My grandmother was so impressed with his strength, she asked him to go out with her. The rest, as they say, is history."

"That's a pretty cool story," Blade replied.

"Which brings me to the question of how the two of you first met?" Cade blurted. This walk down memory lane was the perfect opportunity to find out a little about their past relationship.

Both Reena and Blade frowned. Neither said a thing.

Okay. So, why had Blade been so gung-ho last night about her sweet pussy? And why did he possess other sexual knowledge about her if there wasn't some kind of serious thing going on?

"Something I said?" he prodded.

Uneasiness swept through him and he didn't like the flicker of darkness in Reena's eyes.

"It is private," Blade said, tossing Cade a cool gaze that asked him to back off.

"Actually, I should tell him, Blade. I owe both of you the whole truth. Why don't I make us some coffee and we can talk?"

She stood, turned and headed back toward the kitchen, sighing heavily.

Nope, she was not looking forward to this confession.

Chapter Nine

Up until a few minutes ago, Reena had been damned irresistible in tight jeans and a navy-blue sweater that perfectly hugged the curves of her breasts. But as she stood silently, staring out the nearby window, her arms crossed over her breasts, she appeared serious and untouchable. Maybe she was thinking about those hunters who'd roughed her up the other day. Blade was surprised she hadn't shown herself to be more deeply affected by that experience. She was probably just good at hiding her emotions.

Except for now.

His gaze drifted to Cade, who was also watching her with concern. He had probably never been a threat to her. Most likely, if Blade hadn't come along, she and Cade would have gotten together sometime on the trail back to civilization. She would have been dead months ago if Blade hadn't developed this sexual desire for her and hesitated pulling the trigger the two times he'd had the chance. It seemed like such a long time ago. So damn long.

Will winced at the sudden jolt of pain zipping through his chest, compliments of the bullet wound that still ached whenever he moved too quickly. He tried to ignore the discomfort and shifted in his seat, returning to studying the satellite phone he'd partially pieced together. The sizzle of pain reminded him that he was recovering from a bullet wound and shouldn't be thinking about having sex with her again. Not until he was a hell of a lot more healed.

"You've been fiddling with that all day. Any ideas if you can fix it?" Cade asked in a low voice so Reena wouldn't hear. Blade knew the last thing Cade wanted was for Reena to get on the phone and call the Resistance. If the Outlaw brothers discovered Cade's bounty was Tyler's good friend, there would be hell to pay.

"I'm pretty sure the damage can't be reversed," Blade said truthfully and gazed over at Red, still staring out the window. His balls tightened in awareness of her beauty and his protective instincts concerning her made his heart pick up speed.

"She looks stressed," Cade commented.

"Fucking her 24/7 would take care of that problem, but I don't think she'd want that."

Cade chuckled. "She just might if last night was an indication."

Blade gritted his teeth as his cock twitched against his pants. Memories of her sensual whimpers stroked his senses, the powerful orgasm he'd experienced in her sweet, tight mouth.

"By the serious look on her face, having sex with us again is the farthest thing from her mind."

"Do you have any idea what she wants to discuss?"

Blade let out a low, deep sigh that didn't loosen any of the tension tightening his body. He suspected he knew what Reena wanted to talk about. If his suspicions were correct, he may as well give Cade the lowdown and soften the blow by a few minutes.

"Most likely, her time as a pleasure slave would be my best guess."

Cade's mouth dropped open in shock. His face went a bit pale behind his healthy outdoor tan. It appeared Cade hadn't been briefed on that short period of her life.

"Are you serious?" he asked in a strangled voice.

Blade shrugged and returned to working on the radio. He wished he'd just kept his big mouth shut.

* * * * *

Cade reeled from this newest tidbit of information. Reena had been a pleasure slave? But he quickly reined in his surprise. Reena's father had mentioned he'd lost touch with his daughter while she'd been in the Terrorist Wars. Cade knew women had been forced into weekly R & R sex with the soldiers. Her father had said he'd tried to protect her for as long as possible, but then he'd lost contact with her.

Is that what Blade had been referring to? Her time in the Wars? Before he could question Blade further, Reena thrust a mug of black coffee in front of his face and the moist steam whispered against his cheeks. When he accepted the coffee and looked up at her, his gut clenched at the torment etching her facial features. For a woman in her early twenties, she suddenly appeared many years older. She was a woman of vast sexual experience—good and bad—and he got the feeling she was about to tell them the really bad part.

Suddenly he wished he was anywhere but here.

* * * * *

Reena didn't want to explain her past to the two men. But the intense way they'd been looking at her all day made her realize she had to say something. Their we-want-to-have-more-sex-with-you stares and her own cravings to experience more pleasure with them made her want to remind them she wasn't some dainty virgin who was just starting to explore sex. She was experienced and she'd put her life in danger on many occasions for the Cause. If she needed to die in order to help free women from the insane Claiming Law, the same that gave men the right to rape women and take them as wives against their will, then she was quite willing to make that sacrifice.

At least she had been until last night. Before then, she'd used sex to gain something. During the Terrorist Wars she'd disciplined herself into not thinking about what happened to her on a daily basis. Instead she'd turned her emotions inward, hidden her dreams, forgotten her desires for a man to love her and cut off all ideas of having kids and a family. She'd buried it all deep inside. Concealed her dreams somewhere safe, where no insane Claiming Law or X-virus or R & R could reach and ruin them.

She'd turned cold toward men. She'd lost her innocence and trust because of what she'd been forced to endure. But in such a short time, Cade and Will had snuck past her defenses.

They'd allowed her to trust again. Trust in strangers. With that trust, hope had been bursting through her all day. Hope for all women. Because if two guys she barely knew would put their own lives at risk to save hers, this meant all men weren't as bad as she'd originally believed.

Sure, Cade had an agenda to keep her alive so he could get his bounty, but Will didn't. He could have shot her in that camp with all those hunters and left Cade to fight it out with those men. Cade could have killed Blade when they'd discovered her missing and come after her alone. But he hadn't. The two men, working on opposite sides—one to kill her and one to take her in—had banded together against bad odds to rescue her.

She had hope for man again and this was the best she'd felt in a long time. But before she let her hopes grow, she needed to tell them the truth. People said "the truth shall set you free." She hoped they were right in her case.

Emotions, thick and raw, welled up as she sat down upon the chair she'd occupied earlier. Both men stared expectantly at her as they nursed their coffees. Once again, they looked at her as if she was just some normal woman they could have sex with.

She closed her eyes and breathed deep, gathering her courage. She hoped one or both men would reassure her that whatever she said wouldn't change things. Better yet, she hoped they urged her not to tell them anything.

They remained silent.

She opened her eyes. Both men were smiling encouragement at her. Gosh, they were both so cute. One dark-haired, the other fair. Her rescuers. Her guys.

She shook away those thoughts and concentrated on what she needed to say.

"During the Wars, I was forced to serve many soldiers," she said. If the men were shocked, their faces didn't show it and this encouraged her to continue. "I went into the R & R program unwillingly, as many other surviving women did. We were required to have sex with our colleagues, subordinates and bosses.

"We were sexual chattel, comfort women for soldiers, our rights stripped away. We were put on a weekly schedule to work eight hours a day. Half an hour for each man. At night we were bedded by superiors and slept in their beds. Our health was of the utmost importance. Condoms and spermicide, as well as other forms of birth control, were mandatory. Video surveillance was 24/7. I learned to cope. I learned to please. I learned to hate."

She stopped speaking as a quiver of rage made its way into her voice. It was very difficult to maintain eye contact with both men and, despite them trying to appear strong and indifferent, Will's fists were clenched in anger and muscles spasmed in Cade's cheeks as he ground his teeth together.

"I also learned to listen. While they fucked me, the men's guards were lowered. I pumped them for information. Anything and everything I found useful about them, I tucked away in my brain, because I knew someday I would use the information against them. And I did. Since I came back to the United States, many military installations have been taken out under mysterious circumstances because of what I learned during those days."

"So, effectively, you became a spy," Cade said.

"It's why the government wants me. They don't want to talk to me about a compromise. They want to know what I know."

"Which is?" Blade asked.

"I have told my people enough to keep the Resistance active for quite some time. Most of what I know has been filtered through the ranks." Reena wasn't afraid of the information getting out. It would just make the government shake in their boots. "As with most of the members of the Resistance, I went undercover, too. Where the opportunity exists to gather more information on powerful men, we go in and get it using any means necessary—and that includes sleeping with them." She turned her attention to Will. "That's why I was at the Pleasure Palace when your SKULL men thought they were rescuing me. My getting caught and sent there was a well-orchestrated plan. While at the palace, I was a sex slave for a couple generals from whom I was able to pump some extremely valuable information regarding White House security. Last month's suicide bomber inside the presidential palace was compliments of yours truly."

"Twenty people died and more than a hundred were injured," Cade replied.

She detected the disappointment in his voice and was glad she'd told him. Told both of them the truth about who she really was, what she'd done and, hopefully, give them an idea of what she was capable of doing.

"Do you feel guilty over those people being killed and injured?" Blade asked.

Her heart caught at that unexpected question. Damn him. Guilt, thick and hurtful, bubbled up from somewhere deep inside of her.

Shit. She thought she had a lid on that emotion.

"She doesn't need to answer that. It's written all over her face," Cade said roughly.

"She wouldn't be human if she didn't," Blade replied, keeping his gaze fixed to her face.

"Why are you telling us this?" Cade asked. His soft words smoothed over her tattered heart. She'd expected his disappointment to linger, but Cade seemed more concerned for her over the horrible thing that had happened. They still didn't know the whole story.

"Because you two saved my life. You should know who you saved."

"Do you not think your life is worth saving?" Blade prodded.

She couldn't help but wince as the question lanced through her. Yeah, she'd thought that a couple of times.

"Is that why you've been biting off everyone's head? Is that why you came out here alone?" Cade asked. "Because the guilt of that suicide bomber, who acted on her own, was eating you up inside?"

"How do you know all of this?" she asked him. "It isn't common knowledge that the woman went rogue on us."

Cade shrugged casually. "I overheard someone talking. Someone in the Resistance."

She wondered if he was talking about his brother Tyler and Tyler's woman Laurie. He did live with them. They probably talked, maybe even in front of Cade. Laurie and Tyler had suggested Reena get counseling to deal with the renegade suicide bomber. Reena had trusted only a handful of women with the information she had discovered while sleeping with that general, and one of those trusted women had rolled on her, turning into a suicide bomber. The break in trust had shattered Reena's ability to read the women in her most trusted group. If she couldn't trust those closest to her to follow orders and remain mentally and emotionally stable, then who the hell could she trust?

"Yeah, I guess that's why I'm being a bitch," she acknowledged.

"I wouldn't say you're a bitch." Blade chuckled, setting a part of the satellite phone down on the floor near his seat.

"Definitely not a bitch," Cade remarked. He winked at her.

She liked the searing way their gazes slid over her entire body. It made her feel just a tad better. After revealing both her vulnerable and evil side at the same time, they still looked at her in the same appreciative way. Even with all the blood of those people on her hands.

"If you didn't order a suicide bomber to go in there, then the deaths are not your fault," Cade continued in a soft voice that wreaked havoc upon her senses.

"She did what she did based on what I told her. I should have read my people better. She was one of my strongest women. I trusted her," Reena confessed.

"Even the strongest of us can snap, Red," Blade soothed. "I've seen it a few times. People you least expect to roll take matters into their own hands. You can never be a hundred percent sure of the mental stability of someone. It's the chance you take when bringing someone into your confidence."

"This empathy coming from a man who wants me dead?" Red blurted. She wanted to know if Blade still truly wanted to kill her. Had the sex they shared just been sex? Or something more than that?

Beside her, Cade stiffened as if sensing an argument.

Anger spark in Blade's eyes and she read a distinct warning to back off.

"He's not going to hurt you. Ever. Right, Will?" Cade's voice was cool and demanding.

Blade snapped his gaze to Cade. "If I wanted to hurt her, she would have been dead months ago—that first time you stopped me."

What in the world? "Okay this is getting weird, guys. Exactly why are we discussing something that happened a few days ago as if it were months?"

Cade inhaled as if preparing to answer, but Will spoke first. "I've been on your ass for months, Red. Recently I've realized that if I'd truly wanted you dead, you would have been a long time ago."

God.

"When?" She needed to know how he'd been able to get so close to her. It was a matter of security, not to mention what the hell kind of guy she was dealing with.

"One of your visits to the Outlaw farm," he said.

"How did you find out I was there?" But she didn't need to ask. She knew. God, how could she have been so stupid?

"You were one of Laurie's husbands when the Barlows had her. So, what? You decided to keep an eye on her and saw me?"

He closed his eyes and cursed softly. Beside him, Cade frowned. Jealousy sizzled through her at the idea of Blade wanting to be with

Tyler's woman. Blade would have slept with her, but Laurie had told her the Barlows had not permitted it, at least not until she became impregnated by a Barlow. Thanks to the birth control pills she'd kept hidden beneath the floorboards of her bedroom, she hadn't become pregnant.

But did Blade have feelings for Laurie? She was a very nice woman. Reena wouldn't be surprised if Blade had fallen in love with her.

"Are you in love with her?" she whispered, the sting of hurt lancing her.

"I developed a deep care for her," Will acknowledged.

Beside him, Cade cursed softly.

"But I know she belongs to Tyler and Hunter. I've accepted it and moved on."

"Moved on...what, to me?" Reena asked, not able to stop herself. She didn't even know this guy. She shouldn't give two shits about him, but a dangerous attraction sizzled between them. One she would like to explore further, despite him almost having killed her. He could have too had Cade not stopped him. Such fierceness in both men made her adrenaline roar. Oh man, did she like to live on the edge or what?

Blade's Adam's apple bobbed crazily as he swallowed. To her surprise, he smiled. The smile reached his eyes and they glowed with a magnificent sparkle that made her tummy flip-flop wonderfully all over the place.

"I'd much rather be fucking you then shooting you," he replied.

Sincerity etched his voice. Blade had turned from enemy to ally. She could trust him.

She turned to Cade. "And what about you?"

"I'm with Will. I'd rather be fucking you than turning you over as my bounty."

"I'm not an easy fuck to catch, gentlemen," she quipped, trying to deny the wild flare of heat whipping through her body. The unmistakable lust-filled sparks shining in their smiles made it clear what they wanted from her.

"You can't just expect me to have sex with you at the drop of a hat," she complained, loving the way they were looking at her.

"You didn't seem to have a problem when you thought the both of us were unconscious. You owe us, Red." Cade's voice was strangled and low. Oh sweet heavens, were they going to throw *that* at her every chance they got?

"Maybe she should pretend we're both unconscious again?" Blade chuckled.

Both men stood and moved in front of her. Their gazes were fierce with seductive intent and Rena almost bolted from her chair. But to go where?

Outside the storm continued to rage and she couldn't very well fend them off in here. Not that she wanted to.

She shuddered as Cade held out his hand to her. His eyes were darker now and a muscle spasmed in his right cheek as if he were fighting for self-control. Instinctively she held out her hand and his fingers intertwined erotically with hers. He pulled her to her feet.

His eyes flared as he let go of her hand.

"We want you, Reena. Both of us want to take you. Do you want us?" Cade asked.

"Yes," she answered without hesitating. Oh man, she was not going to like herself in the morning for being so weak.

Cade's palms firmly settled on her upper chest, near her neck. For a split second, she remembered the other night when Blade had shown up at their campsite and Cade had told him not to sit too close to her for fear Blade may break her neck. Would Cade break her neck instead?

That crazy idea vanished as his fingers pressed against the bottom of her chin and he tilted her head upward.

"You're way too easy to catch, Reena. Way too easy," he whispered.

"Maybe I want to be caught," she answered, sighing with anticipation as Cade's head lowered and his warm mouth slid possessively over hers.

Reena swore her entire body orgasmed.

"Easy, Red," Will whispered from somewhere behind her.

She whimpered into Cade's mouth as Will's body embraced her backside. She was effectively sandwiched between two big, muscular bodies. Their hard muscles caressed her curves and their erections pressed against her—Cade's pushing hot and swollen into her lower belly and Will's bulging against her ass.

"Do you ever wear a butt plug?" Will asked as Cade broke the kiss. She breathed heavily. Her breasts were swollen, her nipples sensitive. Her clit pulsed and she ached to pull on her labia rings in order to give her pussy lips that extra sweet pleasure-pain she loved.

"I've been surgically enhanced," she admitted.

Their harsh, surprised intakes of breath had her creaming.

"And you thought you knew everything there was to know about your subject," she whispered in a sultry voice.

These days being surgically enhanced was something that was "in" for women. Groups of husbands ordered the procedure for their wife. It could mean larger breasts, tummy tucks, bigger lips or a nose job. In her case, because of her assignment at the Pleasure Palace, she'd been enhanced with labia rings, nipple rings, a bellybutton ring and the muscles in her anus had been made just a little looser—permanently. This gave a man's cock an incredibly tight fit without having to plan ahead with an anal plug.

So if Will and Blade wished to double penetrate her, and she sure wished they did, she didn't need any prep—except, of course, for some lube.

"You're the ideal woman for more than one man, aren't you, Red?" Will whispered against her neck.

Appreciation laced his voice and curiosity shone in Cade's eyes as he gazed at her.

"So you've been double penetrated before?" Cade asked.

She detected jealous hostility in his voice. She could lie and make him more jealous, but she figured it best to tell the truth.

"I have been with more than one man at the same time," she admitted.

Disappointment shone clearly in Cade's eyes. Will's face was unreadable.

"I've had anal, but I've never been double penetrated."

Both men cursed. Animalistic and territorial. Her senses grew bright and alert as they eagerly touched her, exploring her body while removing her clothing. Their confident hands caressed her sensitized flesh and their soft mouths brushed sensually over her shoulders, her neck. One mouth kissed along the length of her collarbone while another kissed a fiery line down her spine to the curves of her ass.

Her eyelids drooped so heavy she couldn't even open her eyes to see who was doing what to her body. She cried out as the mouth kissing her front dotted over to her bellybutton ring and pulled so sweetly. Her mind whirled as their hands and fingers caressed her hips, her inner thighs, her waist.

Automatically she spread her legs wider, allowing them full access.

"Lube?" Blade's voice came from behind her.

Gosh, she had lube, didn't she? She couldn't gather her thoughts. Couldn't fathom whether or not she had lube in the cabin. Why would she? She'd come here alone. She whimpered her disappointment. No, she didn't have any.

"Margarine," Cade hissed. "Saw some on the counter."

"Always be prepared." Will chuckled.

The confident set of hands that whispered over the curve of her hips disappeared. Will had gone for the lube. They would begin fucking her soon.

Sweet mercy! She could barely wait.

"Your pussy looks so beautiful," Cade whispered from between her legs. She managed to part her eyelids ever so slightly. Cade knelt on the floor in front of her. His head was near her belly and his teeth started a wicked pull on her belly ring. With his hands, he began stroking her inner thighs. Up and down. Rubbing nice and hard.

Shivers rocked her. Made her legs tremble. Made her gasp and pull on her nipple rings.

"Labia," she managed to choke, wanting to have those rings pulled as well.

Her legs tensed as his hand slipped up to tug on her labia rings. He pulled and spread her pussy lips at the same time.

Sweet burn. Oh, she liked this so much.

She kept pulling her nipple rings and whimpered as cool, lubed fingers slipped against her sphincter. Her ass clenched around one slippery finger as Will entered.

"Perfect," he moaned.

Cade answered with a groan.

"She's opening nicely. Whoever did her knew what he was doing," Will said.

Need swept through her. She wanted them to fuck her. But Cade had different things in mind.

"Let go of your rings, baby. Keep your hands to your sides," he muttered.

Reluctantly she let go of her rings and gasped as his mouth kissed an intoxicating line up her belly. She did as he said, holding her hands to her sides, and then yelped as Cade's two palms smeared cool margarine over her breasts. The slippery texture of the lube let him move his palms fast and steady over her perky breasts, sparking tingles over her skin. Suddenly he pulled on her nipple rings harder than she'd just done, sensitizing her rosy peaks.

Another thickly lubed finger dipped into her anus and she groaned as two of Blade's fingers gently probed and explored. The violent need for an orgasm rose quickly, taking hold, and had her frantically gasping for them to take her. She moaned long and hard and the sultry sound was like an aphrodisiac to her ears.

"She's ready," Will growled. His fingers slipped out of her, leaving her open and desperate for her back end to be filled. The rip of plastic split the air, followed by the crunch of foil. The slurp of lube had her panting as she envisioned Will smearing margarine over his entire engorged shaft.

Between her thighs, her pussy grew warm and sopping as she awaited Cade to take her. Sexual hunger sliced through her like sharp pleasure blades. The incredible vibrations flared around her in a whirlwind, drowning her, making her vulnerable and needy with greed. The moment Will's cock head slipped into her ass, she knew he had found a home inside of her.

She cried out, distraught as he withdrew. But just as quickly, Cade entered her pussy, invading her channel, making her muscles stretch with an exquisite burn.

Oh, this is so right.

He withdrew, leaving her desolately alone, but then Will entered her anus, his cool, lubed cock pushing a little harder and deeper. Suddenly, she felt wonderfully grounded. As if everything was right in the world. Crazy thoughts, yeah, but there they were, laid out bright and clear in her mind. She needed and wanted these two men in her life.

Reaching out, she settled her hands on Cade's waist and held on tight. As Will withdrew, Cade took her mouth, his lips melting possessively over hers. He entered her again, his cock throbbing as he sank deep. He pulled out and Will plunged deeper than ever.

Every swollen inch of his heated flesh pulsed inside her. Then too soon, he withdrew.

Reena's senses swirled as both men took turns entering her. Their thrusts were wicked, powerful and oh so lusciously possessive. Each stroke into her tender ass and needy pussy ignited a hailstorm of tremors that sucked her closer and closer to an orgasm.

Oh! How she craved to climax with these two men. Their thrusts were well-timed and furious. Their hands held her steady as their bodies pummeled her. Hard muscles slammed into her soft curves.

In an instant, she slipped inside the wonderful contractions. They exploded and engulfed her with breathtaking speed. The sensual jolts snapped through her rising passion like lashes of electricity and she shattered into a million pieces. Her mind splintered and her self-control vanished.

She free fell into a world of pleasure. It grabbed her, caressed and engulfed her with a magnificence she'd never known before. And she finally understood she would never be the same again.

* * * * *

The three of them existed that way for days. Cade had no idea how many days or nights were filled with their intense lovemaking. All he knew was he and Will were healing quickly and life beyond the cabin walls didn't exist. Inside was warm heaven. Outside, cold hell. Quick trips to the woodpile for firewood or to the porch with pots in hand to gather snow to melt into water became the norm.

The coldness in Will's eyes disappeared and the evil depression threatening Cade after he'd been shot vanished. Life was good.

Tying Reena down, fucking her, loving her, enjoying her wild, sensual whimpers as he and Will double-penetrated her on a nightly—hell, on a daily—basis became life.

He trained his mind to believe their time together would never end. Reena belonged to both him and Will. There was no way he was going to let her leave. Ever.

But he was delusional. Stupid. Naïve.

He didn't care. This freedom rocked. As far as he was concerned, this ecstasy could last forever. It had to.

* * * * *

Will couldn't get enough of watching Reena while she slept. It was the only time he let his emotions wreak havoc on him. He'd almost killed her. Twice. Now this jewel of a woman belonged to him and Cade. The most beautiful woman in the world. And he—the suicidal moth drawn to her flame. He'd eventually get burned by her. How could he not? Every other woman he'd loved had either died, found another man or—in Laurie's case—found other men.

Why should this time around be any different? He sensed Cade felt differently. He seemed confident she would always belong to them. It showed in his easygoing, laid-back attitude. No fucking worries for Cade Outlaw. Blade wished he could be like that. Wished he could just live hour by hour without thinking about reality.

Truth was, though, he just couldn't settle down, because last night while Cade and Reena had slept, he'd been working on the satellite phone. And he'd fixed it. Out on the porch, he'd gotten a signal. All he needed to do was tell Reena and Cade.

Problem was, he didn't want to tell them anything. He didn't want to leave here. He didn't want to leave her. Ever.

Chapter Ten

Early the next morning, after another wild night of hot sex, Cade awoke to discover Blade staring out the back window. From the angle of Blade's head, Cade could see the frown on his lips. Until now, Blade had always been the last one out of bed. The guy seemed to need a hell of a lot of sleep. So having him up and frowning the way he was didn't sit well with Cade, and his gut twisted at this deviation from the norm.

Irritation slammed into him like a freight train.

Reluctantly he moved away from Reena's warm, naked body and got out of bed. Slipping on his underwear and jeans, he donned a pullover and joined Blade. Gazing out the window, he inhaled at the sparkles of early morning sunshine dusting the pristine white snow. Pine trees were draped in white and the sky was so blue and bright it actually hurt his eyes. He averted his gaze from the scenery.

"It's way too early in the morning to be pissed off. What's wrong?" Cade asked as he moved to the kitchen. He grabbed a mug, spooned some instant coffee into it, and then grabbed the aluminum teapot off the hot woodstove. He poured himself a full cup, dashed some sugar into it and stirred before rejoining Will.

"The storm's over."

Cade almost choked on his coffee. "And you're just getting that? The storm's been over for days, my man."

"We're running out of food," Blade replied and a cold wave of worry washed away Cade's amusement.

"I know." He'd seen it coming for days. Reena had brought in just enough food to last two weeks for one person. They'd located some unspoiled dried food in the cupboards—years old, but still good. But they were down to just coffee, a couple of tins of canned meat and a package of raisins.

"We have to think about what happens next. Any ideas?" Blade asked.

"I know how to hunt and skin. We'll have meat. I can go out later and look for something to tide us over for a few days. But sooner or later SKULL is going to wonder what happened to you. They'll also want an explanation why you didn't kill her."

"Been thinking on that. The only way they aren't going to send another assassin to take her out is if we pretend she's dead."

"So we'll pretend she's dead," Cade countered, instantly liking that idea.

"There's only one flaw in your plan, gentlemen." Reena's drowsy voice floated over from the bed.

"What's that?" Blade asked.

"I'm not going to play dead. Ever."

* * * * *

Raw anger surged through Red. She'd been following their conversation and wasn't pleased with Blade's suggestion of her playing dead.

Tossing aside the blankets, she sat up and ignored the flare of excitement in the men's gazes as they latched onto her nudity.

"I am the leader of the Resistance. I was given that position for a reason and it's because I do not bow down. To anyone. I will not abandon my people. I will go ahead with my plan and my women will resist and protest this abhorred treatment."

"And guess what you'll get for your troubles, Red? A bullet between the eyes," Blade said coolly.

She truly didn't like his tone. Confident. A premonition?

"Because that's what's going to happen, Red," he said. "Lots of people want you out of the way."

"Screw them. Women want their freedoms back. If we become baby machines then at least we want the right to choose our men and how many husbands we take," she snapped. "And we'll keep causing civil discord until we get our way."

"How about I present your case to the government," Cade interjected. "Blade can come with me. We'll speak for you. You can stay here where it's safe."

Damn them both!

"Safe and a coward."

"Red—" Blade said, but she held up her hand to silence him.

"There's one thing you two don't know about me. When I make up my mind, I will not change it. I will not back down to the United States Government. I will not stop our demands. I will not have an audience with that dictatorship and I will not play dead. Not even for you two."

She took the utmost satisfaction in their silence. Perhaps they were actually listening to her?

"Now please, gentlemen. Let's make love, not war. Yes, the storm has stopped outside, but it doesn't *have* to stop inside...despite our lack of food."

"If you aren't the most stubborn—" Cade began.

"Most headstrong—" Blade interjected.

"Pigheaded, most gorgeous—" Cade said.

"Sexy seductress."

"Who needs an orgasm so she can start her day," Reena purred, smiling at them. After they'd quickly undressed and joined her beneath the covers, she didn't waste any time reaching out and wrapping her hands around each of their shafts. She grinned when both men groaned as she squeezed their flesh.

"Christ, most women prefer coffee in the morning, but this one wants an orgasm," Cade gasped.

"She's too demanding, don't you think?" Blade countered.

"Gentlemen, please," Reena soothed. "I want my orgasm."

She sucked in a deep breath when both men bent their heads and each took one of her nipples into his mouth. Heat zapped through her breasts. She moaned her delight.

Perfect. Absolutely perfect.

* * * * *

An odd sound shifted through the layers of Cade's sleep. He didn't really give a shit. Either Reena or Blade, or maybe both of them, were moving around inside the cabin.

She was an independent, sexually active woman. He finally understood times were different now. Traditions were gone. Group sex was the new norm. And Red could have sex with whomever she wanted.

Over my dead body, an angry voice roared from deep within him. He'd allow only Blade to be with her—besides himself. No one else.

The unmistakable crunch of someone skiing in the snow somewhere outside the cabin snapped him back to reality. He opened his eyes and it took only two precious seconds to realize Blade and Red were still asleep in the bed with him.

Shit!

"We've got company," he said as he threw the blankets aside and tried to remember where he'd left his weapons.

He drew a blank. He'd become slack while lying around this cabin.

Dammit!

The weapons were stashed in a back room. In an instant, Blade and Red scrambled with lightning speed from beneath the blankets. Before he could blink, Blade was tossing them guns and knives. Yeah, Blade was a heck of a better contingency planner than he was.

"Anything?" Cade asked as he joined Blade at the ice-frosted living room window. He'd smudged a clear spot near the side and was peering out.

"A ski line in the snow. Looks like one set. He came in from the north and headed past the cabin toward the west. Already gone."

"Hunter?" Red asked as she sidled in beside Cade. Her female scent tickled his nose and he wanted to take her again, but that sure as hell wasn't going to happen now. He concentrated on what was transpiring outdoors and immediately spied the dark ski tracks laced through the snow.

"Could be just a hunter," Cade admitted, but he doubted it. Something, a premonition, nagged at him that trouble floated in the air.

What a bummer. And he was really liking it here.

*****

"We leave first thing in the morning. First light," Blade said as he got dressed. He didn't like the idea of staying the night. Didn't like the idea of someone lurking around out there without introducing them self. Sure, he or she could be just a hunter as Red suggested, but he didn't want to take any chances with her life.

Not take chances with her life? Oh man, how was he going to explain all this to SKULL? To hell with them. He should have quit them long ago. He needed to protect Red.

"We should go now," Red said as she buttoned her top and then threw on a sweater. She shoved her hands under her red hair, lifted it out of the sweater and down to her shoulders like a flaming waterfall. Oh yeah, he liked the way her hair fell like that.

"I feel like a coward hanging around in here. I need to get back to my people," she complained.

She felt like a coward? Heck, that comment stung like a son of a bitch. He thought she'd been enjoying herself getting fucked by two men.

"Could it be a Resistance scout? Checking up on you?" Cade asked. He was fully dressed and peeking out another clear spot he'd smeared through the lacy frost on a back window. His gun was out and pointed up at the ceiling, his body tense and ready for action.

"Gentlemen, if people from the Resistance were here, we'd know it. Whoever is out there has a fire going just beyond the trees to the west."

Blade stiffened at her casual announcement. He caught Cade's surprised glance and they both joined her at the window she'd been covering.

She moved away, allowing Blade to peek out first. Sure enough, just beyond the trees a thin spiral of gray smoke was meandering into the quickly darkening sky. He moved aside so Cade could look.

"Someone from SKULL?" Cade asked.

"Doubt it," Blade answered truthfully. "Sure, they could have sent someone to search for me. But I never gave the coordinates where I was and if by chance they'd discovered we're here, Red would already be dead. Any sniper could have taken her out the minute she'd stepped by one of the windows. Besides, a SKULL assassin wouldn't be sitting nearby with a smoky fire. Whoever is out there wants us to see them."

"I suggest we go and take a look then," Red said, and Blade and Cade joined her in strapping on their weapons.

Blade grabbed his rifle. One thing for sure, friend or foe was not welcome here. They'd totally ruined another hot night with Red. And he for one was quite pissed off about it.

* * * * *

They waited until complete dark and for their eyes to adjust before the three of them—wearing old snowshoes—slipped out the back door of the cabin.

Gun in hand, Reena stomped outside last. The cold late-November air slamming deep into her lungs made her gasp. The snow wouldn't be melting any time soon. An odd sense of loneliness swept over her as she moved into the nearby tree line. Branches creaked overhead and a volley of snaps and crackles flew through the air as the ice shifted beneath the snow on the nearby lake.

From somewhere to her left came the soft swish of Blade moving through the woods on his snowshoes. She focused on their plans. Blade would flank her on the left and Cade on the right with her coming right down the middle, running parallel to the ski trail created by the intruder.

Uneasiness curled through her tummy over what had transpired. She'd become cozy with two men who'd meant her harm in the beginning but had given her so much pleasure since. Now they were out of sight and a raw, deep emotional ache grumbled inside of her. She just wanted to see them again. Wanted to make sure they were okay.

Okay?

Reena pulled up short. Good grief! What was the matter with her? They were grown men. Professionals with weapons. They would be fine. Wouldn't they?

She frowned in annoyance and started shuffling forward, following the ski trail, keeping her eyes and ears glued for any noise or movement. Of course they would be fine!

Stop thinking about them and concentrate on keeping yourself out of harm's way.

Whoever was out there had kept their campfire going at an even pace. As if they wanted to be seen, just like Cade had suggested. Or maybe this was an ambush? There could be others around, using this one person to give a fake sense of security.

Okay chill, Reena.

They'd gone through all these possibilities back at the cabin. Going out to confront the situation—no matter the dangers—was the best way to go. Unfortunately, now she wished they'd simply hightailed it out of here and gone the other way without checking on the newcomer...and without looking back.

The moon was rising, washing the snow in an eerie blue glow. The wind was picking up too, a cold breeze that snapped through her clothes and made her shiver. Man, what she wouldn't give to be back in that warm cabin again.

As she neared the campfire, she made out a figure huddled in front of the flames and wondered if maybe it was just a dummy propped up as a decoy. But then it moved and Reena tightened her grip on her gun as the person reached into a nearby packsack for something. Probably a gun. She really should shoot first and ask questions later. But ambushing someone wasn't her style. He could just be an innocent person.

She wondered if Blade and Cade were already in their positions and decided to chance that they were. Before the person could pull out whatever they were searching for, Reena stomped behind a tree for cover and called in a loud, commanding voice. "You! In the campsite! You are surrounded! Raise your hands so we can see them!"

Reena held her breath as the figure did as she instructed. She tensed as Cade and Blade simultaneously erupted from their respective positions and covered the intruder with their guns. She shuffled into camp, joining the trio.

Both men were silent as they stared at the newcomer and, as the person turned to face her, Reena gasped in surprise.

"Maggie? What the hell are you doing here? We could have killed you! Do you have a death wish?"

Maggie—the person Reena had left in charge of the Resistance when she'd decided to go into temporary seclusion—smiled at her. Her startling blue eyes glittered with happiness and, without warning, she threw her arms around Reena, holding her tight.

"I was wondering when you'd break free of your bonds and come out of that cabin for a visit," the woman said and grinned widely.

"You two know each other?" Cade asked as he lowered his weapon. Blade, on the other hand, wasn't as trusting and kept his gun on Maggie.

"Maggie's my right-arm man," Reena explained and returned her attention to her good friend, confidant and bodyguard. "Why didn't you use our secret call and let me know you were here? You scared the crap out of us."

"And interrupt your ménages?" Maggie chuckled as she gazed up and down first at Cade and then Blade, raising her eyebrows the way she always did when pleased about something.

Ménages? Reena's cheeks warmed. Exactly how long had Maggie been lurking around out here? How did she know they were having sex? Maggie was a pretty good tracker and had a lot of patience. This was one of the reasons Reena had picked her for her top bodyguard. But why hadn't she made herself known?

Maggie had been with Reena since the Resistance started. Unaffected by the X-virus, Maggie and her twin sister Jolie had pretended they were sick and dying along with their mother and grandmother. Their overprotective brothers had insisted. They'd all been told rumors of the government taking unaffected females into government labs, and their brothers didn't want the same thing to happen to Maggie and Jolie.

So the two sisters hid from everyone. Living as recluses in their grandfather's home, not daring to go outside or even look out the windows. It had been hell, but they'd learned the art of patience and admitted hiding had been worthwhile because the last thing they'd wanted was to be Claimed. When their grandfather and brothers joined the Resistance, they'd brought Maggie and Jolie in too.

Unfortunately, Jolie, a plastic surgeon, had been kidnapped while on assignment. Rumor had it she'd become a sex slave to some powerful men in Saudi Arabia and had subsequently been killed. Maggie had been devastated.

"I've brought some huge news," Maggie said. And by the way the woman's blue eyes flared with barely contained excitement, Reena knew the news must be big.

"Brace yourselves for this one, guys. The Unites States dictatorship has fallen."

* * * * *

By the stunned shock on both Will and Cade's faces, the two men were still reeling from the news Maggie had dropped about half an hour earlier. As the four of them sat at the cabin table nursing coffees, Cade and Will listened intently and with obvious extreme interest to Maggie's tale.

"The International Initiative, or the II as they call themselves, walked right in and took over." Maggie laughed. "A military coup. Just like that. Or so we've been told. And I haven't even gotten to the best part yet."

Reena wasn't sure she wanted to hear any more. It was all so overwhelming. They had a new government. Dare she hope this government would be better than the last one that'd taken power in a similar fashion?

Her tummy did somersaults as she tried to figure out what all this would mean for the Resistance. They'd secretly been studying the government and toying with the idea of overthrowing the dictatorship themselves. The Resistance's plans had now changed. They had a new enemy to infiltrate and would have to start all over collecting information on them. Maggie had said they were a relatively new group—the II. A group Reena had never heard of.

"They have sent a formal invitation to the Resistance and other factions who wish to free woman. They want liaisons from all pertinent groups to attend a meeting to discuss the future of women and girls in the United States. They want our input into a global plan. Everything is on the table, including the Claiming Law and women's rights."

Shivers swept through Reena. She should've been jumping for joy at this news, but she couldn't conjure up any excitement or happiness. Perhaps because she'd been fighting for so long and she'd grown cautious. Maybe too cautious?

All three of them were watching her carefully. The men waited for her reaction and Maggie bubbled with an abundance of joy that surprised Reena.

"Did it ever occur to you this might be a trap, Maggie?" she asked her friend.

Shock splashed over her friend's face and her mouth dropped open in stunned disbelief. Guilt raced through Reena for bursting the woman's bubble.

"Been thinking the same thing," Blade said in a cool, controlled voice.

"Was hoping someone else would broach the subject, myself," Cade replied. "Didn't want to bring anyone down." He sipped his coffee, averting his eyes from Maggie, who shot both men and then Reena a scalding glare.

"A trick? You think this is a trick?" she snapped.

Oops, the bubble had burst.

"The government could have made up the ruse in order to draw all leaders out into the open," Blade suggested.

"Okay so listen, guys. I didn't fucking well hoof it all the way in here just to get a load of pessimistic bullshit from you three," Maggie snarled. She turned her attention to Reena. "And you should know the Resistance better than this. We wouldn't accept anything at face value. Our people confirmed the story. It's happened. Change is coming whether you like it or not. I realize you came out here to help you get over your burnout." Maggie let her gaze wander to Cade, then to Will and then back to Reena. "And I would be pissed off, too, having been interrupted with these two men—who, by the way, you haven't formally introduced. Not that I don't know of them. But let me get to the point before any introductions and explanations. Either you send someone on your behalf to this initial meeting, Reena, or I'm bloody well going in your place. This is history in the making, damn it! I, for one, don't want to be left out in the cold. I've been there for too damned long. I want to get on with my life."

Reena smiled inwardly at Maggie's spunk. Her feistiness was another reason why she'd picked Maggie as her right-hand woman.

Lately Maggie had been understandably sad about her sister's death and Reena was glad to see a little of the old Maggie shining through.

"Okay chill, Mag," Reena said softly. "I want you to debrief me tonight. We leave first thing in the morning."

* * * * *

"Do you think what Maggie said is legit?" Cade asked Will, joining his friend outside on the front porch. Maggie had brought a knapsack full of food and the two women were preparing dinner while catching up on Resistance information and gossip. The gossip part was when both men excused themselves.

"As legit as anything can be these days." The frown Will had been toting since they'd been interrupted by this Maggie chick only deepened.

Yep, Blade was just as pissed about Reena returning to the Resistance as Cade.

"You've heard of this group?" he prodded.

Blade nodded. "SKULL thought they were irrelevant. Obviously they were wrong."

"Red seems intent on going to the meeting on her own, forgoing a liaison. What's your take on that?"

"Over my dead body," Blade growled.

"Good, then we're of the same mind."

Cade smiled. Having Will work with him was good. The two of them should be able to convince Reena of the dangers. She was more important than ever to the Resistance. She would have to be protected at all costs.

Fuck. If he didn't miss his guess, he and Blade had just joined the Resistance.

* * * * *

The four of them had a feast of fried steak, boiled potatoes and fresh green salad. Due to the excitement, Reena didn't get more than four hours of sleep during the night. She'd nestled between Blade and Cade, but out of respect for Maggie they hadn't had sex. The need to reach out and touch them, to have the two of them make love to her again, made for a restless night at best.

As the gray light of dawn cracked through the frosted windows, Reena awoke and was the first one out of bed. A moment later, Maggie's sleepy voice uncurled from beneath the bundle of blankets piled on top of the pull-out couch in the living room.

"Morning," she said cheerfully. That was Maggie, always happy first thing in the morning.

Tyler had mentioned how irritatingly cheerful their brother Mac could be in the mornings. Perhaps Reena should play matchmaker and hook up Maggie and Mac? She shook those thoughts aside. She had more important things to do, such as get ready to attend the meeting the II had set up for the day after tomorrow.

Last night had been fraught with arguments between her, Maggie, Will and Cade. They had been adamant about her not going in person. But she'd faced dangerous situations before and she would face more in the future. Now was not the time to hide.

Besides if the II was smart, they wouldn't take her out. If they did, the Resistance would only turn her into a martyr, and martyrs were harder to fight than a real woman willing to negotiate.

"Morning," Reena replied, keeping her voice low so the men wouldn't be disturbed. She quietly stoked the woodstove with kindling and old newspaper. It took only a few seconds for the hot coals inside the stove to light. Gray smoke curled and then bright orange flames erupted, quickly devouring the paper.

"It'll be a few minutes for the coffee. Did you sleep well?" Reena asked. She placed a couple split logs onto the crackling fire and quickly closed the stove door.

"Like a rock. This fresh country air beat the crap out of me." Maggie chuckled and stretched her long johns-clad arms out from beneath the blankets. She quickly stuck them back underneath. "Too cold," she grumbled, keeping her voice low. "No wonder you cuddled up with two hot guys to keep warm."

Reena rolled her eyes. Maggie wasn't about to let her forget she'd shacked up with a couple of hunks.

"You're pooped from skiing through all that snow. I only went half a mile last night and my legs are killing me," Reena complained.

"But you should be in great shape. Especially your legs, curling them around your lovers' waists while..."

Maggie wiggled her eyebrows and, despite the heat flaming her face, Reena maintained firm eye contact with her friend.

"Which leads me to my question," Reena said. "Exactly how long were you lurking out there and why would you think anything was happening in here?"

Maggie smiled knowingly, sweet dimples popping along her cheekbones.

Oh damn. She'd been around long enough, that for was sure.

"You really should pull your curtains," Maggie suggested. "All I needed was my powerful binoculars, a melted patch in your frosted windows and settling on a perch off a nearby cliff and I could see everything, sweets. You were okay and entertaining a couple of hunks, so I just gave you a little bit of fun time while we kept an eye out for enemies. It wasn't easy, I might add. With the fall of the government and us getting cold asses out there, I was biting off everyone's head, just like you'd been doing before you left. God! How do you run everything on a daily basis without going nuts?" Maggie shook her head in frustration. "We waited until we figured you were running low on food before I came in. Anyway, I didn't know your men were so handy they could use margarine as lube."

Shit!

Reena's face grew even hotter. She laughed quietly at being caught with her pants down and two men literally thrusting into her.

Maggie's voice turned serious. "Anyone could have been watching, Red. You should have been more careful. We came across a camp littered with frozen dead bodies. The only reason we saw them was because an arm had frozen poking right up out of the snow. Scared the daylights out of me. A little digging around and we found more bodies. I'm assuming you had something to do with that?"

"We did. Those men caught me. Cade and Will saved my life. I figured I was safe with them here," Reena admitted. A sweet warmth raced through her at bragging to Maggie about her two men.

"Well hell, girl, as long as you had some fun. That's really all that counts, right? A little R & R—"

"Maggie," Reena warned. The last thing she wanted was for Maggie to compare R & R with what she'd experienced with Cade and Will. R & R had been forced on her. What she had with Cade and Will was special and to be treasured.

Maggie shoved her blankets aside and began dressing. "Okay, okay. Sorry. We were all just so worried about you when you didn't check in at the predetermined times..."

"Like I said last night, the phone was busted. Blade's been trying to fix it. He hasn't been successful."

"There was nothing wrong with it when I tried it outside. I got a signal right away," Maggie said.

Reena blinked in surprise.

"You guys had gone to sleep and I snuck out for a pee. Took the phone with me to see if I couldn't figure out what was wrong. But it works fine. Didn't you ever try it?"

No, she'd trusted Will when he said he hadn't fixed it. Reena froze as Cade and Will's soft snores grew louder...along with the beating of her heart.

"Are you sure?"

"Yeah, of course I'm sure. I was able to make contact with HQ and let them know you're okay. Will did a good job of putting it together."

An icy coldness swept through Reena. She mentally backtracked to when she'd last seen Will working on the phone. Actually, he hadn't been near it since a couple of days ago. Blade had fixed it and never told her?

"By the weird look on your face I take it you didn't know?" Maggie asked, suspicion lacing her voice. She stood beside Reena, her eyebrows scrunched in a severe frown.

Reena shook her head as the cold sank deeper into her body. Did Cade also know the phone was working? Maybe he'd forgotten about the phone, just like she had. They had been kind of busy. She'd never noticed whether or not he had questioned Blade about it. Maybe they *were* in cahoots together?

Had Blade called in her whereabouts? Was SKULL sending another assassin because Blade couldn't kill her?

Reena stared at the two men on the bed. If Blade or Cade was expecting company, they wouldn't be sleeping so soundly, would they? Unless they thought they had her in the bag, so to speak?

Beside her, Maggie produced a gun and Reena's blood ran cold as Maggie aimed the barrel at Cade.

"I can take them both out right now. Just give me the word," she said quietly.

There was an icy calm to her voice. Maggie wouldn't hesitate to kill the two men Reena had so quickly grown to care for. Maybe their connection even went beyond caring and gratitude? Maybe love?

Oh get over it, Reena!

Caring and gratitude only. That was it. How could she not care for two men who'd saved her life?

Reena reached out and placed her hand on the barrel of the gun, pushing until it pointed at the floor.

"No, that won't be necessary. I have another idea."

* * * * *

It was really hard to pretend nothing was wrong as they packed. All Reena wanted to do was ask Will about the satellite phone. Or Cade. She almost did several times, but she held back, hoping Will or Cade would tell her.

God, why was she being so childish? A simple question would solve the issue. But if she asked Cade and he said no, Will hadn't said anything to him, he could be lying. If he said yes, Will had told him, then she'd be hurt they hadn't told her.

Another reason for remaining silent—she didn't want to tip them off that she knew. She preferred the element of surprise. The best defense was a good offense. She should be angry. Instead sadness clung to her to the point of wanting to cry.

Stupid woman. Be strong. Be tough. Let the plan play out as you've laid it. Action first. Questions later.

She bit her bottom lip and hoisted her knapsack onto her back and buckled the belt. The others were standing out on the veranda waiting for her. She suspected Maggie had arranged their departure to give Reena a few moments alone to say goodbye to her grandparents' cabin. She didn't know when she would be back. Or even if she *would* come back.

She gazed at the pull-out sofa, neatly tucked in again. The cots had been put away and the kitchen had been cleaned to perfection. It appeared as if they'd never been there. As if this part of her past had been erased.

The woodstove continued to pump out heat, but the fire would be dead in a few hours. The cabin would once again freeze over. Just as cold as she felt regarding her men.

Her men.

Yeah, she'd been in total dreamland about them. She smiled wistfully. Maybe it *had* been a dream, but it had been wonderful while it lasted.

She turned and, without glancing back, walked out the door.

Chapter Eleven

"Something's up with Red," Will said in a low voice as Cade snowshoed beside him. Up ahead, the two women disappeared behind a clump of snow-draped balsam trees.

"She was too quiet while we packed," Cade replied. "She tried to act normal, but I could see right through it. Maybe she's just mulling over what we argued about last night."

Hope tinged Cade's voice and it whispered through Blade as well. Maybe Cade was right. Maybe she was rethinking her stance on personally going to this meeting the II had set up. Or maybe something else was going on...

"But I think there's more to it." Cade echoed Will's thoughts.

"Maggie probably knows. When I get the chance to talk to her, I'll pump her for information," Will said.

He reached into his pocket and grabbed a bottle of water. He gulped the ice-cold liquid, enjoying the way it slid down his parched throat. They'd been snowshoeing along the back road for a couple hours and his wounds were aching, but it was a good ache. It meant he was alive.

"Pretty nice out here, isn't it?" Cade asked as he produced his own bottle of water and took a few swallows.

Blade nodded. "A far cry from the heat and sand we encountered during the Terrorist Wars."

He enjoyed the white-blanketed trees and the spectacular way the sunshine sparkled off the snow drifts. The silence was deafening except for the soft hiss and crackle of snow melting beneath the hot glare of sunshine.

The gentle whisper was much better than the report of gunshots as bullets left the barrel of his rifle and splattered someone's brains. Yep, he could get used to this peace and quiet.

The crunch of snow broke the silence as Cade began to snowshoe ahead, following the trail the women had carved. The four of them had been taking turns with the lead.

Every half hour the first person in line—who had the hardest job of stomping down the snow—would go to the end of the line. This gave everyone an equal opportunity for a small rest.

Right now Maggie was in the lead. When she dropped back to the end of the line, he'd talk to her about Red. But the instant he and Cade rounded the sharp curve where Red and Maggie had disappeared moments earlier, several men and women came out of the nearby trees and completely surrounded them.

He didn't know who was more surprised, him or Cade. Several guns were pointed at them and a sharp slap of anger twisted through Blade.

"Hands off the weapons!" A man dressed in white-and-gray camouflage fatigues shouted.

Immediately Blade loosened his hand from the handle of his gun. Hell, he didn't even remember reaching for it.

Two women he'd never seen before—also dressed in head-to-toe camouflage white—moved toward them. Quickly, they frisked both him and Cade, alleviating them of all weapons.

"The Resistance, I presume," Blade muttered. He sought out Reena and Maggie, who were watching from behind the group.

He caught Red's gaze and saw her anger was aimed directly at him. What the hell was she so pissed about?

Maggie was saying something to Red and she nodded. She turned her back to them and started snowshoeing down the road. Farther ahead several more people, heavily armed, dressed in camouflage, waited for her.

"Reena! Don't do it!" Cade shouted from beside him.

Her shoulders stiffened momentarily and hope raced through him as she hesitated.

Come on, Red. Talk to us.

His hopes plummeted as she continued walking.

Dammit!

"She's going to that fucking meeting," Cade said. Anger twisted his voice.

Blade cursed violently and the people surrounding them released the safety catches on their weapons.

Cripes! Jumpy bunch, aren't they?

"We trusted you, Reena!" Cade shouted. He made a move to start snowshoeing after her, but Blade grabbed his elbow, stopping him cold. Despite Blade's anger at Red for being so damned stubborn, he had to admit he was impressed with the weaponry of her entourage. Maybe she'd get lucky and get out of that meeting alive, but he didn't think so.

* * * * *

It was hard to keep from sobbing as Cade's angry shouts split into her like bullets. The betrayal flaring in both men's eyes over how Reena had called in her entourage just about killed her. But, Maggie reminded her, these two men were virtual strangers, and until they could prove themselves trustworthy within the group they needed to be carefully observed—just like everyone else—before entry to the Resistance.

Still it didn't sit well, not having them by her side as she and her people were ushered into the south entrance of the White House for her impending meeting with the new dictatorship.

She was so tired of this shit. Hiding. Fighting. Wanting life to get back to normal. She'd done a total one-eighty over the past couple of weeks having Cade and Blade in her life. Their time together had been so normal. Well, if a ménage à trois was normal. Which it was for her now.

The normalcy had dulled her instincts and clouded her judgment. She'd been swept up in the other Resistance members' hopefulness—that maybe things would change for the better if Reena showed up at the White House.

To her surprise, she found her father standing farther down the hallway. He was alone.

Despite their rocky relationship over the years, happiness at seeing him bubbled up inside of her. When he held out his hands to her, shock shifted through her. He never did that. Never showed emotion. Even when he'd been told by her doctors she had the X-virus, O mutation, he hadn't so much as flinched. He'd just held a cool, expressionless face.

Now, as he held out his hands to her, he was smiling. Was he actually happy to see her?

Something burst inside of her and she flew into his arms. She swore this was the first time he'd ever hugged her in her life. It was a wonderful hug. She eventually pulled away. Not that she wanted to, but she had so many questions.

"What are you doing here, Dad? No one could tell me if you'd been killed during the coup or what had happened to you." She brushed away a sudden swell of tears that irritatingly appeared, blurring her vision. She'd assumed he was dead. But here he was, alive.

"He's one of you now," a sharp, unfamiliar male voice called from behind her.

Her entourage was already on top of him, their rifles aimed at the lone figure who'd walked out of a nearby room. The man was dressed entirely in black. She knew from her briefing he was the new president's top security man. They called him "the man in black" because of the way he dressed as well as the way he ran White House security. Anyone who questioned their leadership was sent to the dungeons below the White House.

His eyes were dark-brown, almost black. He wore a thick black mustache, had bushy black eyebrows and was bald.

"You are Reena Wilde. The woman the Resistance calls 'Red.'"

He smiled, but the smile did not reach his cold eyes. Inwardly, Reena shivered. A man's eyes were the mirror to his soul. And this man's soul was dark and untrustworthy.

She stiffened her shoulders. "I am the leader of the Resistance."

He extended his hand.

She ignored it. "I'm here for the meeting."

"Ah yes, the meeting. Unfortunately the meeting has been canceled. For *all* of you."

A hissing erupted from several areas around the hallway. She didn't see anything, didn't smell anything, but instantaneously lightheadedness crashed into her.

Damn!

She went for her gas mask as the others struggled to retrieve theirs as well.

"Your masks won't work." The man in black chuckled. "You need the same pill I just took for protection. The gas is a fast-acting paralyzing agent. But don't worry. You'll still be able to breathe."

Shit.

She struggled to remain standing as dizziness assailed her. Her father grabbed her arm, but too soon they both dropped to their knees.

"You are now my prisoners." The man laughed.

"Bastard." She'd been so stupid to come here. She should have listened to Cade and Blade. Should have listened...

A gun blast echoed dully in her ears and warm liquid splashed against her face. Shock numbed her as splatters of blood rained down all over her coat.

"Reena..." Her father gasped softly from right in front of her. In slow motion, he collapsed to the ground and lay still as a corpse. He was dead.

Oh God. Why?

She wanted to scream. But no words escaped her mouth. She couldn't even move her lips.

"Your father's death is your first lesson in obedience. If you don't behave, the same will happen to your entourage. One at a time." The man's words were slow and distorted.

Blackness swooped in and claimed her.

* * * * *

A horrible sound reverberated through Reena's unconsciousness, prodding her back to reality. She came awake with a pounding awareness and bitter panic that had her gasping in anguish. The last thing she had seen before she'd blacked out had been her father's sightless eyes.

No. No. No. This can't be happening. It can't be. He can't be dead.

He'd hugged her for the very first time...and for the last time. She inhaled on a strangled sob. She had to keep quiet. Had to figure out where she was and what was happening.

A ghastly wail permeated the air, capturing her full attention.

Someone was screaming. Nearby. The agonizing screams dropped abruptly, followed by several sharp slaps that were definitely flesh on flesh. A woman sobbed and guilt ripped into Reena. One of her own people being tortured? Who?

She inwardly moaned and then tensed when the woman screamed again. Torture? It had to be. Had to be.

Okay. Okay. Calm down. Calm down!

She jerked at the sharp slap of flesh hitting flesh again, which was quickly followed by the woman's wretched sobbing.

Reena lay on the floor and stared through the darkness for what seemed an eternity, listening, trying to figure out who it could be. And where she was.

Putrid dampness made her shiver and the ice-cold cement floor beneath her wasn't helping. She cursed softly as she tried to move, but couldn't. Her shoes and socks had been removed and her ankles were bound tightly. Her arms were behind her back and her wrists were tied.

She wiggled her fingers and pain ripped through them. At least she could move them. She froze. She wasn't wearing any pants.

Oh God. No.

Calm, Reena. Calm.

She lay still and took a mental inventory of her body. Her feet were icy cold. Her thighs, too. She wore panties. The cloth hugged her stiff hips. Her coat and sweater had been removed. She only wore her bra and thermal underwear top...and her panties.

She didn't think she'd been raped. She wasn't sore. But that didn't mean anything.

Panic began to well. Goose bumps scrambled up her arms when the woman cried out again. A throbbing silence followed.

The woman began pleading.

Reena shivered uncontrollably. She wanted to puke. Quick-paced footsteps echoed from down a hall and she struggled to calm her breathing. The footsteps stopped just a few feet behind her.

"Is she awake yet?" came the man in black's voice.

Anger ripped through her and she wanted to scream at the son of a bitch. To kill him with her bare hands.

"No sir. She hasn't moved," came the answer.

An abrupt, agonized shriek filled Reena's head and her heart thudded insanely fast against her chest.

"And our other guest? How is she doing? Cooperating?"

"No sir," another man answered.

A heavy sigh, and then a long moment of silence followed.

"Tell them to kill her."

No. No. No. Reena wanted to shout and bring their attention away from the woman. She didn't want any more people to die. Her father was dead.

Dead. Oh God.

The tight rein on her anger spiraled out of control.

"Stop!" Reena called, surprised at how loudly her voice echoed in the room.

"Wait," the man in black said calmly.

Reena moaned as she rolled onto her back and arms. Pain shrieked through her shoulders. How long had she been lying here? Hours? Days? Her legs were so cold they hurt.

A bare light bulb flickered on immediately above her, blinding her. She closed her eyes, begging for the dark again, but then quickly remembered the woman in danger and forced herself to reopen her eyes.

She blinked rapidly against the bright intensity, turned her head to the left and found the man in black standing not more than five feet away. Heavy metal bars separated her from him but, oh man, she wanted him so dead.

"Don't...kill...the woman. Please," she begged.

Number one rule in the Resistance: if you're caught, never show sympathy for your fellow prisoners. Your captors will use it against you. And here she'd broken the number-one rule.

Stupid, Reena. Very stupid.

"Our Reena is awake. Bring her up to the quarters. And give the other woman a reprieve. I'll issue further orders after I speak with Ms. Wilde."

Reena tensed as the footsteps started up again, moving away from her. She jerked as a key grated noisily and a door creaked open. The guards entered her cell in a flurry of footsteps.

"Perhaps a quick fuck before we take her to the man." The guard chuckled.

Panic slammed into her and she took a speedy inventory of the two men who leered at her. They both wore green camouflage fatigues, rifles slung over their shoulders and holstered pistols at their waists.

"The man wouldn't approve," she said quickly as a rush of panic took hold again. "He wants me. Untouched. I belong to him. Understand?"

The guards' eyes widened. They said nothing as one of them undid the ropes around her ankles and the other continued to leer longingly at her panties.

Oh yeah, she was going to puke. She swallowed bitter bile and tried to figure out a way to escape. If she'd been in better shape, if she could have moved her legs and they weren't so useless and heavy and cold—or maybe if she still didn't suffer the aftereffects of the gas she'd inhaled—she could have easily twined her legs around the guy's neck, broken it and killed him.

Unfortunately, she was too weak to do anything but curse as he tugged her left shoulder and pushed her roughly onto her belly. Together they grabbed her bound wrists and lifted her to her knees by the rope.

Pain sliced through her shoulders as they yanked, but she refused to scream. She wouldn't give these sons of bitches the satisfaction. In moments, they had her standing on her wobbly legs and stuffed their hands under her armpits, forcing her to keep her balance. She bit her bottom lip as the circulation began to move in her arms and legs. Fire burned painfully and she still refused to cry out. Refused to give them the pleasure of seeing her in pain.

They dragged her out of the cell. Ahead, an endless row of metal-barred cell doors lined both sides of the hallway. They stopped her right in front of the cell immediately beside hers.

"The man says to stop for now. He'll give further orders later," one guard said into the dark cell.

The woman sobbed and cried out as someone slapped her.

"I said no more!" the guard called.

Shadows moved inside the room and a moment later the barred door creaked open and two burly guards came out. Reena gasped as she spied the woman standing against the back wall. She was naked. Blood dribbled along her inner thighs. Tangled long black hair hung over her face.

Reena didn't recognize her.

"You two want a go at her? We can take over and deliver this bitch for you." One of the new guards leered at her and she knew exactly what he wanted to do to her.

Creep.

Oh, this was great. These men were just as bad, if not worse, than the ones they'd replaced in this new so-called government. The women of this country would get nowhere trying to negotiate with this new regime.

"We'll take her," the guard who held her by the left armpit said. "You stay and watch that one. The man said she has a reprieve."

The two burly guards frowned. One closed the cell door with a brutal clang as if he was quite pissed off, and each man took a spot on the opposite sides of the door.

Inside the cell, the woman began to wail. The intense sobs made Reena shake again as the two guards practically dragged her down the hallway and up the stairs. Down several more hallways, up more stairs and they finally entered an elevator.

As she stood between the two men, she kept her gaze moving, searching for any clue to her whereabouts or for any way out of this mess.

Cade and Will kept entering her mind. They had rescued her and she wished like hell she hadn't ordered them to be locked up until her return. She shouldn't have treated them so badly. Would she ever see them again so she could apologize?

Tears stung her eyes. She closed them and saw her father's sightless gaze as he slumped to the ground. Her fault. His death was her fault. If she hadn't come here, he'd still be alive. His death was her fault.

Another sob built in her chest and she choked it down.

She had to get a fucking grip! This *wasn't* her fault. She wasn't the one who'd pulled the trigger. The man in black had. She had to forget the dead and figure a way out of here and rescue her people. Then she needed to get back to the Resistance. Back to Cade and Will.

The Resistance would continue their plans to take out the government. She would not stop until all women were free and horrors like what had happened to that woman in the cell were squashed.

Reena pressed away her fear for her own safety and fought to steady her breathing. One thing was certain. If she died today, she would take the man with her. She smiled inwardly. Yeah, killing him would certainly make her day.

* * * * *

"Someone's coming," Blade muttered from his perch on the top bunk of the cell they'd been languishing in for hours.

Cade tumbled out of his bed, the familiar anger roaring through him like a damn cannonball. To his surprise, the door swung inward and Maggie stepped inside. Her face was pale, she visibly shook and she'd left the door wide open behind her. No one else followed.

Escape time.

Blade must've realized her mistake because he flew out of bed. They tackled Maggie at the same time, rushing her to the ground, pinning her beneath them. She squirmed helplessly for a few precious seconds before she finally gave up the fight.

"You fucking idiots," she breathed as Cade snatched her pistol from her shoulder holster. Blade moved off of her and patted her down for any other weapons she might have. He removed the knife strapped to her inner right ankle.

Maggie groaned in frustration. "Come on! If I wanted you guys to stay here, do you think I'd be stupid enough to leave the bloody door open?"

Cade and Blade looked at each other.

"She has a point," Cade acknowledged.

"Or she's the fucking idiot and forgot she shouldn't come into a cell with a couple of really pissed-off men," Blade replied coolly as he pressed the point of her knife against her jugular. "I bet she'll look nice in a red necktie. Want to find out?"

Maggie's eyes widened and Cade detected an instant of fear before she quickly concealed it behind a cold, defiant mask.

"Something has happened to Reena. We need your help."

Cade's finger tightened on the trigger of the gun and Blade's hand twitched ever so slightly. A thin trickle of blood appeared at the point of the knife where he'd pressed it against her neck.

"You better not be lying," Blade whispered in a voice so icy cold shivers even traveled down Cade's spine.

"Hell, you better be lying. If something happened to her, I'll fucking kill you right now," he growled as a nasty kind of fear took hold of him.

Maggie frowned. "She was double-crossed at the meeting. None of the entourage returned."

Blade cursed and removed the knife from against Maggie's neck.

"Details. Everything you know," Cade snapped. He kept the gun trained on her head. "If you leave anything out, you're dead."

* * * * *

A man's laughter erupted down the hallway the moment Reena and the two guards stepped off the elevator. Actually, *they* stepped off the elevator and she was hauled off. Her damn legs still weren't working right and she spent almost all her concentration stumbling along the plush white carpet.

It was different here than in that stinking cell. Fresh air and mild scents of disinfectant hung in hallways which were lined with framed erotic pictures—women in bondage, some being flogged and others being caned, while still others were in restraints and ropes.

She swore the floor was heated beneath her bare feet. By the time they stopped her at the end of the hallway, wonderful warm air had embraced her and her legs moved with much more fluidity.

Her hopes soared. Maybe she could get out of here after all. Her hope died when one guard knocked on the door and the man in black instructed them to enter.

One guard slid an electronic key into the door lock and pressed an awfully long password into a nearby keypad, keeping his body in front of it to make sure she couldn't see. Despite not wanting to, she began to tremble as the door opened and the guards pushed her into the room.

It didn't take long to figure out the room was one of a suite. Several open doors led to other rooms and she counted at least five bedrooms, all lavishly appointed. The main room where she stood was intricately decorated with crystal chandeliers, flushed pink carpeting and white furniture.

There was nothing she could use as a weapon. The man stood beside a couch, leering at her. He wasn't wearing a gun.

Her gaze flew back to the bedrooms, past the open doorways. Beautiful women dressed in gorgeous, sexy gowns sat on the beds and stared out at her with glazed, curious stares.

Her blood froze. She recognized those stares. She knew what this place was.

A brothel. Damn!

The man in black swept his hands in a large semicircle. "Welcome to my personal lair, Ms. Wilde. This will be your new home."

Reena ignored the wild adrenaline roaring through her and gazed around, pretending she'd expected something like this and wasn't pleased.

"I've seen better," she said coolly, putting on airs, tilting her nose in a snobby fashion in hopes her attitude would irritate him.

He grunted, akin to that of displeasure, and then snapped his fingers. The two guards quickly left.

Well, there goes your only possibility of grabbing a gun and shooting your way out.

The stakes were one on one now. All she needed was her hands untied and she would kill the bastard who murdered her father.

"Ah yes, your short stay at the Pleasure Palace," he murmured.

"I guess you've seen my resume, but you must not have read the part about my performing better with my hands untied."

The man chuckled lightly at her wry comment and she tensed as he circled her like a vulture. His breath came faster and was raspy by the time he rounded her front. Thankfully he didn't touch her. If he had, she wouldn't have been able to handle it.

"Your hands won't be freed until you're under my full control, Ms. Wilde." He pointed to a syringe filled with blue fluid set on a nearby glass table.

Shit! Sex drugs.

"Being under your control will be boring for both of us." She forced herself to smile at him as sweetly as she could under the circumstances.

He smiled back, once again the smile not reaching his eyes.

Okay, so he was getting the picture. It encouraged her to plod ahead with her quickly formulated plan. She gazed at the open doors that led to the bedrooms occupied by the women.

"The women in those rooms. They look very pretty. They also appear quite bored. I could teach them a thing or two, things they could do to make you happy."

Like putting a bullet right between your eyes.

His eyes widened. She noted his irritation when he shifted uneasily.

"I heard your laughter as we came off the elevator. A bored laugh. I can make you groan instead of laugh. You'd prefer that, wouldn't you?"

She lowered her voice to the sexy whisper she reserved for getting information out of men. Those assignments were necessary, yet quite distasteful.

But this one, by far, was the worst. And if she had to seduce her way out of these restraints, then so be it. It was the only way to break free and get back to Cade and Will.

Just thinking about the two of them made her heart leap with hope. Surely she wouldn't end up in here for the rest of her life? Never see Will and Cade again? She wouldn't live long here. She knew that. Once the man in black tired of her, he'd have her killed or dumped back into that cell as fodder for those guards, just like the other woman she'd seen down there.

"So you have sympathy for my girls. You wish for them to please me?" His eyes snapped with a deadly fire.

She had his interest. "Yes, of course. If you're pleased, then we're pleased. Everybody is happy."

He backhanded her across her face. The pain seared into her flesh, making her stumble backward. She collapsed onto a sofa.

She tried to get up, but thought better of it when he moved in front of her, standing with his legs pressed against her knees, blocking her way. Her gut churned at the satisfied smirk on his face. She resisted like hell the opportunity to slam her foot against the tender area between his thighs. He'd kill her for sure.

She wasn't ready to die. Not until he was dead first. She owed her dad at least that. She squashed another well of emotions when she thought of her father. He was gone. She had to deal with her loss another time.

"Don't even consider whatever you are thinking, my beautiful red-haired slut." He grinned as he began to unbuckle his pants.

Oh God.

"You'll lie on the couch and enjoy your first lesson in submission." His eyes were darkening with lust as he lowered his zipper.

Reena could barely breathe as she quickly went through her options. She could either do what he said or die trying to escape. She decided on the latter.

Pistoning her legs, she smashed her heels directly into his groin. He sharply inhaled as surprise and pain sliced through his eyes.

The man gurgled and dropped to his knees like a stone.

Perfect.

In a flash, she circled his neck with her shins.

"I don't like guys who scream like girls, asshole." She twisted her legs and grimaced at the gut-wrenching crack. Broken neck. The man's body went limp. She shuddered and let go and he flopped over like a rag doll.

Clapping hands made her lift her gaze toward the door where several men stood, all dressed in dark clothing like the guards who'd brought her to this room. Her stomach twisted in a sickening lurch, but then she recognized Tyler and Mac Outlaw.

They stepped inside.

"It's about time you showed up," she managed to say. Relief made her entire body go into tremble mode. She opted to remain sitting on the couch until she could slow her pounding heart at surviving such a close call.

"Couldn't have done it any better myself, Red." Blade smiled as he stepped into the room.

"That's our girl. She knows how to take care of herself. I don't know why we were worried." Cade chuckled as he also stepped inside.

Huge relief splashed through her at seeing the two of them, and it took all her effort to fight back her tears at how they—once again—came to her rescue.

Cade moved forward, his rifle trained on the several women who now stood in their doorways, peering out curiously. Their hands smoothed over their breasts and thighs as they watched the men fan out and check the rest of the rooms.

"The building is secure, ladies. Get whatever you need and come with us. Be ready in three minutes," Cade called.

None of the women moved.

"They won't go. They need their next fix," Reena replied as she leaned forward and Will untied her wrists.

The women were hooked on the sex drugs. She could tell in the way they were touching themselves and the erotic way they stared at the men with glazed eyes. They would stay here and wait for their next fix.

She'd been one of them during her stay at the Pleasure Palace and she knew how it could be. For her, it had been very hard to get off those drugs and she hadn't even been on them very long. That's the main reason she'd stayed at the SKULL safe house and had sex with those men. It had been her way of getting off the drugs.

Her shoulders screamed like fire as she moved her arms forward.

Fuck! That hurt!

Blade began a quick rub on her right arm, grimacing when she whimpered in pain.

"Sorry," he whispered.

"You better be," she teased. "How did you find me?"

"Mac has a lot of pull with people in this new government. He did some quick snooping and found out where this guy had you."

"I need to thank him," she said.

"Thank him if we get out of here alive," Blade said. "We only secured this building, not the compound surrounding the White House. All hell could break loose at any second."

"Your people have a back entrance to the camp secured." Tyler moved in beside Blade and began to rub her left shoulder. Fire raced through her arm, but she held back a moan of pain.

Mac Outlaw stayed at the door, looking out as if he fully expected company.

She sucked in a breath as more pain flared, compliments of her circulation beginning to move faster.

"My entourage. Where are they?" She grimaced, fully expecting an answer that they'd been shot dead.

"We've released them. They were down in the dungeons. We got several other prisoners out. We got them all." Tyler rubbed her arms harder. "They're okay. Some were tortured, but they'll be fine. They are already on their way out. Hold on." For a moment, he put his finger on his ear as he listened to his ear mike.

Her people were okay. Thank God. And that other woman was free. But Reena's momentary happiness was shattered as she thought about her dad.

Damn! He *was* dead. She wouldn't have a body to bury. But she could handle this. Yes, she could handle his death. She had to.

Tyler grinned. "Copy that."

His grin widened as he gazed at her. "Everyone made it out safely. The entrance is still secure. Now it's our turn. Ready, pumpkin?"

Reena nodded shakily. "I was, like, ready yesterday, Teach."

Blade and Tyler grabbed her arms and helped her to stand.

"We need to find her something for her feet," Blade called as he glanced down at her lack of footwear.

"Pants would be nice too," she blurted.

"Already on it." Cade dropped a pair of expensive-looking low-heeled silver shoes to the floor in front of her and handed Blade some clothing.

"Compliments of one of those women." Cade indicated a very pretty, tall black- haired Asian woman. She smiled at Reena with overly bright-red lips.

"Thanks," Reena replied and quickly donned a pair of silver, baggy pants and a matching silver long-sleeved top before she slipped into the shoes.

Geez, she'd be a neon target going outside in these clothes. But heck, beggars couldn't be choosers and right now gratitude and happiness embraced her. Will and Cade and the others had come to her rescue.

Gosh, did she ever owe them. Big-time. She should never have doubted them. She'd have to plan the biggest thank-you party for all these men. That is, if they got out of there alive.

* * * * *

The instant they left the building a heavy line of gunfire exploded toward their number-one escape route, a gate north of the compound. Cade cursed. Pulling his mike closer to his mouth, he impatiently waited for an update. He didn't have to wait long. Maggie's anguished cry erupted over the line.

"The bastards found us while we were leaving. It just happened. Your north escape route has been compromised. I repeat. The north route is unsafe. Do not come this way."

The other three men swore softly as they received the same information through their mikes. Blade pointed a finger at Reena, then at Cade, and then held up his hand, motioning for Reena to stick with Cade and remain at the back exit of the building.

Blade, Mac and Tyler disappeared around the building.

"What's wrong?" Reena asked as she snuggled up against him. His body reacted favorably to all her sweet, hot curves, but his trained mind kept his attention on getting them the hell out of there. Alive.

Another line of gunfire crackled, closer this time. The ground shook from an explosion and Reena curled a hand around his shoulder to steady herself.

"Too close," she muttered, her gaze flashing with fear for a split second, and then to determination and defiance as she kept an eye on the corner of the building where the other men had disappeared.

"I'd say you're too close," he replied, trying to lighten the mood.

She grinned at him and squeezed his shoulder. Her eyes sparkled with a magnificent fire and it was as if he'd been sucker-punched, but in one hell of a nice way.

"I'm sorry I didn't trust you," she whispered.

"Yeah well, Maggie explained about the satellite phone. Will and I will make you so sweetly sorry when we're alone again. You can count on that, Red," he promised.

She laughed. "Looking forward to it, Outlaw. Looking forward to it."

"You better."

She grew serious. "I need a gun."

Cade had his pistol out of his holster before she even finished her sentence. In their hurry to get out of the building, they hadn't even thought of arming her.

"What's the matter? You don't trust us to protect you?" He chuckled as she palmed his pistol, released the safety and swung upward. He had to admit, she knew how to handle a weapon.

"You're not used to a woman wanting to protect herself, are you?" A smile nudged the sides of her sweet pink lips.

"The confident way you protect yourself makes you sweetly sexy," he admitted. "But that doesn't mean you have to keep getting into trouble at every turn, okay? Because I can't handle how it turns me on and not being able to get relief."

She laughed again, the sound as pure and bright as the sun shining down on them.

"Chopper coming in." Will's voice erupted in his ear.

Cade tensed.

"It's ours," Mac replied. "Plan B."

"Fuck, yeah!" Tyler roared.

The report of gunfire snapped all around them. Just then Blade appeared at the corner and waved them over. Cade grabbed Reena and they quickly followed. He sighed in relief at the huge camouflage-green chopper landing not more than one hundred feet away.

A couple of men hung out of the open door, their submachine guns sputtering sparks as they took out some snipers on the adjoining rooftops. Mac, Tyler and Will kept up the rapid fire, allowing Reena and Cade to sprint to the chopper.

Pings ricocheted off the wall of the chopper, alerting Cade to more gunfire. Practically throwing Reena up to the two men inside, he twisted around and began shooting at a close figure rounding the corner of a nearby building. The man went down and lay still.

In quick unison, they all jumped into the chopper, each covering the others' backs. Cade was the last man inside and he swore he'd never been so relieved when the chopper was successfully airborne and out of range from gunfire.

He had a good reason. Hell, he'd never been so in love with a woman before and suddenly everything in life seemed to matter again.

He couldn't wait until he was alone with her. He and Will would show her exactly how pissed off and damned glad they were that she was safe. He could hardly wait.

* * * * *

The squeak of a key grating in the door quickly alerted Blade from where he and Cade were lounging on the sofa. Both of them dashed into a back room and quietly waited. It had been two weeks since their escape from the compound and Reena had been avoiding them. Okay, maybe avoiding was too strong a word. A busy lady didn't have much time to sexually accommodate both him and Cade.

Well, that was about to change. It had taken them two weeks to finally convince Maggie to trust them enough to give them a key to Red's place in the Resistance's compound so they could plan a private surprise for her. Finally, this afternoon, Maggie had come through for them. Against her better judgment, she told them with a wink.

He and Cade were now full members of the Resistance. Will had sent a message to SKULL telling them he'd resigned. He didn't expect any arguments. He was out and that was that.

"She's undressing," Cade whispered over Reena's soft humming and the rustle of clothes being removed.

"We'd better follow suit," Will answered in a low voice.

He grinned into the darkness as he began to peel off his clothes. They were in an unheated back room and it was damp and cool. Yet this did little to alleviate the heat flashing across his skin and the tight pull of his swollen balls and throbbing cock.

Ever since getting Reena to safety, he'd wanted to be around her as much as possible. Had needed to see her laughing eyes, touch that flaming, silky red hair of hers and just know she was safe.

He knew Cade felt the same way. Maybe more than Blade in the way he constantly made "ga-ga" eyes at her.

"She's got the shower running." Excitement laced his friend's voice.

Will's grin widened. Time to get their naked asses in gear.

* * * * *

Reena knew the instant they entered the bathroom. Their shadows loomed on the other side of the frosted shower door. She'd been expecting them. Of course Maggie had told her they wanted the key to her place. So Reena had stalled for as long as she could. She'd teased them by avoiding them and taking care of her own orgasms. Finally, today, she could stand the wait no longer.

Truth be told, her masturbating just didn't compare to how fantastic Will and Cade made her climax. For days she'd been wound up tight and all she'd been able to think about was some red-hot sex and total satisfaction. The satisfaction that could only be achieved with Will and Cade.

Damn them!

Because of them she'd once again begun snapping at everyone. Maggie insisted she get laid. Maggie was right.

She needed sex, and to tell the truth she wanted to see Will and Cade again. Wanted them touching and loving her.

She gasped as the glass door slid open and a hand snapped around her wrist. Instinctively she tried to pull away, but Will stepped into the shower stall.

Wow! She'd forgotten what a big, tall man he was. He took up a lot of the space in the tiny, confined area. The shower spray splashed against his backside as he faced her.

He grinned. "So you finally decided to allow us to see you, you little minx," he growled.

"Hey, good things come to those who wait," she chirped and inhaled as he pushed his naked body against her breasts, backing her against the wall with a rough thud.

"And I've waited a hell of a long time." His voice had lowered and his gaze darkened as he licked a bead of water off his lower lip. "If you'd hung around that first night we were together, you would have had a lot of good things happen to you. But you took off."

She gasped in surprise. "I took off? You're the one who left the room."

He shook his head and she cried out as his fingers slipped between her thighs and he began a sensual rubbing on her clit.

"I went outside. Needed to cool down. Had I stayed... Let's just say it was too intense and I didn't want to hurt you."

He'd come back fully expecting her to be there? But she'd taken off, hurt burrowing through her, thinking she'd never see him again. Boy, had she ever been wrong.

"I guess I should have stayed," she whispered.

"And you could have shown me that, yes, this relationship could exist, because I remember whispering it could never be."

It could never be... His last words spoken to her before he'd dressed and walked out that door.

"I'll show you now that it can be," she whispered and brushed her lips against Blade's firm, dewy mouth.

"You'll show both of us." Cade grinned over Blade's shoulder.

Excitement burst through her at seeing Cade. Her heart swelled and the bubbly happiness swirling inside her made her think she just might explode.

Blade grabbed her wrists and brought her forward and away from the wall. He stood her in the middle of the shower and then quickly brought her arms up over her head where—to her stunned amazement—black leather wrist cuffs dangled from a chain in the ceiling. A chain attached to a little hook. How in the world had she not seen that hook?

"Hey, those cuffs weren't there a minute ago," she complained as Blade continued to hold her arms up while Cade quickly cuffed both her wrists.

"A minute ago, Blade wasn't being a decoy." Cade chuckled. "We were in here earlier and drilled a strong little hook into your ceiling. While he was distracting you—the sly fellow that he is—I hung the chain and cuffs on the hook."

"Sneaky boys," she chastised and laughed.

"Men, not boys," Cade growled as he stepped in behind her and grabbed her by the waist. His hands seared her like molten lava as he held her still.

"She's all yours, Will."

"She's all ours, Cade," Blade corrected. "All ours."

Reena shivered at his deep, territorial tone.

He stepped in front of her and she inhaled sharply as Will reached down and placed his hands on her inner thighs, encouraging her to spread her legs.

To her shock, Cade pummeled the shower spray against her butt. She had one of those hand-held sprayers and he'd placed it on the strongest jet. He pressed one of her ass cheeks open and aimed the spray right at her sphincter.

The pummeling was fantastic. She closed her eyes, moaning into the pleasure. Her eyes popped open and she gasped and jerked against the restraints as Will's mouth seared over her pussy. He sucked oh so deliciously hard.

The wicked man had dropped to his knees in front of her, his face buried between her thighs. His erotic tongue laved her clit and plunged in and out of her vaginal opening until her legs were trembling.

He moved his face away and pulled on her labia rings so sweetly hard, she groaned at the burn. He let go and stood in front of her, licking his lips. "You should have trusted us, Red. Trusted us about the satellite phone."

"You should have told me," she quipped.

Excitement flared in his eyes. "I didn't want to give you an excuse to leave. I wanted us to stay at the cabin forever."

"Me too," Cade whispered as he nuzzled his bristly cheek against the crook of her neck and shoulder. He moved the spray away and she cried out as the rush of water pummeled her sensitive clit. Blade now held the device!

Both men chuckled.

Damn them!

She moaned as Cade reached around her right shoulder and grabbed a bottle of lube off the soap dish. Gosh! How had she missed that lube being there? One of them must have been placed it there while she'd been distracted. These men truly were devilishly sneaky. She'd love having them around and would really enjoy their surprises.

She'd have to remember recommending that women be allowed the option of having more than one husband when the Resistance won the fight against the government and took over running the country. Having Will and Cade by her side, things just might be more bearable as they continued their fight against this latest dictatorship.

Cade slipped his lubed cock into her bottom and the fullness of his penetration had her gasping and moaning at the pleasure-pain. His hands came around and he began pulling on her nipple rings. Nice and hard. Perfect.

Will kept the shower spray on her clit and she cried out her warning as the knots of tension uncurled deep inside her and raced toward a fast-budding orgasm.

Will cursed. The pummeling spray moved away and a clatter erupted in the stall as the shower device hit the wall.

Her breaths came fast and hard as foil was ripped and a condom sheathed Will's swollen shaft. Seconds later, Cade slid out of her as Will plunged his juicy, big cock into her vagina.

Beautiful!

The two men settled quickly into a mind-shattering rhythm. Their rock-hard bodies crashed against her as they made love to her. Being sandwiched between her two solid men gave her a sense of protection and love, and her long-buried dreams of settling down with a man—make that two men—began to blossom again.

Everything in her life was right. Suddenly beautiful.

As they plunged in and out of her, their rough guttural groans rocked through her like lightning bolts, carrying her away into the land of an intense pleasure she craved. These men were a precious gift and Reena had to treasure them.

She would. Always.

Her pussy and anus clenched around the thick intrusions. Convulsions grabbed her, held her, and she lost all control.

She free fell into her emotions, tumbling into exquisite pleasure. Somewhere far off, Cade and Will moaned their releases and all her resistance to the old ways vanished.

The three of them would be one.

Forever.

The End

Want more Jan Springer Adult Romances?

Mini Catalog

Kidnap Fantasies Series

In the land of the rich and famous, the top-secret Kidnap Fantasies is the answer to discreet and naughty downtime.

Book One

Jade's Fantasy

When ex-downhill skier Jade's two sisters give her a Kidnap Fantasies questionnaire, Jade is aroused at the prospect of having no-strings fun in the sun with a stranger whose only job would be to fulfill her every intimate fantasy. Although she knows she's too shy to send it in, she secretly pours her deepest wishes into the questionnaire.

Soon the questionnaire mysteriously vanishes and Jade's fantasy man appears on her luxury yacht in the form of a sexy handy man who gives her an intimate toy-filled holiday she'll never forget.

———————————————————

Book Two
Christmas Lovers
(can also be found in the Merry Ménage Kisses Boxed Set)
Sergeant Connor Jordan, wounded overseas and sent back to the States to recuperate, just cannot stop fantasizing about the sexy nurse who cared for him. When his brothers give him a holiday gift certificate to Kidnap Fantasies, a top-secret fantasy organization, Connor knows he'll use their gift, if only to help him forget his wickedly delicious attraction to Nurse Sparks.
Nurse Tania Sparks has always been purely professional with her injured soldiers...until sinfully sexy Connor Jordan enters her hospital. He makes her body throb with an intense desire she's never known

before. The last thing she wants is to get involved with the injured warrior. So what's a woman supposed to do to relieve her naughty frustrations? Call Kidnap Fantasies and have them supply her with a lookalike man who'll help her forget her sexy soldier...

When Tania and Connor unexpectedly come together at a secluded mountain chalet, their love explodes in a ménage of passion, sensuous desires and a happily forever after.

Contains ménage scenes.

Book Three

Zero to Sexy

Because Santana hides from something bad in his past, he lives only for the moment and doesn't dare dream of a future. He exists within the sensual world of Kidnap Fantasies, a top-secret escort world where he explores his sexuality and enjoys pleasure with both men and women.

But it is love at first sight the instant he sees Amy at his good friend's wedding. She's got future written all over her. He knows she is a hunger he must deny, so why is he whispering "you're mine" to her at the wedding?

The instant Amy Sparks sees the handsome African-American at her sister's wedding, she knows in her heart that he's everything she's ever fantasized about in a lover—but before they can connect, he mysteriously disappears. Upon discovering he works for Kidnap

Fantasies, Amy knows how he'll make all her intimate fantasies come true...

When Santana's next Kidnap Fantasies assignment turns out to be Amy, he knows he must protect her from his past and he can be with her only this one time...

Reader Advisory: Includes a sizzling ménage scene and some male-on-male sensual interaction.

_____

Boxed Sets

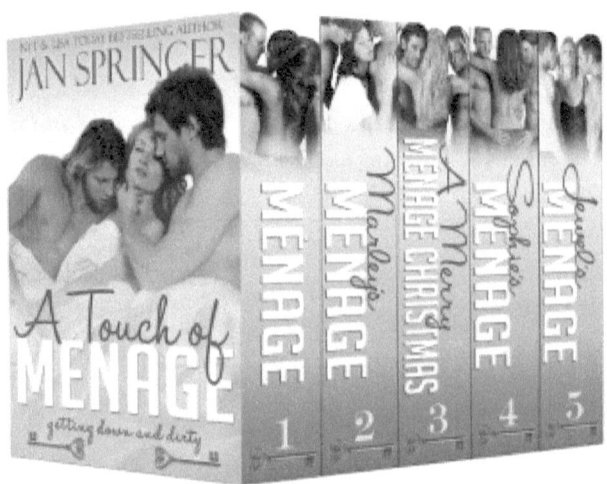

SIX Erotic Romance Ménage Stories! INCLUDES A BONUS MÉNAGE EBOOK

BONUS MENAGE BOOK: "Cowboys for Christmas," Book one of Jan's new Cowboys Online series. Jennifer Jane is getting THREE Cowboys for Christmas. What more could a girl want?
Jennifer Jane Watson has spent the past ten Christmases in a maximum-security prison. The last thing she expects is to get early parole along with a job on a secluded Canadian cattle ranch serving Christmas holiday dinners to three of the sexiest cowboys she's ever met!

~

Step into The Key Club's Ménage Nights where naughty fantasies come true and two men are hotter than one. Includes FIVE bestselling The Key Club stories; Ménage, Marley's Ménage, A Merry Ménage Christmas, Sophie's Ménage and Jewel's Ménage.

The Key Club Series
Ménage - Book One

Sandwiched between constant deadlines, erotic romance author Claire
Miller, enjoys an occasional unwind at The Key Club. And this time
she's going to indulge in a yummy ménage.

Marley's Ménage - Book Two

Single soon-to-be mom Marley Madison has had some wicked cravings in her day, but being pregnant has made her cravings downright naughty. She wants a sizzling ménage and she needs it bad.

A Merry Ménage Christmas - Book Three

Dr. Kelsie Madison can't remember the last time she's had no-strings sex, and that's her clue she's been working way too hard. It's time to unwind at the Key Club by indulging in a yummy Christmas present for herself...a red-hot ménage.

Sophie's Ménage - Book Four

It's Spank-Me Ménage Night at the Key Club and Sophie is finally taking the plunge back into the spank scene...but she didn't expect her two ex-boyfriends to be there too.

Jewel's Ménage - Book Five

She thought she would never trust a man again...
Until one rainy night, two hunky truckers come to Jewel's rescue,
igniting delicious desires for a red-hot ménage a trios.

Jaxie's Ménage - Book Six

A close encounter with death pushes Jaxie into making one of her
most intimate fantasies come true...

A Homecoming Ménage Christmas - Book Seven

Rachel has a very naughty secret, and she's way too embarrassed to let anyone know about it. When The Key Club throws a Santa Fetish Ménage Night, it's almost too good to be true. She has to figure out how to participate without anyone finding out!

Pleasure Bound Box Set
The Complete Series
Books 1 - 6

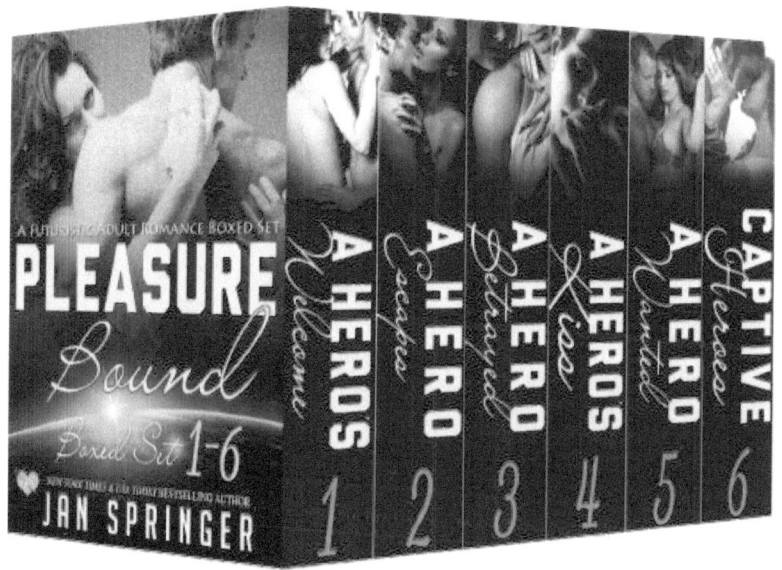

A Futuristic Adult Romance
Books 1-6

This PLEASURE BOUND BOXED SET is an EROTIC ROMANCE SET and includes the first SIX books in the Pleasure Bound series.
TOP-SECRET MISSION: Explore a recently discovered planet in outer space.

DISCOVERY: A sizzling trip into the realms of bondage, BDSM, pleasure-pain, betrayal and...love.

Inside this Boxed Set:

During a top-secret mission to a newly discovered planet, the six Hero siblings are thrust into a sensual world of erotic violence, unconventional romance and sizzling sex.

A HERO'S WELCOME

Pleasure Bound, Book One

Jan Springer

Being shot and held captive isn't what astronaut Joe Hero had in mind when he agreed to a top-secret mission to explore a newly discovered planet for NASA.

But a man would have to be dead not to fall for the sensual female doctor in charge of his care.

One night of scorching passion in the arms of the stranger from another planet is enough to convince Dr. Annie there's more to males than she's been taught by the Educators.

Who is this sexy hunk and why does she welcome him into her bed and her heart *every* chance she gets?

A HERO ESCAPES

Pleasure Bound, Book Two
Jan Springer
Queen Jacey has always fantasized about bedding a male.
But taking one for her enjoyment is strictly forbidden. That is, until an attractive well-hung stranger from another planet forces her to overcome her training and her beliefs.
Being held captive and forced to mate with a gorgeous Queen isn't exactly what astronaut Ben Hero expected when he agreed to explore a newly discovered planet for NASA.
Escaping *should* be his top priority but making sizzling love to Jacey *is* all he can think about.
When he discovers she's also being held captive, Ben's protective instincts kick in big time.
Suddenly they're on the run, irresistibly aroused, and wrapped in each other's arms every chance they get!

A HERO BETRAYED

Pleasure Bound, Book Three

Jan Springer

Astronaut Buck Hero didn't count on being held captive or becoming infected with passion poison when he agreed to explore a newly discovered planet for NASA.

If he doesn't get the cure soon he's going to be one *very* dead man.

Fugitive on-the-run Virgin has just rescued an infected male and needs to administer the cure - a twenty-four-hour sex marathon. Then she'll turn him over to his enemies in order to gain her freedom.

But her well-laid plans go into orbit when she discovers she's fallen in love with the stranger from another world.

A HERO'S KISS

Pleasure Bound, Book Four
Jan Springer
During a secret NASA mission to locate their brothers on the faraway planet of Paradise, the Hero sisters become separated after they crash-land...and find unexpected romance with the tormented male warriors of the species.

Jarod and Piper

Being injured and infected by sensuous swamp water isn't what Piper
Hero signed up for when she agreed to search for her three missing
brothers. But when she's rescued by a dangerously sexy man who
makes her so hot that she can't even think straight, Piper is glad that
she came.

Jarod Ellis has sworn off women. But he's captivated by Piper Hero, a
woman who claims to be related to the Earthmen he has vowed to
protect with his life. Although he mistrusts her, she sets free a carnal
inferno of needs he's never experienced during his previous life as a
pleasure slave.

Despite her intimate fantasies coming true, Piper knows she needs to
continue her mission of reuniting her siblings and she'll do it-with or
without the help of her well-hung stud...

A HERO WANTED

Pleasure Bound, Book Five
(Loosely connected with this series)
Jan Springer

Old-fashioned gal needs a man who loves to walk in the rain. Must be well-hung. A homebody, white picket fence-type of guy. Sexual requirements-gentle yet untamed lover. He must be sexually adventurous who will train me to be same. Must be romantic, enjoy toys, interested in mutual light bondage, ménages are welcome.

That's what full-figured, antique shop owner Jenna MacLean wants when she and her best friend outline a want ad just for fun on their weekly girls' night out.

After years of being away from his pretty-plus sized ex-girlfriend, Sully's back in town. When he finds the want ad, he knows he's the only man who can make all of Jenna's sizzling-hot fantasies come true. She's never left his heart and he needs her back in his bed—but he's not going the traditional romantic route. This time, he'll prove he loves her with help from the notorious Ménage Club, a relationship club designed specifically to get estranged couples back together with the help of a third and sometimes a fourth in the bedroom.

CAPTIVE HEROES

Pleasure Bound, Book Six

Jan Springer

During a secret NASA mission to locate their brothers on the faraway planet of Paradise, the Hero sisters become separated after they crash land...and find unexpected romance with the tormented alien male warriors of the species in this ultra-long sci-fi book.

Taylor and Kayla

While searching for her brothers, Kayla Hero is bound and imprisoned by the Breeders— along with a male captive whose tantalizing scars pique her interest. Forced to escape with him, she's irresistibly aroused when she suddenly becomes *his* captive. Wild lust flares in Kayla's eyes— a sensual side effect of the Fever Swamp water she's accidentally ingested. Taylor knows he will enjoy administering the cure — lots of sizzling hot lovemaking!

Blackie and Kinley

Injured and lost in a dense jungle, Kinley Hero is intimidated by the scarred man who hunts her, especially due to the power of erotic submission he holds over her.

Capturing his beautiful female prey, Blackie can't wait to train her as a pleasure slave for the Death Valley Boys. When her captor slips a collar around her neck, Kinley must struggle with lust as a natural submissive.

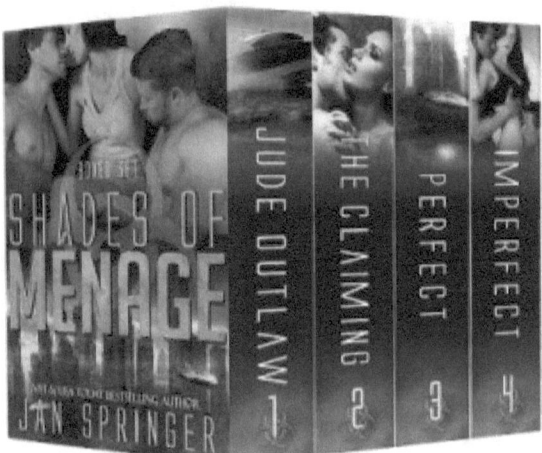

Shades of Ménage Boxed Set: Four Book Romance Ménage Collection

A fast-acting virus has killed a majority of the world's female population. Women's rights are stripped away and The Claiming Law is created, allowing groups of men to stake a claim on a female—as their sensual property.

After five years of fighting in the Terrorist Wars, the Outlaw brothers are coming home to declare ownership on the women they love...and they'll do it any way they can in **Jude Outlaw and The Claiming**.

PLUS

In the future...for population control, each human is embedded with a microchip that suppresses the urge to mate.

*Centuries later,...*A rebel group of young doctors are secretly tampering with their microchips and experimenting with intimacy. Now they search for allies who can help them with their cause – to eventually free humanity in the Dystopian Romance Ménage stories **"Perfect"** & **"Imperfect"**.

A CONTEMPORARY EROTIC ROMANCE BOXED SET

Naughty Girl Desires Boxed Set: Romance, Contemporary Romance, Romance Suspense, Box Set

(m/f only)

What You'll Find Inside Naughty Girl Desires

Jade's Fantasy

Kidnap Fantasies, Book One

Jan Springer

In the land of the rich and famous, Kidnap Fantasies is the answer to discreet naughty downtime.

When ex-downhill skier Jade Hart's two sisters give her a Kidnap Fantasies questionnaire, Jade is aroused at the prospect of having no-strings fun in the sun with a stranger whose only job would be to fulfill her every intimate fantasy. Although she knows she's too shy to send it in, she secretly pours her deepest wishes into the questionnaire. Soon the questionnaire mysteriously vanishes, and Jade's fantasy man appears on her luxury yacht in the form of a sexy handy man who gives her an intimate toy-filled Christmas holiday she'll never forget.

~*~

The Biker and The Bride
Jan Springer

Wrapped in red-hot lust for revenge, Avery plots to murder the man responsible for the death of her son. Her plans are dashed when her ex-husband crashes her wedding and whisks her away on his motorcycle to the rustic Canadian wilderness cabin where they'd once honeymooned.

Police detective Mason is fighting for Avery's love with everything he has.

Armed with whipped cream, handcuffs and his undying devotion, Mason vows he will make Avery love again. But it's only a matter of time before the man she'd planned to kill hunts them down...

~*~

Sinderella Sexy
Jan Springer

By day, she's a dedicated gynecologist.
By night, Dr. Ella Cinder, escapes reality by secretly performing in her own erotic, adult version of Cinderella, aptly retitled Sinderella.

When sexy colleague Dr. Roarke Stephenson shows up in the Sinderella audience on the same night her Prince Charming stands her up, Ella seizes the opportunity to make Roarke into her Prince Charming for one carnal night of extremely naughty fun in front of an audience.

But at the strike of midnight, Ella knows she must face the harsh reality that Roarke must never learn her secret life and they can never be together again. Until then, she'll make sure he'll never forget their night of sensual play.

Dr. Roarke Stephenson is immediately captured by the lusciously curvy actress who hides behind a mask and is known only as Sinderella. For some insane reason, she reminds him of his klutzy co-worker, Ella. But that's not possible. Ella would never have the nerve to do the wickedly delicious things Sinderella does to him...or would she?

~*~

Nice Girl Naughty
Jan Springer

Blind since the age of nineteen, Summer has blossomed into a famous wood carver. When she's almost killed by a serial killer, she's whisked away to a secluded wilderness cabin by the man she once secretly loved.

Summer can't get enough of touching professional bodyguard Nick Cassidy's thick, powerful muscles and all those other hard, yummy male body parts that she has always longed to explore.

For years, Nick has stayed away from his best friend's kid sister, nice girl Summer. Now he's back, and sweeping his gorgeous redhead into the naughty cravings he's always had for her. With passion blinding him, Nick doesn't realize their hideout isn't safe—until it's too late.

Please note: The titles in Naughty Girl Desires have been previously published.

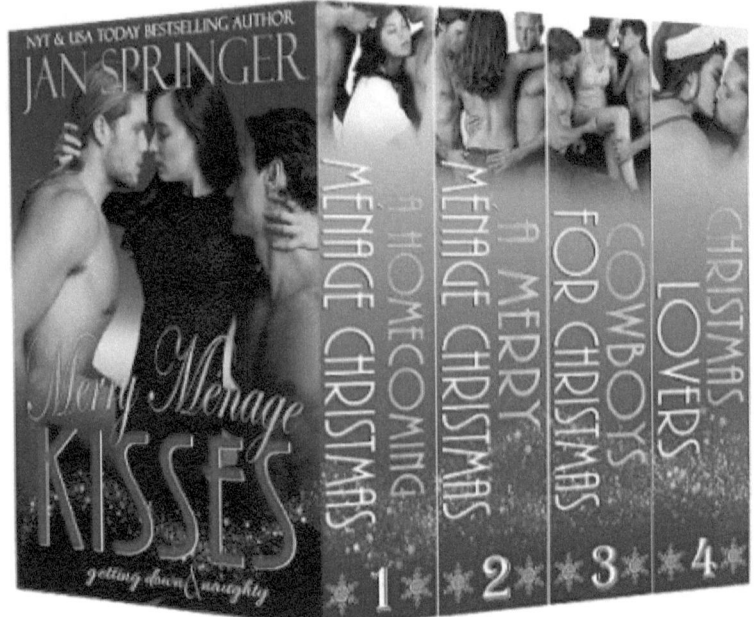

What You'll Find In The
Merry Ménage Kisses Boxed Set
Wrap yourself in four sexy holiday themed adult romance ménages.

A Homecoming Ménage Christmas

Jan Springer

Rachel has a *very* naughty secret and she's way too embarrassed to let anyone know about it. When The Key Club throws a Santa Fetish Ménage Night, it's almost too good to be true. She *has* to figure out how to participate without anyone finding out!

Key Club bartenders Rob and Ron Simpson have fallen head over Santa hats for quiet, nice-girl Rachel. But she has no clue how they feel about her. But she *will* know, because Rachel is coming home from a trip to Europe and the twin brothers are going to give her the best Homecoming Ménage Christmas ever. They'll do it with the help of some naughty toys, the Red Room, a safe word and...Santa Claus.

A Merry Ménage Christmas

Jan Springer

Dr. Kelsie Madison can't remember the last time she's had no-strings sex and that's her clue she's been working way too hard. It's time to unwind at the Key Club by indulging in a yummy Christmas present for herself. Something she's never experienced before — a red-hot ménage.

ER doctor Ryder Greene and his roommate, physiotherapist Dixon Flynn, love sharing their women. They've had their eye on cute Dr. Kelsie Madison for quite some time, but she's a workaholic and she never has time to play.

When they learn she'll be at the Santa Claus Ménage Night festivities, they'll make sure they're the ones kissing Kelsie under the mistletoe.

And if they get their wish, Kelsie will be taking them home for Christmas.

Cowboys for Christmas

Jan Springer

Jennifer Jane (JJ) Watson has spent the past ten Christmases in a maximum-security prison.

The last thing she expects is to get early parole, along with a job on a remote Canadian cattle ranch serving Christmas holiday dinners to three of the sexiest cowboys she's ever met!

Rafe, Brady and Dan thought they were getting a couple of male ex-cons to help out around their secluded ranch, but instead they get an attractive and very appealing female.

In the snowbound wilds of Northern Ontario, female companionship is rare.

It's a good thing the three men like to share...

They're dominating, sexy-as-sin and they fill JJ with the hottest ménage fantasies she's ever had. Suddenly she's craving cowboys for Christmas and wishing for something she knows she can never have...a happily ever after.

Christmas Lovers

Jan Springer

Sergeant Connor Jordan, wounded overseas and sent back to the States to recuperate, just cannot stop fantasizing about the sexy nurse who cared for him. When his brothers give him a holiday gift certificate to Kidnap Fantasies, a top-secret fantasy organization, Connor knows he'll use their gift, if only to help him forget his wickedly delicious attraction to Nurse Sparks.

Nurse Tania Sparks has always been purely professional with her injured soldiers...until sinfully sexy Connor Jordan enters her hospital. He makes her body throb with an intense desire she's never known before. The last thing she wants is to get involved with the injured warrior. So what's a woman supposed to do to relieve her naughty frustrations? Call Kidnap Fantasies and have them supply her with a look-alike man who'll help her forget her sexy soldier...

When Tania and Connor unexpectedly come together at a secluded mountain chalet, their love explodes in a ménage of passion, sensuous desires and a happily forever after.

Contains ménage scenes.

For more Jan Springer stories, please visit http://www.janspringer.com

---

Jan's Newsletter

Hi! If you would like to get an email when my books are released, you can sign up here:
Newsletter: http://ymlp.com/xguembmugmgb
Your emails will never be shared and you can unsubscribe whenever you like.

Discover Other Titles by Jan Springer
http://www.janspringer.com

~*~

About the Author

Jan Springer writes full-time at her home nestled in cottage country, Ontario, Canada. She enjoys hiking, kayaking, gardening, reading and writing. She is a member of the Writers Union of Canada and the Romance Writers of America. She loves hearing from her readers.

A Word From The Author

Hi! Thank you for purchasing this book. Word of mouth is important for any author to succeed. If you enjoyed this story, feel free to leave a short review at the place where you bought it. I would really appreciate it. I look forward to bringing you more stories in the near future. Thanks!

If you would like to contact me or personally send me feedback, you can reach me by using my contact page at:

http://janspringerauthor.wordpress.com/contact/

Here are other ways we can connect:
Jan Springer Website at http://www.janspringer.com
Instagram – http://www.instagram.com/janspringerauthor
Facebook - https://www.facebook.com/janspringereroticromance
Twitter - https://twitter.com/janspringer @janspringer
Pinterest - http://www.pinterest.com/janspringer1/
Jan's Blog - http://janspringerauthor.wordpress.com/blog-2/
LinkedIn - http://ca.linkedin.com/in/janspringerauthor/
Google Plus - https://plus.google.com/u/0/
101527334949931513035/posts
Jan's Newsletter - http://ymlp.com/xguembmugmgb
Goodreads - https://www.goodreads.com/author/show/
260628.Jan_Springer
Happy Reading,
Jan Springer

Don't miss out!

Visit the website below and you can sign up to receive emails whenever Jan Springer publishes a new book. There's no charge and no obligation.

https://books2read.com/r/B-A-WGQ-VCKK

BOOKS 2 READ

Connecting independent readers to independent writers.

www.ingramcontent.com/pod-product-compliance
Lightning Source LLC
Chambersburg PA
CBHW020556180626
46810CB00007B/2532